Edward Payson Jackson

A Demigod

A novel

Edward Payson Jackson

A Demigod
A novel

ISBN/EAN: 9783337000363

Printed in Europe, USA, Canada, Australia, Japan

Cover: Foto ©Andreas Hilbeck / pixelio.de

More available books at **www.hansebooks.com**

A Novel

'Ετεχ' ''Εκτορα δῖον·
ILIAD, xx., 240

NEW YORK

HARPER & BROTHERS, FRANKLIN SQUARE

1887

THE THEME.

The Demigod's name was Hector Vyr.

He was evolved from ordinary humanity by a long-continued process of artificial selection, aided by auspicious fortune.

The natural pear is a wretched little rose-hip: art has developed it into a Duchesse d'Angoulême.

The wild horse can scarcely trot a mile in four minutes: artificial selection has produced a Maud S.

The evolution of the Demigod and certain passages from his history are herein recounted—thus, I regret to add, helping to frustrate one of the most cherished purposes of his life. But what secret purpose so noble, what precinct of the heart so sacred, as to be safe from man's profane scrutiny? The general's plans of battle are known to his enemy almost as soon as to his own officers, and the President reads the secret counsels of his Cabinet in his evening paper.

That the publication of this narrative is not the act of perfidy to its hero it may for a while appear, will be proved in due time, I trust, to everybody's satisfaction.

CONTENTS.

I.

KENELM VERE, the great-great-great-great-grandfather of our hero, was a wealthy English physician, who lived in Amsterdam in the very height of the famous *tulipomania*. He became infected with the prevailing madness, which in his case soon changed to an entirely different form. Instead of attempting to evolve new varieties of tulips, his thoughts ran on the improvement of his own race. Failing to divert the general enthusiasm into this new channel, he suddenly disappeared, and nothing was ever afterwards seen or heard of him. One of his letters is still extant, however, in which he declares his intention to make a home for himself in the purest atmosphere of Greece, to take to wife the handsomest and wholesomest barbarian that money can buy, and to enforce among his children the strictest code of mental and physical health.

"Natur," he writes, "hath not desyned Man to be a beaste of prey. Y^e devouring of flesh is but little better than Caribalism [cannibalism]. It planteth foul humours in the blood and lewde lusts in y^e

heart. My children shal not be of this sorte, I promise thee. Neither shal they cherish ambitions, the which burn vp the powers of ye minde and bodye like a consuming fyre. Natur, lyke water, doth seeke her own level. Genius doth seldome beget genius. Wherefor they shall be trayned vp to voyde all maner and degree of notorietie. Nay, my yonge Impes shal sware to giue their lyves and powers to harmonious self-nourture, to the ende y^t they may leaue a goodlie heretage of mental and phisikal health to their descendents, as ye master of an en-tayled estate doth sware to transmit it with en-creased seigniories to his heirs.

"Moreouer, they shal sware to impose a lyke obli-gation vpon their children. So shall futur genera-tions see whether a Man be as good as a Tulype or no. Did not the lawes of auncient Sparta breed vp a race of gyantes? What hath ben don, can it not be don agen? Aye, and better yette."

For several years after Dr. Vere's disappearance his friends tried to reopen communication with him, but no clew to his hiding-place could be obtained, and he was at last given up for dead.

Two centuries have buried him deeper than the nethermost Troy.

II.

AT THE PARTHENON.

It is one of those days in Athens when the faintest cloud would be but a blemish on the blue vault of the sky. Every shrub on Hymettus and Pentelicus shows sharp and distinct through the crystalline air. Even Parnes and Cithæron seem an easy walk, while Parnassus, seventy miles away, cuts the horizon like a knife of pearl.

Among the ruins of the propylæa are lounging a little party of American tourists, whom we will present in due order.

On one of the broad marble steps sits Major Warren Paul, a robust man of fifty, with closely cropped hair, which shows only a sprinkling of its original black, ruddy face flanked by full, granite-colored whiskers, and the general forceful air of a political demagogue or of a railroad manager. He would make but an indifferent specimen of either, however, except in the haranguing of a mob of communists or strikers; for though he possesses energy enough, it usually expends itself so entirely in words that it is followed by an inglorious reaction, and thus his acts are apt to be whimsically inconsistent with his speech. At home he will abuse a political candidate in terms that even a campaign editor would hesitate to use, and then go straight to the polls and vote for him. In his family he will storm like a madman over their extravagance, and then make up for his brutality by buying them luxuries they would never dream of buying for themselves. But this foible of his had its peculiar advantages. Without it a far less unruly tongue would have cost him all his friends; few men, however, were more popular than the loud-mouthed Major Paul. It was even the cause of one of the proudest triumphs of his life.

He had entered the army with the rank of captain. For a while his company was a proverb of discipline; but the men soon discovered that his verbal cartridges were always without ball, and then his company was a proverb of anarchy. What was to be done? Have him put on the general's staff? have him detailed for special duty? Not for worlds—his colonel and fellow-officers would not lose so good a fellow from the regiment. Happy thought—promote him to the majorship!

He has an ear for round, ringing words, like a musician's for the concord of sweet sounds, and I half think this is the true explanation of his frequent philippics. A sonorous polysyllable or phrase will always catch his attention, often at the expense of the connected thought, and you will soon hear him rolling it over his tongue as an expletive, in ludicrous defiance of its meaning. "Boswell's Life of Johnson!" he will say, for instance, as any one else would say "Good gracious!" Time was when he swore,

not for the wickedness of the habit, nor often to give
vent to his less amiable emotions, but simply on account of the rousing resonance which unfortunately
belongs to most of the more common "swear words."
Since his wife's death, however, which had by some
persons been attributed to Divine indignation at his
fearful blasphemies — as if Providence would hesitate to visit his transgressions directly upon his own
head! — he had tried to break himself of the habit,
and now swore big, but for the most part innocent
words, as a man chews gentian or slippery elm in
lieu of tobacco.

A little below the stair-way, on a battered plinth,
in the shadow of the pedestal of Agrippa, that with
its ugly height dwarfs the mutilated beauties of the
marbles around it, half reclines a tall, graceful young
lady, in whom a casual glance scarcely discovers the
daughter of the gallant major. Closer observation
reveals certain turns of the eye and tricks of gesture
so curiously like his that you almost wonder why
they do not make him as enchanting as they make
her. There is, too, an occasional vigor, perhaps I
should say luxuriance, in her speech even more strikingly suggesting the relationship between them. She
is in a state of sound health, which, in the good old
times, would have been unpardonably vulgar, but
which, in these bad new times, is more than offset
by rich color of cheek and lip, clear light of happy
eyes, and firm roundness of figure.

A young man is seated cross-legged on the ground
near her, playing a *solitaire* game of "jack-stones"

with chips of marble, which, for aught he knew, may have been fragments of the famous Athené of the Inner Temple. His face is a curious jumble of inconsistencies. The general cast is that of the conventional pirate—low, heavy brows, eyes dark and deep-set, nose strongly aquiline, lower jaw square and firm, and, as if the owner aimed at completing the picture, a long, drooping black mustache. But the effect is spoiled, or rather redeemed, by an expression of jocular good-nature, in strange contrast with the forbidding form and color of the features. You miss the skull and cross-bones from the black flag, and see only a cap and bells in their stead. For the rest, he has a long, athletic, though slightly round-shouldered figure, and slender, shapely hands, displayed to peculiar advantage in their present idle employment.

Both he and his fair companion wear garments of those coarse, neutral-tinted materials so curiously becoming to people who can wear satin and broadcloth when they choose, and which conduce so inevitably to ease of speech and demeanor, just as satin and broadcloth conduce to stateliness and formality. There is little enough of stateliness or formality between these two, at all events, for they are engaged in a more than half serious quarrel; though, for that matter, they would be as likely to quarrel in satin and broadcloth as in tweed and serge. Happily, their quarrels never last long, and leave no more clouds than a summer shower.

She has entered upon the propylæa with her shoes

removed. This must not be understood to mean that her little feet are actually nude, like those of old Cecrops and his daughter a few rods distant, but must be interpreted as simply describing her mental condition. He, on the other hand, has tramped in upon that consecrated ground like an irreverent Moslem. She has been trying to inspire him with something of her own awe and admiration of the ruined glories around them, while he has been profaning them and exasperating her with stale puns and other witless nonsense.

"Robert Griffin!" she exclaims, at last, "I really didn't know you were such a shallow, soulless creature!"

"Oh, Madeline," he drawls, catching three stones on the back of his hand and then in his palm, "I'm afraid you mean to insinuate something derogatory."

"Ugh! you poor, miserable—"

"*Poor!* By Jove, that's too much! I've *some* feelings, you heartless traducer!"

"I wish I could touch them," she retorted, through her white teeth. "I wish anybody or anything could."

"Well, if *you* can't, you may be sure nothing else can. What do you mean (toss), you little frump, by calling me poor, when you know I've got (toss) Eastern Pacific enough to buy that old knock-kneed, broken-backed (toss) church that you admire so much?"

"You *dare* to speak so of the Parthenon?"

"Pooh! what is there to dare? where's the danger?"

"'Fools rush in where angels fear to tread.'"

"Plucky fools! It seems, however, that *one* angel dares to tread here as well as one fool— There, by George, I've missed it again! Just hand me that jack-stone behind your heel, will you?"

"*You* talk of buying the Parthenon! You ought to be ashamed to mention your disgusting bonds in its presence—you sordid, blasphemous wretch!"

"Come, I say! *I* can call names as well as you. You snaky-haired Medusa! You blood-thirsty cannibal! Oh, for breath to tell thee what thou art! But consider a little, my darling cousin, my sweet-brier-rose—you won't find those same bonds so disgusting in a year or so."

"Yes, I shall—and their proprietor, too, unless he changes in a great many respects. And, by-the-way, I don't wish you to speak to me or look at me in that way, Robert. You know very well you have no right."

"Haven't I, indeed?" cried Griffin, throwing away his jack-stones, and leaping up in mock fury. "We haven't been promised to each other almost from our infancy, have we?"

"Most certainly not," she answered, looking him squarely in the face. "Whatever papa may have said, *I* have made no promises, and I don't think I ever shall."

"What treason is this? Wasn't it for that very purpose we took this tour together? Wasn't this close and constant association to knit our souls inseparably together? Mine is already knit; isn't yours?"

"I only wish you knew how utterly distasteful such speeches are to me. You turn everything into nonsense, even your professed love for me. How can I believe in your professions, or place any value upon them? This close and constant association is producing exactly the opposite effect to that which you and papa pretend to hope from it. I am really serious, Robert."

Her looks and tones confirmed her words.

"Would you be better pleased with me," Griffin asked, "if I were like young Spooner, whose fondest hopes you so mercilessly nipped in the bud?"

"I should be immensely better pleased with you," she replied, with an angry flush, "if you sometimes showed that you had one-tenth of Dr. Spooner's heart and soul."

"Pity he hasn't a head to match," sneered Griffin.

"Well," the little vixen darted back, in her high key, "no one can accuse *you* of any such want of symmetry. But," she added, as an instant but needless antidote, "we were not talking of Dr. Spooner, we were discussing a much more interesting subject —we were discussing *you.*"

"Oh, *me.* Why will you always be lugging in such deep and abstruse subjects, when I am trying to rest my mind by a little light conversation?"

"I don't know where we could find a lighter subject," she answered, laughing in spite of herself.

2

"Nonsense. You know I am full of heart and soul, Madge."

"Take care, sir. You may really wish to use those sacred words seriously some time, and find yourself like the soldier in battle who has broken his weapons in reckless play."

She said this with an air of solemn warning that impressed even him.

"Words are never weapons, Madeline," he replied, with a sudden accession of gravity and even dignity. "Weapons are solid facts. No amount of play can harm facts. You know my heart — what more is necessary? What do words amount to, anyway? They're nothing but nitrogen and carbonic acid gas."

"I know that's your valuation of them, yet I know of no one who uses them more volubly than you do."

"Well," he returned, with a portentous sigh, "I've got to *breathe;* I may as well breathe through my glottis as through my nose."

"You forget that you are not the only one concerned."

"Oh, I *bore* you? That's terrible. I thought I only shocked you."

"Words must have some meaning to possess even that power."

"So I haven't even the power to *shock* anybody?" —threateningly.

"You needn't try"—in alarm.

"You should have seen Aunt Eliza this morning. I had blundered into some of my imprudent speeches, and she went so far as to say no *gentleman* would speak like that. I told her I didn't profess to be a gentleman, that it was only another name for imbecile. She said I was not only no gentleman, but no Christian. I replied that I made no pretensions to either title, that Christians were either hypocrites or fanatics. I thought the poor old virgin would go mad. '*What are you?*' she shrieked. 'A laughing philosopher,' said I; 'a mere animal with senses to enjoy, and with just prudence enough to avoid crime and disaster.'"

Madeline listened to his story without a smile. "I am more than half convinced," she said, "that you gave her your true genus and species."

"'Course I did—*Homo Perditus.*"

"Then, of course, you cannot reasonably expect me to have anything more to say or do with you?"

"I suppose not"—with a sigh of resignation. "Henceforth we must be as if we had never met."

"Good-by."

"Good-by. Try to think of me as I was in the innocent days of my childhood."

"I shall try not to think of you at all."

She rose and walked leisurely towards the stairway of the propylæa. The major had by this time left his seat on the steps, and had disappeared on the plateau of the akropolis. Griffin sprang up and overtook Madeline.

"Where are you going?" he asked.

"I'm going to find papa."

"May I go, too?"

"If you'll stop your abominable, tiresome nonsense."

"Now, isn't that rather hard on a poor fellow who has only been doing his best to entertain you?"

"Can't you see, you poor, dear boy, that you have been going about it in exactly the wrong way? Can't you get rid of the absurd idea that what you call fun is entitled to precedence over everything else, and at all times? Can't you realize that there are *some* things too sacred to be trifled with? Instead of increasing by your sympathy the pleasure we might both enjoy here, you only— I confess I cannot understand your insensibility to this wonderful scene, with all its associations. How can you look upon those ruins, and desecrate them with every-day chatter, especially every-day puns? I should think their very names would make some impression upon you."

She had stopped walking during this appeal, and now seated herself on one of the steps. Griffin was absently tracing the figures in the sculptured rubbish which lay around them with the end of his walking-stick.

"Hang it, Madeline!" he said, bringing the stick down with a whack upon one of the marble blocks, "you must remember I'm not made of such refined clay as you are. I'm only an every-day sort of fellow, and can talk only every-day talk. If I were promoted to a regular member's seat on High Olympus, I should probably forfeit it the very first day by some vile pun. I suppose it only shows the coarseness of my nature, but, to tell you the honest truth, I never believed that people who talk classical rhapsodies really *feel* as they talk. They only want to show how exquisitely æsthetic they are. I—I—don't mean *you*, of course."

"I don't profess to be made of finer clay than you are," returned Madeline, well pleased that he was at last reduced to seriousness, "but as to saying what I don't feel—well, if you choose to think me such a hypocrite—"

"Didn't I just say I didn't mean you?"

"I really *do* feel a great deal more than I can express. I don't see how any one can help it—here. I never was in any other place that affected me as this does. Nowhere else have I ever felt such a glow of tender emotions. Don't interrupt me, please. Let me talk to you, for once, as I would to any one else. The Parthenon, especially, seems to me like a vast, noble intelligence clothed in a form of perfect beauty, lamenting its own downfall. I have no words to express the exquisite sorrow that fills me—the longing to see it restored in all its symmetry and grandeur—and to think that only two centuries ago it was almost uninjured! I feel like speaking with bated breath in that sublime presence. It seems as if the great shade of Phidias hovered in the blue air over it."

"Like the Spectre of the Brocken," interposed Robert, his face lighting up with self-appreciation, "big only because it is so far off. Come, now, I call that a mighty good comparison. I don't suppose

Phidias was much ahead of some of the great artists of to-day, do you?"

"Well," returned Madeline, impatiently, "if that is your real judgment, I abandon you as an incorrigible."

Griffin's brow contracted a little. "I suppose I *am* a lamentable specimen of ignorance and vulgarity. I don't understand how you can condescend to associate with such a peasant."

"Oh, fudge! I know very well you don't really feel as you talk, as you say about classical rhapsodists. You only talk as you do for the sake of exasperating me."

Griffin reflectively poked the stones with his stick a few moments, and then said,

"Perhaps you are right. I don't pretend to understand myself very well. As I said a little while ago, the subject is altogether too profound for me. Uncle Warren talks just as I do, only a great deal more so."

"Oh, papa! I don't mind his sneers any more than I do his scolding. Everybody knows the more he abuses a thing the more he really respects it. There's nothing he berates more than the classics and the classic countries, yet you know he wanted you to go to Harvard, and here we've been in Greece longer than in any other country since we left Boston. He spent a long time yesterday at the Theseum, and I have no doubt we shall presently find him worshipping the Parthenon. Let's go up and see."

So saying, she sprung up again, and led the way through terraced colonnades, an avenue of beautiful desolation, past great monoliths prone and stained with the mellow gold of centuries, until they stood within the ramparts of the akropolis. Close at hand rose the rocky tower of Lycabettus. A little farther on, the silver of vast olive-groves gleamed in the sunlight, threaded by the white line of the Piræus railway. Away in the horizon waved the mountains of Morea, and the blue Ægean lay around its islands. Within the parapet lay scattered everywhere shattered columns, friezes, drums, fragments of the entablature, and sculptured marble in every stage of mutilation. From the midst of all this the Temple of the Virgin soared into the vivid blue, like the palace of a dream.

"What did I tell you?" exclaimed Madeline, with a laugh, waving her hand towards a portly figure with its back towards them, motionless as the Colossus of Rhodes, and in a similar attitude. "*Now* will you pretend you don't admire classical ruins?" she cried, startling her father from his reverie.

"Great Thomas Jefferson, how you scared me! I thought you were one of those old she-gods come to life again!"

"Not a very strange mistake," said Robert Griffin. "I've often thought so myself."

"Thank you both," laughed Madeline, "particularly for the 'old.' Papa, dear, I beseech you not to say 'she-gods' again; it's altogether too Saxon an expression for this place, which you know you reverence in your heart. Didn't we just catch you worshipping at the shrine of Athené?"

"H'm'ph! you may call it worshipping if you like. It's the way a good many worship at our modern shrines. I was estimating the outrageous waste of material and skilled labor here. That building alone must have cost half a million dollars, and what, in the name of the Young Men's Christian Association, was it ever good for but to look at? But that's all those old Greeks lived for. They were a set of preposterous, effeminate coxcombs. They ate pickles and chalk to tone down their muscles into smoother outlines. They thought it was vulgar to have the muscles of *men*, and so only the statues of barbarians and satyrs show anything like real manhood. Talk about their being a noble type of humanity! Baxter's 'Saints' Rest!' your true Greek athlete was a pretty, rose-water-sucking *monstrosity*. '*Athlete!*' Head of Heliogabalus! I'd bet on Madge in a fair fight with one of 'em!"

Her father's coarseness afflicted poor Madeline even more than her cousin's frivolity. As far as she was concerned, their ravages were worse than those the classic precincts around her had already suffered; for while Time and Turk had mutilated and defaced only the marbles, her companions seemed bent on annihilating the very soul of poetry and romance that other iconoclasts—Lord Elgin and all—had left intact.

"I don't know why you brought me here," she said, turning away with a grief and anger she rarely felt towards her father. She walked slowly towards the eastern parapet, complaining to herself: "Why couldn't they let me enjoy it as I wanted to? Men have no more feeling or sense than a stone. I never will go anywhere with either of them again!" But soon her thoughts were diverted by the glories of the eastern landscape, which the sun was painting in a thousand brilliant hues. It was not long before she was descanting, with all her wonted enthusiasm, to the two penitent delinquents upon the mysterious, ragged relics of the Pelasgic Walls, the stately ruin of the Temple of Olympian Zeus, the decrepit old Ilissus tottering along at the foot of Hymettus, and the proud Lycabettus, with skirts of green velvet and long, soft train of shadow.

In an hour or two the party descended. Passing the inspection of a bright-eyed soldier, whose duty it was to see that no relic was carried away, they wound through the grove of huge aloes beneath the southern wall of the akropolis, thus avoiding the miserable huts, built of mud, stones, and many a sculptured fragment once precious, that skirt the western base. They found the narrow, horribly-paved streets thronged; for, as usual, all Athens was out-of-doors. Whatever they see, Athenians must *be* seen—rich or poor, young or old, beautiful or ugly, in embroidered silk or dirty linen, they must be seen. So they were all there—gay *palikars* in their crimson jackets and snow-white *fustanellis;* black-eyed ladies in jaunty gold-tasselled fez; beggars in their rags, and Franks and Greeks dressed like Franks in sober black and gray.

The picturesque Greek costume is fast giving place

to the unromantic coat and trousers of Western Europe; but there are certain classes who will, for many years to come, proudly wear the scarlet jacket and white fustanelli, as we still find, here and there in our own country, the blue swallow-tail and bright buttons of a past generation.

As our friends drove past long rows of one-storied, tumble-down shops and dwellings, towards their great hotel in the Square of the Constitution, Major Paul told, with much satisfaction and many congratulations, of a new guide and interpreter whose services he had secured, Professor Markos Tsáras—a real professor, mind you — late of L'Arvarion, formerly of the island of Corfu, "where Greek and English are spoken in equal purity."

III.

THE PROFESSOR.

Professor Tsáras, or Daskalomarkotsáras, as he was called for short in his own language, was a thin, nervous little man, with a suggestion of the typical Greek beauty in his straight nose, dark eyes, and olive cheeks. He was impulsive, inquisitive, cunning, polite, keen at a bargain, and intensely patriotic—at least in words. Living in a country totally unable to support its large proportion of professional citizens in a state befitting their occupations, he was as poor in purse as he was rich in education. There were no subjects upon which his nimble tongue ran more unceasingly than his own attainments and the injustice of Fortune, who lavished her favors upon the ignorant and the stupid, and withheld them from those who, like himself, had the brains to appreciate them. Like most of his countrymen, he was quite ready to turn an honest *drachma* in almost any way that offered, from translating a book to running of errands; so, when Major Paul applied to him for a trustworthy dragoman, he immediately proposed himself, with the most flattering recommendations.

When Greek meets Yankee in the way of trade, then comes the tug of war. It was a good-natured warfare in this case, however, and at last the terms were satisfactorily arranged. Tsáras agreed to act as interpreter and guide, and to provide food, lodging, and transportation for the party at ten dollars *per diem*, not including *baksheesh* to servants, drivers, etc.—by no means an unimportant item.

"Monsieur Paul," he said, shaking his head with most impressive meaning, "I congratulaïte you for the excéllent contráct you have maïke. I shall saïfe you more as my remuneraïtion each days. You are ver' acute, Monsieur Paul, but you know not how terríble you shall be cheat if you shall try to maïke the contráct with Greek *oikodespótai* and *agogiátai** you'self."

The party made several short excursions to Eleusis, Marathon, Sunium, the summits of Hymettus

---

* Landlords and muleteers.

and Pentelicus — and then the major signified his desire to visit Sparta, and that most magnificent of all the Greek ranges, the Taygetus.

"I want to see the people who live among those mountains," he said. "I have heard that they are the direct descendants of the ancient Spartans, and that they have inherited the strength and hardihood of their ancestors. If that is true, they must be a most remarkable people, sir, and I want to make their acquaintance."

They were seated in a café in the Square of the Constitution, smoking nargiles and sipping Cretan wine. A Bavarian band, just outside, was playing Greek and German airs, to the great annoyance of some palikars, who, with true Greek inquisitiveness, were vainly trying to divine what the distinguished-looking Frank was saying. What to them were the tuneful strains of the Hymn of the Revolution—

"Δεῦτε παῖδες τῶν Ἑλλήνων,
Ἄνδρες φίλοι τῶν κινδύνων,
Ἡ πατρὶς σᾶ προσκαλεῖ"

—but a cover to some possible treason on the part of their learned countryman or of the foreigner? They could hear the "Δεῦτε" at any other time.

"Yeas," replied Tsáras, highly pleased. "I can tell to you wond'ful stoaries of the Mainotes. They perrformed prodigee of valor in the Revolution. You shall faind glorious examples of the Greek raäce among them, and you shall be convince that we are not the degeneraäte pipple the wörrld thing we are. Aah yeas, we have gret many heroes in Greece to-day, gret many unknown Leonidas. Mbotzaris was not the las'—no, Monsieur Paul—we have gret many more hero as braäve laike Mbotzaris. Have not you hearrd the naäme Vyr?"

"Vere—Vere? Oh yes. It's an English name."

"Engleesh! *O diábolos!*—no; *Greek.* It is the naäme of a wond'ful familee among the Mainotes. P'raps we mus' not belief all those stoaries which comes to us of the familee Vyr, becose some of those stoaries be laike—aah—mirácle. For instanz: one young man is call the modern Herakles. His rilly naäme is Hector Vyr, and it shall not be a difficúltee to—aah—arraänge Twelf Laäbors of his exploit which shall resemble those laäbors of the old Herakles. One taime, it says, he purrsued a band of klephts ten kilométres, and he knock them down this all distanz with the bodee of a klepht which he have kill with his onlee hands!"

"Pooh! I can beat that," said the major, contemptuously. "Haven't you ever heard of the American Herakles, Davy Crockett, and how he used to kill Indians with flashes of lightning from his eyes?"

"Aah, you maäke the joke with me, Monsieur Paul; but I tell to you the only truth, laike as it is tell to me. No klepht have the braävery to come near to his filds or to his orrchards. Hector Vyr shall never lose sheeps, and he pays not—aah—what you call—"

"Black-mail?"

"Yeas. Hector Vyr never pays black-mails!"

"Why, then, in the name of Bunyan's 'Pilgrim's

Progress,'" asked Major Paul, "doesn't he come forth and drive the cussed venomous vermin from your country altogether?"

"Aah, Monsieur Paul, that is the mos' straänges' thing. Yeas. He shall not be induce' to leave his home. With all his power and his braävery, he have not the ambcction. The Hellenic Gov'munt have maäke to him the offer to command in the arrmee, but he shall not accept not any offices in the arrmee, not in the *Boulé*."

"But I should think *patriotism* would call him out, if ambition didn't."

"Aah," replied Tsáras, shaking his head, "not any man ûnd'stands Hector Vyr. He is wond'ful modest, laike he is wond'ful strong. It is difficûltee to evén see him; for, although he have not the fear to faäce a arrmee of enemee, he shall run from a visitor laike as he shall run from the *diáboloù!*"

"Then we shall stand rather a slim chance of seeing this demigod of yours," suggested the major.

"'Slim?' Aah, you min *little* chance. Yeas. If we shall see him we shall be fortunaäte more as any man at all."

"Except the klephts."

"Yeas, except the klephts. They shall be more fortunaäte if they do not see him."

"He has a very convenient habit for a *demigod* in these days," remarked the major, in a somewhat sarcastic tone. "We have sharper eyes and more critical tests than they had in the time of Homer."

"You do not belive? Well, we shall see. You

shall leave my countree with différent thoughts as when you have came here, Monsieur Paul."

" Very probable, professor. By-the-way, speaking of klephts, I suppose you mean *brigands*."

" Yeas. But all the klephts are not necessaüry brigands. The naüme klepht min rillee *mountaineer*, which mos' often are wandering shepherds, *blacho-poiménes*. They live in the stronghold of the mount-ains unt'l they have exhaust the grass for their herds, and too friquént the booty for theyself. Then they go 'way very queeck to other stronghold. The principal rizzon that it is difficúltee to exterrminaüte them is becose they are so acquaint with the countree that they easily escaüpe from those purrsuit. Whaile their enemee climb toilfully upon one mountain, they fly easy away laike the birds to other. They shall go fiftee, sixtee kilométres in one naight, over mount-ains which other men shall faind impassable. The Hellenic Gov'munt is—aah—asperse mos' únjustlee for rizzon of the klephts. The naütions mus' have the sympathee for us, but they have not the sympa-thee. They say the mos' terrible slander agains' us. They say, ' Greece is the Caüve of Adúllam, and the Greeks are a naütion of assassin.' Listen, Monsieur Paul ?"

He took from his pocket a scrap of newspaper, and read, " ' Greece is geograüphicallee a part of Turkey ; moraüllee a continuaütion of Hades ; social-lee an offshoot of Soho Square. The land is in the hands of brigands ; the-only law observed is the law of pillage ; the only king recognaized is King Death !'

"Those, Monsieur Paul, is the sentimént of a countryman of the Engleesh hero, Lorrd Beeron, who was our braäve friend—one gret philhellene. What you thing of me if I shall say New York is a continuäätion of Hades, becose multitude of thiefs haide in her bad strits, which laugh and wag their head at the gov'munt? We mus' not be censure becose Engleesh and Américan travéllers are robbed in our mountains, no more as you mus' be censure becose Greek travéllers are robbed in your bad strits, Monsieur Paul."

"That is hardly a fair comparison, professor," replied Major Paul, with a frown. "We have no organized bands of cutthroats roaming over the length and breadth of our land. If we had, by the Infernal Blacksmith, we should declare war, and sweep them into the Atlantic Ocean!"

"Declare war!" almost shrieked Tsáras. "Do not *we*, too, also declare war? It is war without begin and without end. But Greece is not all overweave with railway laike your countree. We have all only mountain and valley. Our only roads are—ah—ravines in the mountains, and the channél of rivers which have dry ûp. Every plaäces have caäves and thickets which cannot be—ah—penetraäte, where the klephts hide theyself in one little moment. Some taime we have draive them away farr to the north; but the Turk *skylloi* (dogs) they recive them with open arms, and when we have come to our homes, the klephts they come too, also.

"Also we are not strong laike your countree,

Monsieur Paul. We have not yet recoverr ourself of the Turkish oppression. We are braäve and patriót, but we are little nùmber. The naätions mus' not slander us, they mus' hellup us, Monsieur Paul, *they mus' hellup us!*"

Tsáras spoke with much show of feeling. His gestures were numerous, and in the most impassioned passages he arose from his seat and walked back and forth by his side of the table.

"But I have heard," said the major, after a reflective silence on both sides, "that you do not always punish your robbers, even when you catch them."

"Punish our robbers? aah, we are too sof' in our heart. The Greek pipple be heroes, and they love heroes. The klephts are not laike the Engleesh thiefs — they be laike hero. They were force' to haide theyself in the mountains from the Turkish *diáboloi*. They were saäfe there, Monsieur Paul, and they fly away down upon their oppressors laike the eagle fly down upon the jackal. Each klepht were laike the Switz hero, Willum Tell. They were the mos' braäve in all the arrmee of the revolution; and when the war finish, they faind their homes all gone, they faind their beezness all gone. What mus' they do — what mus' they *do*, Monsieur Paul? They mus' eat, they mus' have house, they mus' have garment. They have learrn to love braävery in the mountains, and — they stay in the mountains. They were heroes which faight for liberrty — they are klephts which faight for meat. Is it not the jùstice?"

Major Paul felt but little admiration for the flam-

3

ing eye, the erect figure, the ringing tones, and the impassioned gestures of the speaker. His prevailing feeling was one of disgust and irritation at the abominable cause the little professor was pleading. Controlling himself, he said as quietly as possible,

"So your people admire the robbers, and are even said to feed and shelter them, and help them to escape from their pursuers, when they have any."

"Aah, Monsieur Paul, are not we a ûnhappee pipple? The *oikodespótes* knows if he tell the gov'munt, or if he refuse meat and hellup, his sheeps shall be robbed away, and his house shall be bûrn with faire. It is better he pay — ah — black - mails than he be ruin."

"What do you say to the charges against your government of being in collusion with the rascals?"

"Pardon. I do not ûnd'stand."

"Why, your government, or at least prominent members of it, are accused of secretly helping the brigands and sharing in their plunder. What do you say to that, professor?"

Tsáras's cheek flushed darkly.

"Monsieur Paul, all those is black lies of the Engleesh goddams! The Hellenic gov'munt does all what he is able. And he has done gooddill, Monsieur Paul. He has swip away the piraäte from the tsea, and many taime he has draive the klephts to the top of the mountains. He gives protections all which he is able; he sends soldiers with the travéller, and he demands no recómpense for the protections. We are not rich laike to you, Monsieur Paul, but we have helluped to pay the ransom of foreign captives, although it is not our obligaätion. When Lorrd Muncaster and his friends were captive, King Georgias offered his royal bodee for the hostaäge. What can we do more? But it is not enough. The naätions say the saäme black lies as if his Majestee and all the Greeks are klephts. Oh, Monsieur Paul, shall you not have the compassion with us? Is it not one gret infamee?"

Major Paul had no disposition to tempt further the little Hellenist's patriotic ardor, particularly as the inquisitive palikars had moved their chairs nearer, and had evidently gathered some inkling of the nature of the discussion, although probably not one of them understood a word of English. He readily assented to the injustice done to the Greek nation, and in characteristic language expressed his sympathy.

"But," he added, his thoughts taking a more practical turn, "I must say, professor, this talk has not stimulated my appetite for an excursion to the Taygetus. To tell the truth, I feel a little— How do I know that I sha'n't be gobbled up, as Muncaster was?"

"Oh, my friend, have not fear. You shall be saäfe there laike as you are saäfe in Athens. The klephts never come into the Peloponnése. They are all in the North. The Mainotes are a rude pipple, but they are honést and also they are hospitaäble. No travéller takes the escórt when he goes among them. But the Hellenic gov'mnnt shall give to you the escórt, if you shall ask him, as I have said to you." Then, drawing his little figure up to its full height, he concluded with the reassuring reminder: "*I* shall be your guide, Monsieur Paul!"

When the subject of the excursion came up in the family circle, no one was more enthusiastic in its favor than Madeline. The country of the old Spartans! The mountains where they left their sickly babies to perish! The rocky, pathless wilderness! The Morea and the Ægean spread out before them like a panorama! The mules and the pack-saddles, and a thousand romantic adventures! The brigands, too, the brigands! "Oh, papa, when shall we start?"

"When shall *we* start!" cried her father, when he could recover his breath; "who said anything about *your* going?"

"But I *am* going, am I not?"

"Great Blue Dragon! I should as soon think of your going for a soldier! No, no, my pet; you and your aunt Eliza will study art and architecture in Athens, while Robert and I take this little trip by ourselves."

"Professor Tsáras assures us it is perfectly safe," timidly ventured Aunt Eliza.

"What! you want to go, too?"

"I should like to very much, if it would be agreeable."

"*You*, a sensible American woman of forty!"

"I beg your pardon—thirty-nine."

"Well, that's too old for such insane nonsense. One would suppose twenty-one *ought* to be," with an indignant glance at his daughter. "'Mules and pack-saddles!' I *should*— You two have persuaded me to do a great many silly things, but you won't make a fool of me this time. Do you think I'm such a stark, staring idiot as to take you on a journey you couldn't endure for a day? H'm'ph! I should be as bad as your Spartans with their babies!"

"May we go, papa?" Madeline asked, with her most seductive smile. She knew the opposition would soon be exhausted at this rate.

"*No!*" thundered the major; "of course you won't go. 'Mules and pack-saddles!' You'd look well on a pack-saddle, *you* would! and your aunt Eliza— Grandmother of John the Baptist! she'd tumble off more than forty times a minute!"

"Oh no, Warren, I think not. I'm considered a very respectable horsewoman."

"I say you *would!* What do you know about it? Do you think the Greek mountains are like Jepson's riding-school? You talk about brigands!"—turning fiercely back to his daughter— "I suppose you think they're the fascinating gentlemen that sing in the opera—slouched hats with plumes, silk, and gold lace, and slashed sleeves. Ollendorff's Greek Grammar! You'd like an introduction, wouldn't you? You'd find their etiquette a little different from Newbury Street. You wouldn't fall in love with any of 'em, I'll swear—though they might fall in love with *you*—to your everlasting sorrow!"

"Ladies *have* gone plenty of times, and got back safely," urged Aunt Eliza.

This brought on another peal. It thundered and lightened and hailed, until the meteorological magazine gave out, when the usual and expected result followed:

The ladies went.

IV.

THE TAYGETUS.

THE American Minister obtained from the Hellenic Government a circular letter addressed to the various demarchs through whose domains the party was to pass, bespeaking their kindly offices. The Government also sent despatches to the same officials, advising them of the honor in store for them. If there *were* any brigands on or near the projected route, therefore, their game was pointed out to them in ample season.

During the weeks which Major Paul had spent in Athens, he had become friendly with the American Minister, who very gladly showed his friendship by offering his yacht to transport the party from the Piræus to Gýtheion, whence they were to proceed on horseback to Sparta.

Notwithstanding repeated assurances that there was not the slightest occasion for a military escort anywhere south of the Isthmus, Major Paul had persistently asked for one. So, on reaching Sparta he found a lieutenant and six *gens-d'armes* awaiting him.

Apart from its associations, the renowned city of Lycurgus presented but few attractions. Very little of the old city remains. The Americans inspected the ruins of a tomb, alleged—probably falsely—to be that of Leonidas, and an amphitheatre where the Spartans were assembled when the news came of the disastrous defeat at Sellasia.

"They recived the intelligence," said Tsáras, "with indifférence, although it maäde them súbjéct to the Macedonians. They sit still unt'l the trajedce was finish."

Beside these two objects and a temple or two, they saw little except a collection of poor dwellings, whose inhabitants resembled their remote predecessors only in the extreme simplicity of their fare. It is true the modern city has, within the last few years, made a considerable advance in prosperity and civilization; still the prophecy of Thucydides, that from the remains of the two cities posterity would have reason to under-estimate Sparta as much as to over-estimate Athens, has been amply fulfilled.

But when our travellers looked beyond the city they saw enough to admire. Along the west were ranged the five grand, snow-capped peaks of the Pentedactylon. In the east towered Mts. Parnon and Tarax. Between these the fertile valley of the Eurotas stretched up and down as far as the eye could see. The mountains form huge natural bulwarks, and show why no artificial defences have ever been constructed. The strength of the Spartan hegemony, which lived on and on while everywhere else aristocracy was tottering to the ground, was due not more to the laws of Lycurgus than to the topography of Laconia. Sparta, with her river, her garden-like environs, and her gigantic natural walls of defence, formed a stronghold impregnable alike by assault or siege. Her *periœci* starved among the mountains, while, within her own little area, it was easy to keep her foot upon the necks of the helots.

From Sparta Major Paul and his party took up their line of march for the Taygetus. The path led through magnificent groves of olives, mulberry and fig trees, and plane-trees planted in the beginning of the Turkish rule. They soon reached the village of St. John, whose houses were almost hidden in foliage—a very romantic little town. Continuing farther among the mountains, they came to the great rock of Mistra, at the very base of the Taygetus, from which it is separated by deep gorges. Upon this rock is built a city whose paved streets rise, one above another, in the most picturesque irregularity—a densely populated city in the heart of the wildest solitude! Here they spent the night so comfortably that Madeline was quite disappointed.

Early the next morning they found, a little beyond Mistra, several curious old churches, one of which, dedicated to St. Nicholas, was so hidden among rocks, trees, and shrubbery that it was with the greatest difficulty that they penetrated into the interior.

"Well," said Griffin, surveying the scene with undisguised disgust, "we've made a gallant fight, my brave comrades, and here we are in the citadel. Now

let us count the spoils. They certainly are *spoiled*
enough to satisfy even Madge. Item, one ruined
staircase. You ought to admire that, coz, for it is in
worse repair than the Parthenon itself. Item, three
broken candlesticks. Item, a decayed painting of an
angel—or is it a fish ?"

" That's a fair example of your artistic discrimina-
tion," retorted Madeline. " Those are as good wings
as I ever saw. Did you take them for fins ?"

" I didn't know but it might be a flying-fish, you
know. Item, a mouldy portrait of an old duffer with
one eye, a fragment of a nose, and no chin."

" Pardon," broke in Tsáras ; " that is not a ' duffer,'
Monsieur Griffin ; he is a empéror. He is the Empéror Alexius Commenus, who builted the chúrch."

" Robert is nothing, if not irreverent," said Madeline.

" Now for a lecture."

" Don't flatter yourself. I shall wait until I have
a more appreciative audience."

Then she lectured him roundly.

" Monsieur Paul," said Tsáras, after they had finished their inspection of the Church of St. Nicholas,
" what way shall you go ? The way to the north is
four day journey ; the other, across the mountains, is
onlee three day journey, but he is múch more difficúltee."

" Do you know both routes ?"

" Aah, yeas. I know all Greece."

" Well, then, we'll go the shortest way."

The rest of the party voted unanimously in favor of the route across the mountains. They had already become somewhat accustomed to the difficulties of mountain travel, and felt equal to any effort or adventure.

As they entered upon the steep, scrambling, rocky path, the cavalcade proceeded in the following order:

Lieutenant and three *gens-d'armes*.

Major Paul and Tsáras.

The two women.

Cook and assistant cook.

Mules with baggage, including beds and a good supply of comestibles, it being wisely resolved not to trust to the boasted hospitality of the Mainotes.

Three *gens-d'armes*.

Griffin was not confined to any one position. He constituted himself a sort of chief-marshal, and was, by turns, in front and rear, jabbering broken Greek with the escort, calling out diatribes from the major, quarrelling with Madeline, and joking with Tsáras, whose superficial dignity had long since given way to the jaunty young fellow's good-natured impudence.

Everybody was well armed. Even the women carried little revolvers in their belts, which furnished Griffin with the theme for endless witticisms.

For an hour they passed through the wildest glories of nature, rendered doubly magnificent by the purple and gold of morning. At length a wide valley suddenly spread out before them, checkered with olive, mulberry, and orange groves, patches of poplars, willows, and open fields, which ploughs were at that moment gradually turning from green to dark red. Thickly wooded hills stood around the valley, their summits swimming like islands in lakes of rosy mist. Below these were grassy slopes tinted with anemones of every shade, among which groups of peasant children were playing in the sunshine. Here and there on the hills could be seen the tall white fortresses of the Mainotes, among whom a sort of feudal system is still in force, while in the distance gaped the huge black jaws of the Taygetus gorge.

"Now, then, Madeline," said Major Paul, after they had gazed a while in silence, "give us the æsthetic points of this view."

"You nid no better guide as Miss Paul," interposed Tsáras, partly in pique, partly because he would lose no opportunity to compliment the beautiful and sprightly young American.

"Interpreter, you mean, Charles," said Griffin, using one of the numerous English names which he had bestowed on the little Greek. "As a guide to our feet and a lamp to our path, Miss Paul would be a disastrous failure. Your labor is fairly divided. You guide our mules; she guides us. You interpret the language of man; she the language of nature. You are Greek; she is Saxon. You are of the earth, earthy; she is of the heavings, heavingly. Don't be jealous."

"'Jealous,' Monsieur Griffin—it is not jealous: it is admiraätion. Miss Paul is more your guide as I am."

"Dear me!" cried Madeline, "I beg Monsieur Tsáras's pardon for trespassing on his province. I shall do so no more, I assure you, monsieur. In fact, I couldn't if I would. I am literally talked out."

"While Charles is as fresh as ever," added Griffin. "At the start I would have laid two to one on you. You can use the biggest words, but he can wind you, Madge. Let me try *my* hand. Look at that view now. Isn't it glorious? With what calcareous majesty those cærulean—"

"Oh, for the sake of—"

"Look at that ploughman. How his red breeches creep along the furrowed field, like a gigantic lady-bug along a blade of grass!"

"Oh, come, come!" put in the major. "Have done with your nonsense. That's too fine a view—I don't blame Madge for being disgusted with you. Go ahead, Madge, tell us about it."

"Yeas," added Tsáras, "we are attention to Miss Paul's views of the view."

"*Impressions*, you mean, Charlie," corrected Griffin. "'Views of the view' is not good enough for a pun, and it is bad rhetoric."

"I wish that you shall spik Greek, Monsieur Griffin," retorted the nettled Tsáras; "then I shall be so kaind to correct your little mistaüke too, also."

"Thank you, professor; English is good enough for me."

"Order!" shouted the major. "Madeline has the floor."

"Calling a mule's back a floor," began the irrepressible Griffin, "reminds me of the Irishman's—"

"By the Suffering Job! if you interrupt her again I'll pitch you into the middle of the valley! Do you hear? Go on, Madeline."

"Really, papa, I am so overwhelmed by the graceful and elaborate introduction you gentlemen have given me, that I feel altogether inadequate to the occasion. Besides, I am already talked out, and I'm afraid I am *felt* out, too. I've glowed and thrilled, and thrilled and glowed, in spite of Robert's fooleries, till I can glow and thrill no longer, even at such a scene as this. It seems to me less modern than almost anything else we've seen. Those odd, warlike little castles bristling on those rocks, scowling so angrily down on that Arcadian valley, carry me back to the Dark Ages."

The word "Arcadian" roused her father's ire. "'Arcadian!'" he snarled, "of all the swindling—"

"Order!" shouted Griffin.

"Papa is perfectly in order," said Madeline, "I've finished my address."

"Of all swindling, classical humbugs, that word is the meanest! What is Arcadia but a miserable miasmatic swamp? What are the Arcadian shepherds that so much fine poetry is written about but a race of lying, thieving, lazy, squalid scoundrels, that ought to be guillotined without mercy? Oh, *I've* seen 'em!"

"Aah," protested Tsáras, "you spik únjústice, Monsieur Paul. You have sin onlee the East, which is marsh. You mus' visit the Western Arcadia. It is no Stymphaälian marsh there, Monsieur Paul, but

mountains and noble forést. It is laike the Switz'-
land. In the Western Arcadia a rude but manly
raüce keeped their herd of sheeps, and they hunted
the bears, too, also. Arcadia have deraive his naüme
from those bears. You remember the stoary, Monsieur Paul ?—

"' *Callisto Arcadios erraverat ursa per agros.*'"

"No, I don't recall it at this moment," replied the
major, winking at Madeline.

" The Arcadian pipple," resumed Tsáras, " were a
hardee pipple. They lived upon the acorns and the
flesh of the pig, and although they haved not the en-
érgee and the enterpraise, they were ver' strong in
their bodee. They were ver' temperaüte, too, also.
A fountain was at Kleitor which maüke them to haüte
the wines."

"I shall be careful how I drink at Arcadian fount-
ains," muttered Griffin.

"Their bes' young men refused to dwell in Arcadia in so simple laife—but they went 'way to other
etaüte, and they faighted with the both saides when it
was war."

" Are those little castles the former strongholds of
the klephts?" asked Madeline, "or were they to protect honest people from them ?"

"No, Miss Paul. The klephts were never in per-
mánent dwelling, and they never caüme ver' mooch
down here. Those castles were builted in those ún-
settle taimes when every man look upon every man
laike the assassin. You see each of those castles are

on a rock elevaäte—he is on a akropolis by his own self. You see a perféct illústraäition of the mediæval feudal systems. Each of those little white castles are baronial castles in the miniaäture."

" How romantic!"

" And those," said Griffin, nodding towards a party of dirty, ragged urchins, who had been gathering scarlet anemones by the way-side, and were now staring open-mouthed at the passing cavalcade—"those, I suppose, are some of the *barons* in miniature."

" Yeas; I thing it is, Monsieur Griffin."

" Is there no need of such strongholds nowadays?" pursued Madeline. " Are there not still feuds among these rough people?"

" No more feud than it is feud in your countree."

" They'd come handy, though," suggested Major Paul, " if there should be an invasion of northern klephts, wouldn't they?"

" I do not know 'handee.' "

" Useful, convenient."

" Aah, yeas. They would be ver' useful."

Here Aunt Eliza bustled up, and gave signs that she had something to say. Tsáras turned to her with respectful inquiry.

" You really think, Professor Tsáras, that there is no probability of our meeting any brigands, do you?"

" Brigands? No, *kurátza;* no brigands are in the Taygetus. If they are here, they would be afraäid at us with the escórt more than we would be afraäid at them."

"One sight of aunty's seven-shooter would scatter 'em," said Griffin, with an exasperating grin.

"I sincerely hope there will be no test of the courage of *any* of us," retorted Aunt Eliza, with a scornful sniff.

"I don't know. I believe I should rather like the chance of bagging a brace or two of such game."

"It does not occur to you," put in Madeline, "that you might possibly be bagged yourself."

"Well, I should die in a noble cause. I should make a handsome *corpus*, shouldn't I? Imagine me with my marble features turned up to the stars, like a dismantled Greek statue. How would this style do?"

He threw his head back and closed his eyes, pursing his lips into a cupid's bow.

"Robert!" cried Madeline, angrily.

"And you would shed a silent tear or two over my grave, wouldn't you, cousin dear?"

"I suppose you expect me to be overwhelmed with horror and admiration, but I'm not in the least. You think your talk sounds brave, but it doesn't—it only sounds brutal and disgustingly shallow. I know very well you don't want to die any more than the rest of us. You wouldn't joke much if the brigands should really come. I'll warrant you'd be the very first to run."

To tell the truth, I am a little ashamed of my heroine's sharpness of tongue. But what can I do? She's a true daughter of her father, and everybody knows *he* has the best, warmest heart in the world, rave he or storm he never so fiercely.

Griffin's good-nature was usually imperturbable; but this tirade, particularly the closing taunt, appeared to penetrate his thick armor. Without a word in reply, he rode forward and joined the *gens-d'armes*, with whom he remained for hours. Madeline gradually became pensive. Her answers to Aunt Eliza became more and more short and irrelevant. Finally she said, in a low voice, "I'm very sorry I called him a coward. We women don't realize how sensitive they are on that point."

"Oh, my dear, don't fret your heart about that. He'll be back here soon, frivolous as ever. To tell the truth, I shouldn't be sorry if you *had* given him his quietus for a while. I'm tired of his twitter-twatter."

"Don't be ungrateful," returned Madeline, blazing up. "We should all have been stupid enough without him."

The progress of the cavalcade through the valley created an intense excitement among its rural denizens. The farmer left his plough, which, judged from its appearance, might have been the very one left by Cincinnatus in its furrow; the housewife left her loaves, the washer-woman left her linen by the riverside, and one and all came running to see the strangers, to ask who and what they were, whence they came, whither they were going, and wherefore. Among the men there were some of magnificent physique. It would not have been difficult to fancy these the lineal descendants of the famous Three

4

Hundred, had it not been for their speech, which was
the exact reverse of "Laconic."

"Do you suppose your famous Hector Vyr, that
we've heard so much about, is any finer fellow than
one of these?" asked Madeline of Professor Tsáras.

"Oh yeas, Miss Paul. Hector Vyr is a *basiliás*
in compare to them. He is a maighty bodee; he is
a maighty intellects; he is ver' gret beautee, laike
to those statues of old Greece."

"Dear me! We must not fail to find him, on any
consideration whatever."

"Aah, we shall *not* faind him. He would run away
from us, laike as he is a waild man of the forest."

"Then we must run after him, and capture him
for the Zoölogical Museum at Central Park."

"Ha, ha, ha! I thing *you* capture him, Miss Paul.
Not any other shall capture him."

The women in the crowd, as a rule, looked stunted
and labor-worn; but no amount of oppression and
fatigue could mitigate their ceaseless chatter.

When they halted for supper in a valley bright
with oleanders, Griffin had evidently forgotten his
pique. He seasoned, with his usual amount of fun,
the luxurious meal of bread, fresh goat's milk, and
new cheese curd. In the cool of the evening he and
Madeline strolled up the side of a savage hill, furred
with little pines and bristling armies of thistles.
The great, ugly blossoms of tall hollyhocks, growing
wild, stared at them from the way-side. Here and
there on the naked rocks they found the flowers of
the caper-vine.

"Did you enjoy your talk with the guards this afternoon, Robert?" Madeline asked, critically examining one of the wonderful flowers last named, which he had plucked for her.

"Very much. We found each other quite entertaining."

"What could you find to say for so long a time?"

"Oh, there were plenty of things to talk about. They told me all about the discipline in the Greek army, and their scrimmages with the klephts. According to their account of themselves, we have some of the greatest heroes in the world for our escort. I wasn't gone so very long, was I?"

"Nearly three hours."

"Oh no; impossible. It couldn't have been more than two. You ought to be thankful for even that relief." There was a slight perceptible tremor in his voice.

"Robert," burst out Madeline, putting her hand on his arm, "I want you to forgive me for being so unkind and unjust to you to-day."

"Nonsense, Madge. Who said you were unkind or unjust?"

"Not you. You are only too indulgent. It is my own conscience that upbraids me."

"Tell your conscience to keep the peace. What business is it of hers, anyway? If you and I can't have a comfortable, friendly little spat without her interference, it's time she packed up and went home."

"Well, that's like you, Robert. With all my

fault-finding of you, you have one great, admirable virtue which far outweighs all my lesser ones."

"Oh, come now, none of that. I know what I am as well as you. I know I'm a coarse-grained, irreverent chap, without a particle of poetry or sentiment in my composition. I know how I ride rough-shod over all your finest fancies, and continually break up your poetic rhapsodies with my ill-timed nonsense. But what can I do, Madge? I can't very well change my nature. You may have heard a recondite remark in reference to the leopard and the Ethiopian, which applies to my case. If it were not for you, I don't know as I would care to change my spots. As far as I am concerned, I am happy enough as I am. There's an awful lot of drudgery in becoming what you call 'highly cultivated,' and I am essentially and congenitally lazy. As I have often told you, I hate work of all kinds. Why shouldn't I? Doesn't Sir William Hamilton call work pain? What's the nigger's—I beg your pardon — what's the negro's ideal of paradise? A place from whence all kinds of labor are banished, like foul fiends from the Christian's paradise. And, by the same token, is the Christian's ideal very different? 'He has gone to his eternal *rest*,' I believe, is the favorite epitaph."

"Oh, Robert, can't you talk a single hour without being sacrilegious?"

"I assure you nothing was farther from my intention. Isn't what I say true? Don't they say, 'His labors are over?' Haven't you always been taught that heaven is an eternal Sabbath of rest?"

" Rest from trials and sufferings, that means—not rest from labors—that is, occupations."

" Well, labors and sufferings are synonymous terms with me. It has always been so, and I am afraid it always will. I was always at the very foot of my class in college — not, I flatter myself, from any marked deficiency in natural parts, but from sheer, dogged laziness. How in the world I picked up the smattering I have of Greek and Latin is really a mystery, for I do not remember ever studying a lesson in my life."

" Exaggeration always weakens," interrupted Madeline.

" I used the word 'study' in its true sense. I say I always hated work and always shall. And of all kinds of work, 'self-cultivation' is, by all odds, the hardest. I suppose, if I could only make up my mind to the effort, I might in time be able to work myself up to the pitch of appreciating the Parthenon and that old decayed Church of St. Nicholas as you do. But heavens! think of the labor. Imagine the subtle, endless pain Phidias must have endured before he was able to design his statues and his temples, with their Ionic curves and their aërial perspective! Imagine the mental tortures which have spun out the Concord Philosophy, whatever that may be!"

" It is all a mistake, Robert," replied Madeline, earnestly, " a tremendous mistake. It is *not* true that all kinds of labor are painful. There is a vast difference between the labor of the negro slave and that of Phidias and the Concord philosophers,—though I don't profess to know anything of *them* except by reputation."

Robert laughed.

"Well, what amuses you?"

"Nobody seems ashamed of his ignorance on that subject. Even you hastened to assure me of your ignorance, as if you were afraid I should think you *did* understand them."

"Why do you say 'even' I? Have I impressed you as a Blue Stocking?" asked Madeline, quickly.

"Not in the least, my dear cousin; that is, not disagreeably. I have always been a humble admirer of your accomplishments—your musical skill, your knack at verse-making, your exquisite appreciation of art and nature, and all that sort of thing."

"I am afraid your admiration has been cheaply earned. But I want to tell you that whatever of such things I have has been acquired without anything like what you call painful drudgery. I have been conscious only of pleasure."

"Oh, well," rejoined Robert, as he carelessly sent a flat stone skimming over the low trees down the slope, "*you* were born so, I wasn't. That's the difference."

"No," protested Madeline; "the difference is not so much a natural one as it is a different way of looking at things. It is more a difference of opinion than of nature. You and I have conceived different notions of the values of things, that's all. But I say

again to you, Robert, and most solemnly, that you
have made a great mistake. You don't know how
much you lose of the best and sweetest things in
life by your habit of viewing everything in either
a ludicrous or what you are pleased to call a sensible light. If I could only change your *opinions*, I
should have no fears for the result."

"Well," sighed Robert, violently switching off a
big thistle-top with his walking-stick, "perhaps you
are right. As I have told you several times, I don't
pretend to understand myself very well—the subject
is too deep for my limited comprehension."

"And so our talk must end in a stupid old joke!"
cried Madeline, provoked and disappointed.

"Heigh-ho, didn't I tell you I was incorrigible?
You can't carve a marble statue out of a block of
pumice-stone. But tell me, Madge," he said, his
whole manner suddenly changing, "is it going to
make any difference in our—in your— Sha'n't you
love me just as well?"

Madeline clasped his arm affectionately with both
her hands. "You are my own dear cousin Robert,"
she said; "and I love you for your good heart, your
inexhaustible good-nature, your patience under my
numerous provocations. But, as for— It is as I have
always told you, Robert."

He shook off her hands angrily. "And so, because
I can't go into raptures over a rotten old church, or
write idiotic sonnets to the moon, you can't return
as true a love as a man ever offered!"

"No, Robert, it is not that. Can't you believe

me a sensible woman? I know how little poetry and all that have to do with real life—but *poetry* is not the only thing you have just acknowledged that you have no taste for. You—"

She was about to say a very pertinent but humiliating thing, but her good heart forbade, at that time, at least. "If I could feel towards you as you wish," she went on, after a moment's hesitation, "I solemnly assure you that our differences of opinion on any subject would not make the least *real* difference."

"*If* you could—but it is those very differences that prevent you, is it not?"

"I don't know. Your peculiar tastes and inclinations—you can hardly expect me to sympathize with *them*, can you?"

"I understand you perfectly," he answered, bitterly. "You could trust your future to an unromantic man, but not to a lazy one. You are right. Adversity might come. Riches have wings. Yes, you are sensible, Madeline Paul, eminently sensible. Oh, what a fool I have been! what a consummate fool!"

"You read me with your own sordid mind," retorted Madeline, turning pale in the twilight. "If your riches were multiplied tenfold, and I knew with positive certainty that they would increase hour by hour to the day of your death, I would not trust you with my future!"

She stepped haughtily in advance. Griffin followed, silently and dejectedly whipping off the thistle-tops with his stick. Thus they walked on till they came to the steep, rocky bed of a cataract, now dry, lying directly in their path. He sprung to her assistance. As he did so, she caught the mournful pathos in his face and mien, and her heart swelled.

"Oh, Robert!" she burst forth, "I love you dearly, and we might be so happy together, if you only would."

"It isn't the kind of love I want," he replied, hoarsely. "Give me time, Madge. I will change. I promise it. You'll see a different man in me—only give me time—and hope."

She shook her head sadly, pityingly.

"Then I—" he began in a loud, fierce tone, but instantly checked himself. They returned without another word to the encampment.

This consisted of a humble *cafinet* built of stones, and partly covered by an awning of black goat's-hair cloth, in which Miss Wellington (Aunt Eliza) and Madeline were quartered. A few feet distant from the *cafinet* a large fire was kindled, fresh boughs of spruce-fir were brought as an under-mattress for the beds, and on these the men of the party stretched themselves, in the pure, dewless air, cooled by the snows of the mountains and perfumed by the fragrance of the valley, under a sky so clear that the stars scarcely twinkled. The only sounds that broke the stillness of evening were the tinkling of distant sheep-bells, the reeds of shepherds, the soft, clear notes of the cuckoo, and the "*brekekekéx koáx, koáx*" of the frogs in the depth of the valley.

V.

THE BRIGANDS.

WHAT unhappy wight is that who hath never breathed the air of morning in the mountains, having slept in the open air? Let him not die until he hath tasted this most dainty tidbit at the banquet of nature. Till then, he shall not know the full extent of his own capacity for the enjoyment of his physical senses. Till then, he shall never know how blue and purple and golden is the sky, how green is the grass, how white is the snow, how sparkling are the waters—nor how clear are his own eyes, how keen his ears, how elastic his lungs, how resounding his voice, how bounding his step.

Till they had experienced this rare pleasure, our travellers certainly had never known what an exquisite flavor there is to crisp toast and broiled lamb, or what an utterly insignificant task it is to break camp and resume a difficult, dangerous journey.

They passed through a succession of olive orchards, currant plantations, vineyards, and wheat-fields whose dark-red loam was just beginning to turn green. In the glens were little groves of oleander and myrtle. Sage, wild thyme, and mastic shrub thinly covered the "stony shoulders of the hills." At short inter-

vals they halted by the side of little streams to rest
and water their animals, while Aunt Eliza and Madeline plucked bouquets of crocuses and violets, and
listened to tho' loud song of the nightingale and the
softer, more musical notes of the blackbird.

Gradually the country became wilder. Cultivated
fields disappeared, and only an occasional hut of
stones and mud gave evidence of human occupation.
Not far from noon they came to a village of twenty-
five or thirty of these huts. From his gestures and
manner with certain of their tenants Tsáras appeared
to be inquiring his route. The fact that the answering hands pointed in different directions was not reassuring, and, although Major Paul and his party had
by this time become somewhat inured to the prevailing Greek custom of misdirecting and misstating dis-
tances, they began to be seriously alarmed. In reply
to the major's questions, however, the guide said
there was no cause for anxiety; he knew perfectly
well what he was about. But the path grew still
narrower and more obstructed by branches and un-
dergrowth, and finally divided into two branches
equally worn, or rather *un*worn, by travel. Tsáras
and the commander of the escort began to wrangle
on the question which of these branches to take.
Major Paul promptly ordered, Right about, march.

Tsáras remonstrated.

The major repeated his order more peremptorily.

Tsáras entreated.

The major got thoroughly angry, and stormed the
little guide into silence and acquiescence.

But it proved easier to order a return than to exe-
cute the order. After a while they failed to recognize objects which they passed. The path became
more and more difficult, and at last merged into a
flume of blue limestone, which led—no one knew
whither. A little distance at one side of the flume
was the sharp edge of a precipice overhanging a
frightful chasm, to glance into which took the breath
away and made the heart stand still. No one—guide,
escort, or tourist—could longer doubt the truth—

They were lost in the mountains!

The rich color faded from Madeline's cheek; but
her mind was soon diverted from her own situation
by the greater, or at least more demonstrative, terror
of Aunt Eliza. Griffin, who had all day been sullen
and taciturn, was the only one who remained cool
and collected. Major Paul bore down upon the woe-
begone guide like a centaur charging in battle.

"You infernal scoundrel!" he roared, "what do
you mean by getting us into this scrape? Didn't
you tell me you had been over the route?"

"Oh, Monsieur Paul, I beseech you not spik so
loud. I *have* been over the route—but—but—but—
it have been *changes*. The path is no more laike as
he was. I tzwear to you, Monsieur Paul, I have
done the ver' bes' that I was aäble—by my honor,
Monsieur Paul, I tzwear!"

"Done the best you were able! Idiot! Why
didn't you *stay at home?* That would have been the
best you were able, you gesticulating, speech-making,
Homer-quoting ass!"

But fury and resonant reproaches promised no help. A council was held, in which it was decided that two of the *gens-d'armes* should ride as far as possible up the flume, then dismount and make their way on foot until they could command the widest possible view of the surrounding country.

The scouts had scarcely disappeared, and the rest of the party were disposing themselves as comfortably as possible to await their return, when a tall figure stepped forth from the bushes and advanced leisurely towards them.

It was a man of thirty-five or forty, dressed in the Albanian costume—jacket and fustanelli of coarse white woollen stuff, and leggings of leather. From his bare head hung two heavy braids of shining black hair. His face was swarthy, and ornamented with a jetty mustache. He was armed with a pair of silver-mounted pistols and a yataghan. As he advanced he extended his arms and called out in a clear, ringing voice,

" *Kálos orizéte!*"

" He says 'Welcome,'" explained Tsáras, in a low, trembling tone.

The four *gens-d'armes* unslung their carbines and brought them to their shoulders.

" *Alt!*" (halt), ordered the lieutenant.

" *Kýttaxe' piso sou!*" (look behind you), replied the stranger.

Not thirty yards distant the *gens-d'armes* and their party saw a score of dark faces glaring over the thick bushes, each behind a long black tube.

"Robbers, by gorry!" ejaculated Major Paul, springing to his feet and drawing his revolver. "Madeline, my girl, come here."

But the more alert Griffin was already beside the two women, whom he was apparently trying to form into a hollow square.

The brigand, coming still nearer, spoke a few words, which Tsáras translated as follows:

"Throw down your arms, and you shall not be harmed. Attempt to fire, and that instant every man dies, and the women are our prisoners."

The order was sullenly obeyed.

The brigand stood motionless a few seconds, then made an impatient gesture.

"What are your commands?" asked the lieutenant.

"Make the woman give up that pistol, or take it from her."

Aunt Eliza still grasped her tiny weapon, her white lips pressed together in desperate determination.

"It's of no use," said Madeline, wonder-struck at her own calmness. "They have us at their mercy." She disengaged the pistol from the thin, nervous hand, which yielded mechanically to her gentle force, and threw it on the ground with the rest of the surrendered arms.

In the mean time the brigands, twenty strong, closed in around their prisoners, shouting, "*Zito!*" (huzzah), and manifesting in a hundred ways exultation over their bloodless victory.

They were, for the most part, vigorous young rascals, dressed like their leader, save that some of them wore shaggy capotes. They speedily relieved their prisoners of their watches and purses, ordered them to remount, and hurried them along the rocky pathway formed by the flume, five or six brigands being sent in advance to intercept the two *gens-d'armes* who were acting as scouts.

The chief soon opened a conversation with Major Paul, with the aid of Tsáras.

"You see," he began, "that we are well acquainted with your movements. We had the good-fortune to hear of your intended visit."

"Through the Greek Government, no doubt," replied the major, blazing with unutterable scorn and fury.

"Oh no, my good friend. You must not blame the Government. It was one of the Government's *messengers* that informed us—and he not *willingly*, by any means. The poor *gádavos* could not help himself."

The major uttered an inarticulate growl.

"We have been following you for the last four hours," the brigand went on. "You, I presume, are his nobility, the American *Kapitán* Paul?"

"*Major*, damn your impudence!" (It is hardly necessary to state that the less conciliatory passages in the major's remarks were translated with considerable freedom by the less impetuous, more politic interpreter.) "And now perhaps you will condescend to tell me what you are going to do with us?"

"Oh, you will know in good time, your nobility. But don't be uneasy. Make yourselves perfectly happy; we shall treat you like princes."

"That's the very thing we are afraid of," interposed Griffin, who rode immediately behind. "But tell him, Charley, that we are no princes. We are simple American citizens in extremely humble circumstances."

"Yes," added the major, with majestic anger, "and they will have to answer to the American Government—tell him that, too, Tsáras—a government that can depopulate this whole worm - eaten frontier of hell in a week!"

"Ah, you refer us to the American Government. We shall be happy to negotiate with so noble and famous a nation. I am sure they will show a liberality worthy of their wealth and glory. England, France, Germany—all the great nations—are always ready to pay our price for the sake of relieving their valuable citizens from embarrassment. But I beg your pardon. I have not introduced myself. I am the *Kapitán* Peschino, of whom you have doubtless heard. No? Alas, such is glory! I supposed everybody knew the exploits of the *Kapitán* Peschino."

He spoke with honest chagrin.

"Peschino?" asked Griffin, as if suddenly recollecting.

"Ah yes; *you* have heard of me, *Appénte?*"

"Are you not sometimes called his Reverence, *Father* Peschino?"

"No. It is my brother you are thinking of. He

is a priest at Mikro-Maina. It is not strange, however, that you should make the mistake—we are said to be very much alike."

Poor Griffin's face fell. His American jokes would all be lost on that complacent scoundrel.

The procession rapidly ascended the rocky pathway, a brigand at each bridle, until the report of firearms brought them to a sudden halt.

"It is nothing," shouted Peschino to his men. "They have found the two soldiers. Forward!"

They soon came up with the detachment. Both *gens-d'armes* and one brigand were wounded, one of the former badly. Peschino dressed their wounds with considerable surgical skill, graciously accepting Madeline's help. He then called up two of the unwounded soldiers.

"Take four of the mules, with rations for three days, and conduct your comrades home. Remind your commandant that he has not yet sent the three thousand drachmas to the demarch of Mikro-Maina, as he promised, and that I shall hold these two soldiers till he does. When you reach the base of the flume take the path to your right—keep always to your right, and you will easily find the road to Marathonisi. *Kālón kătĕvódion* (farewell); remember to bathe the wounds with cold water every hour—and may God send speedy healing!" .

The march was then resumed. On reaching the upper end of the flume, they struck into a rough, stony path, which, with many windings, up natural stair-ways, over narrow bridges, along the brink of

5

frightful precipices, finally brought them to a level open space. Here they found a large flat rock, above which rose an inaccessible cliff, divided through the middle by a fissure just wide enough to admit of the passage of one mounted man at a time.

This was evidently the gate-way to the robbers' stronghold. Within they were absolutely safe. The heaviest artillery would be powerless against that eternal masonry, and a little band of resolute men could hold that narrow Thermopylæ against any number of enemies, whom it would be but sport to topple over the precipices as they filed slowly up, one by one. Should the garrison weary of the sport, or should provisions become scanty, their enemies would find their stronghold like a last year's bird's-nest. They, with their prisoners, *should the latter live so long*, would be with the birds.

The brigands now busied themselves in the preparation of a sumptuous meal, obtained chiefly from the contents of their captives' panniers. Their own contribution consisted of three or four fine pheasants and sundry bottles of wine (*recinato*), which would have been good but for the villanous resin with which it was abundantly spiced. The flat rock formed an excellent dining-table, to which the confiscated dishes and napkins imparted a wonderfully civilized air, in strange contrast with its wild surroundings. The stimulating mountain air, together with the excitement and fatigue they had undergone, gave the whole party a sharp appetite. Hungry and exhausted soldiers will eat voraciously on the eve of the bloodiest battle. So our unhappy friends, not-withstanding their situation, did full justice to the banquet.

The captors were exceedingly jubilant over their easy and complete success, and they took the utmost pains to entertain their "guests," and to make them forget their uncomfortable predicament.

The meal over, the brigands sung hilarious songs in rough but not unmusical voices. Then they per-formed a wild Romaic dance, which their prisoners witnessed with something akin, at least, to interest.

"Well, your nobility," said Peschino, approaching with the interpreter, "I trust you are not so unhap-py as you expected to be."

"I could answer you better," replied the major, stiffly, "if I knew what you intended to do with us."

"Have a little patience. You shall know all in good time. In the mean time, neither you nor your friends shall receive anything but kindness from us. Cannot you judge my intentions from that? For example, I am going to allow you to be together as if you were at your own houses. No one shall in-trude upon your privacy. Is not that a comfort to you? How do I know what plots and conspiracies you will hatch out among yourselves? Is not that a favor and a great comfort to you?"

"It is indeed, Peschino," replied the major, with a long breath of relief. "I thank you for that with my whole heart, whatever else you may do. But you have little to fear from the plots and conspiracies of two weak women and two unarmed men."

"*Three* unarmed men," corrected Tsáras, with a look of grieved reproach that would have melted a stone.

"Of course, of course—*three* unarmed men." But there was a mental reservation. There should be no *interpreter* of "plots and conspiracies" admitted to the family councils.

As if to prove his good faith at once, Peschino ordered his men away from the prisoners, bidding them keep their distance on peril of his severe displeasure.

"Now, your nobility," he said, with a magnanimous wave of his hand, "you will have the goodness to excuse me for a time. Should you desire anything, it will be easy to find me." He turned to the women, placed his hand on his heart, bowed profoundly, and departed.

VI.

WITHOUT THE GATES.

Tsáras, too, although he yearned for a share in their mutual condolence, was considerate enough to leave the family by themselves around the flat rock. Madeline was the least downcast of the little group. The specious courtesy and kindness with which they had been treated thus far made her comparatively cheerful and hopeful. She spoke enthusiastically of the inestimable privilege they were then enjoying, none of the brigands being in sight, with the exception of a solitary sentinel at a very respectful distance.

"That is the only thing that surprises me," answered her father. "I expected the rascal would keep us apart, of course, until after the 'examination' he has promised. Madeline, have you any idea what I am worth?"

"Ten times your weight in diamonds!" answered the impulsive girl, in whom the transition from despair to hopefulness, however slight, produced a reaction no less surprising to herself than to the others.

"I'm afraid you'd find it hard to realize that amount on the property in the market. Come here and kiss me, you little Zouave. Now answer my question properly, you good-for-nothing rubbish. Do you know how much I'm worth?"

"I haven't the slightest idea, papa. I only know that we have everything that money can buy."

"Eliza, what do you know?"

"No more than Madeline does," sobbed the poor lady, raising her tear-disfigured countenance. "I wish, with all my heart, I didn't know as much."

"Well, I suppose I can trust to your discretion if you should be questioned. You don't know anything, of course, Robert."

"Thank you, uncle, you are pleased to be complimentary."

"Well, I am glad you people can joke, I am sure," said Aunt Eliza, in a tone of the deepest reproach.

"I have always thought those who cannot feel are the happiest."

"Feel!" cried Robert, "what's the use of feeling? We're all in a tremendous scrape, I'll admit. You and Madge ought to have taken Uncle Warren's and my advice. I suppose you realize that *now*. But crying and taking on forever isn't going to get us out of the scrape, is it? Come, aunty, be a man! See how plucky Madge is. She believes, as I do, that we are coming out all right.—What do I know, uncle? Why, you have lately failed, haven't you? You are reduced to the most abject beggary."

"Not too strong, my dear boy," replied the major, with a meagre smile. "Beggars don't travel all over Europe with their families for pleasure. These villains are not fools."

"They are fools enough to leave us to concoct our lies in private, and make them hang together," retorted Robert, airily.

"Oh, don't call them by that name," piped Aunt Eliza. "There is no occasion for— We can say everything that is required for our own advantage and still adhere to the strict truth. I wouldn't tell a falsehood even to save my life!"

"How about the rest of us?" insisted Robert. "Wouldn't you prevaricate a little to save *our* lives?"

"No good ever comes from evil."

"You hear her!" Robert exclaimed, turning indignantly to the other two. "Shall we let this woman sacrifice us all to her fanaticism?"

"You do your own duty, and trust me to do mine, Mr. Griffin!" retorted Aunt Eliza, forgetting her despair in her wrath.

"Didn't you just say that you wouldn't tell a—"

"Neither shall I. I'm not obliged to utter either truth or falsehood, am I? All the robbers in Greece can't make me speak if I *won't!*"

"*Brava!* I apologize most humbly. If you only won't spoil the effect of *my* lies, I shall be satisfied. Remember all: I am a poor devil of a student not worth a continental, and in debt for my education— a precious small debt *that* would be, based on its true value."

"I don't suppose it will make the slightest difference what any of us say," said the major, musingly. "They probably don't expect to get anything out of us by their 'examination.' If they did they certainly wouldn't be idiotic enough to leave us together like this. They'll set their own ransom, without much reference to us."

A gloomy silence followed.

"I don't believe they intend us any very great harm, after all," said Madeline, brightening up at length. "Their leader laughs a great deal, and I never was very much afraid of a man who laughs."

"Harm!" snarled her father. "All they want is our money, of course. They'll rob me and all my friends of every dollar we've got, cash or credit, and then they'll let me go, I suppose, to begin life over again."

"When we *do* get away," he went on, his passion

rising, "I'll see whether there's any virtue in the law of nations! This miserable little government has incurred a mighty responsibility, let me tell 'em."

"Oh dear!" sighed Aunt Eliza. "Don't you believe those soldiers will bring any one to rescue us?"

The major laughed with bitter contempt. "It's my belief that the army, government, and all are in collusion with the devils—pestilence rot their filthy bodies! Yes," he cried, his passion rising higher and higher, "pestilence, consumption, palsy, small-pox, cholera—leprosy, carbuncles, cancers, boils, pimples—"

This feeble anticlimax brought out a general laugh, in which, after a while, the major himself was forced to join. Even Aunt Eliza smiled, so potent an anodyne was her recent anger at her graceless nephew.

"Besides being absurd, you are terribly unjust, papa," said Madeline. "You forget those poor soldiers who shed their blood in our defence."

"Heh?"

"What better pledge of good faith can you ask than their *blood?*"

"Well, perhaps I *was* a little hard on the army. But suppose the whole army should come to rescue us, what could it do in this wilderness? Look at that rock! Besides, long before the advanced guard could scale the mountain, the infernal rascals would have us miles away. I don't want to dampen your good spirits, my darling girl, but we mustn't entertain any nonsensical hopes, for they will make our fate only the harder to bear when it comes."

"Fate! What do you mean? They don't want anything but our *money*, do they?"

"Isn't that enough, for Heaven's sake?"

"I can *work*, you know, dear papa. I can teach and paint and embroider and—"

"Wash and scrub," put in Robert, "and sell apples and peanuts, and do the professional Long-haired Lady, and—"

"Robert can help, too."

However Madeline had been annoyed by her cousin's "ill-timed facetiousness" in days gone by, it was peculiarly welcome to her now. Ever since their stroll together the evening before—which now seemed so long ago—she had felt a tender pity for him that made her resolve never to scold him again, whatever he might do or say. She was deeply grateful to him for having since made no allusion to the momentous conversation that had occurred. To all this was added admiration for the coolness, courage, and wonderful buoyancy of spirits he had displayed all through the trying ordeal they had been undergoing.

"Robert can help, too," she retorted, giving him a beaming smile from her eyes. "He can dig, and carry a hod, and exhibit as the Bearded Lady, and—"

"To *me*," broke in Aunt Eliza, with gloomy asperity, "the extraordinary levity of you two seems absolutely *heartless*, when we're all in such a horrible situation."

"Horrible? I think it is *sublime*," replied Rob-

ert, gayly. " You're always saying 'How romantic !'
—what do you want more romantic than this? Real
brigands, aunty, real brigands! None o' your 'su-
pers,' with false eyebrows and tin daggers. Then
look at that scenery—did you ever see anything
equal to that at the Boston Theatre? It would cost
the management a cool fifty thousand, at least, to
match it! Then look at the company—what could
be better? Besides a chorus of genuine brigands,
with genuine eyebrows, and genuine calves to their
legs, here is a picturesque group of real prisoners in
real distress—"

"Yes," moaned Aunt Eliza, "that's true enough.
Oh, if it were only a play!"

"Well, we can make believe it is, can't we?" replied the undaunted Griffin. " We've made real
evils of imaginary ones often enough·; now let us
make imaginary evils of real ones. There's Uncle
Warren: we'll suppose his vigorous cursing is only
a specimen of matchless elocution—it won't be the
first time such a supposition has been made. Madeline is the heroine, whose beautiful distress is soon
to be rewarded with a thousand dollars and a cham-
pagne supper."

"Thousand dollars! That's an unfortunate reminder, Robert," groaned the major.

"Never mind. For 'out' read 'in,' and it's all
right. Then there's Aunt Eliza—she's the second
lady, in love with the bucolic Professor Tsáras."

"You—aren't you ashamed of yourself?" exclaimed Miss Wellington, in crimson indignation.

"It's only the play, I tell you, aunty," laughed Griffin, gleefully. "I'm reading the cast, that's all. Professor Tsáras, an impecunious but high-souled Argive, with a romantic attachment to the lovely and equally high-souled Heloîse."

"Warren, will you tell him to stop?"

"Stop!" said the major, with a tremendous effort at severity.

"And I order you to stop, too," added Madeline, still more authoritatively.

"To hear is to obey. Next is Roberto Grifino, an—"

"Impudent clown, with a romantic attachment to himself!" breaks in Aunt Eliza, *staccato*. (Applause, in which Griffin himself takes the lead.)

Thus their talk went on, now light and animated, now melancholy, prophetic of the worst, now filled with bitter denunciation of their rapacious enemies. The full realization of their position came upon them only at intervals, in throes. Upon Griffin it seemed to come scarcely at all.

At length Peschino reappeared, issuing from the narrow passage in the cliff. Like an ambitious and hospitable landlord, he had been busy directing the preparations for a reception of his "guests" befitting their supposed station in life.

He was accompanied by the interpreter, through whom he announced to Major Paul that, if agreeable to "his nobility," he would like a private interview before conducting him and his party to their quarters. He led the way to a sort of wild promenade at the base of the cliff, bordered by wild thyme and myrtle.

"Before establishing you," he began, "in what I hope will prove not altogether an unpleasant residence among us, it is well that you should know something of our rules."

The major bowed in haughty disdain.

"As you have already seen, we treat our prisoners with the utmost kindness. We care for their comfort, health, even pleasure. Don't be concerned about the ladies of your party. I swear to you, on the honor of a klepht, that they shall not suffer the slightest indignity, nor more discomfort than our rude life renders unavoidable."

"That will be best for you," answered the major, savagely; "for I swear to you, on the honor of a free American citizen, and soldier of the greatest power on earth, that if any harm comes to them their friends will not rest till they are terribly revenged, if it takes twenty years."

Softened as this speech was in the translation, it brought a fierce, momentary scowl to Peschino's face. He said, however, with a sinister smile, "Speak freely, your nobility. We always allow our visitors to say what they will. It does us no harm, and it adds to their comfort. We welcome anything which will do that. But we digress. I began to tell you about our rules. As I said, we treat our guests with all due courtesy, and we expect similar treatment in return." This was said with an air of gentle rebuke that to a disinterested spectator would have been irresistibly comical. "You see that makes it pleasanter for all parties. We advise their friends of the terms upon which they may be released. These terms we make as reasonable as we can afford."

Major Paul gave vent to his feelings in a snort like that of a locomotive. It made the brigand start back as if in alarm.

"Your nobility is very demonstrative," he said, recovering himself. "Permit me to go on. If the friends are sensible enough to come to our terms, we restore the little trifles which have been deposited with us, and take an affectionate farewell of our guests, to whom, I assure you, we often become strongly attached."

"There is not the slightest doubt of that," grunted the major.

The brigand smiled, showing a row of even, white teeth under his jetty mustache. "You appreciate humor, I see. We shall be good friends in a little while. But"—and the smile gave place to an appalling look—"if, on the other hand, the friends prove to be fools, our guests meet with misfortune."

The captive glared at the villain for a few seconds. Then, with an effort at coolness which proved an ignoble failure, he replied, "Look here. You seem to have some of the elements of civility about you—what do you think of your treatment of honest people that never harmed you, and on whom you have not the shadow of a claim?"

"It is *business*, your brilliancy—honorable, brave

business. You call it crime. It is not crime; it is bravery." *

"H'm! and what sort of terms do you propose?"

"Pardon me. Your question is premature. We cannot decide so important a point without careful consideration. As I have already told you, you must pass an examination before our committee on finance. We have a regular form of interrogatories which you must answer on your oath."

"Oh, you have! But suppose I should refuse to answer?"

"I think you will not refuse, your brilliancy. We have means of persuading that rarely fail."

"You include that in the kind, courteous treatment you promise, I suppose. That is one of the ways you take to make your 'guests,' as you call them, comfortable and happy."

"Business is business, your nobility. We must go through with our forms, you know, although we do so as gently and courteously as is consistent with efficiency."

Major Paul drew a long, deep breath. "Now, Captain Peschino, I think you said you would allow me perfect freedom of speech?"

"Certainly."

"Well, then, give me your attention, if you please —and you, Tsáras, give him every word just as I say it: Of all the insolent, cold-blooded, cowardly, ven-

---

* The identical remark made by one of Arvanitaki's brigands on a similar occasion, "Δεν είναι κακία, είναι παλληκαρία."

omous, *slimy* reptiles that ever crawled, you are the vilest and the slimiest!"

It was of no use for Tsáras to paraphrase. The speaker's face, tone, manner, and gesture were a sufficient and perfectly literal translation of his words.

Peschino paled, and for the third time his eye was lurid with a fiendish light. But his voice was as smooth and mellow as ever as he replied, "We allow perfect liberty of speech, but we always *charge* for it. You will find it, as the innkeeper says, in the account. But pardon me, your brilliancy, you surely do not mean to intimate that we are deficient in manly courage?"

"None but cowards would have sneaked up to us as you did. If you had given us a fair chance, few as we were, we would have beaten you and driven you to your holes!"

"Do you think so? It was fortunate, then, that we did not. Bloodshed would have been very disagreeable. And now, with your kind approval, we will return to your friends, that I may have an opportunity of entertaining the charming young lady whose superior for beauty and spirit, I'll swear, will not be found in all Greece."

The major's clinched hand flew up; but before it fell, the consciousness of his utter helplessness swept over him. His hand and his face sunk together.

It was no part of Peschino's policy to exasperate his captives. He was sincere in his desire to render them as comfortable as the circumstances would permit. He wanted all their money, and with it as much of their good-will as he could get.

"My friend," he said, reproachfully, "you do me injustice. I feel only the most profound respect for your admirable daughter, and nothing shall tempt me to alarm or annoy her in the slightest degree. I mean simply to quiet any fear she may feel as to the safety of herself and her friends."

He approached Madeline and her aunt with the grace of a courtier. "Mesdames, is there anything that can be done to give you pleasure?"

"Oh yes," moaned Aunt Eliza; "let us go home!"

"You shall go very soon, *kurátza*. A day more or less in this mountain air, among this sublime scenery, can be only a pleasure and a benefit to you—especially while you are with friends whose chief delight it will be to supply all your wants, protect you from all harm—in short, devote themselves to your comfort and pleasure. You will find the *Kapitán* Peschino no such ogre as you imagine. Has the *kopeloúda* [dear young lady] observed the expansiveness of the view? That gray peak that towers so proudly above the rest is Mount Taleton; that other, nearly as lofty, but not so pointed, is Belvidere. You should ascend Belvidere, *kurá*. You would see all Peloponnése spread before you like a chart, with the sea and its islands stretching beyond to the sky."

"We have no fault to find with Grecian scenery," responded Madeline, determined not to be charmed by the gallant villain; "it is the *inhabitants* that we complain of."

"Ah, you will think better of us by-and-by "—tenderly. " When the time of parting comes, you will not execrate us as you do now; and when you are once more in your happy homes, surrounded by the elegancies of civilization, you will think of the poor wanderers in the wilderness with feelings of compassion instead of hatred."

"Provided you leave us any homes to be happy in," retorted Madeline, with icy indignation.

" *We* shall be the poor wanderers," wailed Aunt Eliza.

"Ah, mesdames, why will you allow your minds to dwell on that embarrassing subject? Fortune has been bountiful to you, while she has driven us to the mountains, where we should starve if we did not fight against her cruelty. What are a few thousand drachmas to his nobility? He will soon recover them, and be glad, perhaps, that he has shared his good things with his unhappy brothers."

"Would you be willing to advance him a small capital to begin business on?" asked Griffin.

There was no sarcasm to Peschino in this question.

"That shall be fully considered, young man," he said, reflectively, toying with a huge diamond on his little finger. "I sometimes loan money at reasonable usury on good security. That is a matter, however, that rests between the *Kapitán* Paul and myself." He turned again to Madeline. "Have you ever seen such scenery as this in America?"

"I can't think of such things now. I can think of nothing but my poor father. You will not ruin

6

him utterly, will you? He is not young, you see. It
will break his heart—it will break his heart! Oh,"
she cried, clasping her hands in pathetic appeal, "will
you not let us go? You have wealth enough, and
the recollection of your goodness will be a life-long
joy to you. Think what a blessed thing it will be
to you when you stand in the presence of your Mak-
er! You cannot take our gold with you *there*, Peschino—you can take only our blessings for your forbearance, and our prayers for His mercy to your
guilty soul, or our tears for your cruelty!"

As her tall form stood erect on the rock, her hand
pointing upward, her pure, white face looking down
on the dark-faced miscreant, she seemed an angel
from heaven menacing a fiend.

She needed no interpreter. Before her face and
voice, her accusing hand, Peschino's hardened ef-
frontery failed; his eyes fell to the ground, and, mut-
tering unintelligibly, he slunk away.

It was not alone the mesmeric power of Madeline's
appeal that overmastered him. Incredible as it may
appear, he had what he called a *conscience!* His
blood-stained hands were often clasped in prayer before the image of the Virgin, and a tithe of his booty
was always scrupulously set apart for his brother,
the priest of the little church at Mikro-Maina.

Madeline's victory, however, was short-lived. It
modified not a whit the destiny of herself and her
friends. Its only fruit was the promise to the priest
at Mikro-Maina of a generous percentage of the
American *ploúsios's* fortune.

VII.

THE INQUISITION.

As the sun sank towards the horizon, the brigands gathered together their effects and those of their prisoners, and conveyed them through the narrow pass in the cliff. The mules were tothered to the tough stems of the mastic and of other shrubs which grew sparsely around. The prisoners were then filed through the pass. They found it at least a hundred and fifty yards in length, and from two to fifteen or twenty in width. The sides formed nearly perpendicular walls of solid rock, varying from upward of two hundred and fifty feet at the entrance to less than one-tenth of that height at the other extremity. A rivulet coursed along its entire length, breaking into numerous little cascades and pools, and rendering the passage slow and difficult.

On emerging they saw a cluster of little huts, with chimneys, glass windows, and other conveniences of civilization, by no means an unwelcome sight. They had supposed that they were already at the summit of the mountain; but now they saw still another ascent stretching up before them, and terminating in a long, impassable ridge. In the deep valley between them and this ascent they saw a flock of sheep quietly grazing.

Major Paul gazed around in hopeless wonder.
"This is a mountain fastness, indeed!" he exclaimed.
"No hope of a rescue here. We may as well resign
ourselves to our fate. Nature seems to have designed it expressly for such incarnate fiends as you
are!"

"What does he say, Tsáras?" asked Peschino, exultingly.

"He says, 'This is, indeed, a mountain fastness.
There is no hope of rescue. We must resign ourselves to our fate. Nature has designed it expressly
for your safety against your enemies. You have
chosen very judiciously.'"

"No starving here, you see," said the delighted
brigand, pointing to the herd and the rivulet. "Good
shelter, plenty of arms and ammunition, books, pens,
and paper, cards, chess— You play chess, your nobility?"

In spite of himself, the major's face broadened.
He was passionately fond of the game.

"I see that you do; so do I. That will help to
kill a few days."

"Till the other killing begins," muttered Griffin
to himself.

"Now," said Peschino, "come and see how you
like your quarters."

The cleanest and most comfortable cabin was al-
lotted to Miss Wellington and Madeline; the next
best to Major Paul, Tsáras, and Griffin. They were
allowed the use of their own beds, on which they
slept soundly, notwithstanding the fatigues and ex-

citements of the day, their present anxiety, and, almost the worst of all, the boisterous hilarity of the brigands, which lasted half the night.

At dawn they were aroused by loud explosions close at hand.

"The soldiers! the soldiers!" exclaimed Aunt Eliza, springing out of bed, running to the door in her *robe de nuit*, and throwing it wide open. A couple of brigands happening to pass at that moment, modestly turned their faces away, one of them pointing to an invisible object in the horizon. In spite of this delicate and highly respectful conduct, however, the scandalized lady, forgetting that a mountain hut was not "built upon honor," like her mansion on Commonwealth Avenue, slammed the door together with such violent indignation that it fell from its hinges. The innocent but now wickedly-laughing objects of her wrath were constrained to come and make the necessary repairs, the two fair tenants meanwhile hiding behind the high-posted bedstead which had been provided as an especial luxury for them. Every little while, for hours afterwards, Madeline shook with laughter at the recollection of the embarrassing but comical incident.

The explosions which had caused the excitement proved to be only the customary discharge of firearms after an expedition, preparatory to cleansing and reloading them.

After a breakfast of toast, broiled lamb, and excellent coffee, Peschino invited his "guests" to ascend the cliff through which they had passed and witness the glories of sunrise in the Taygetus. In admiring the magnificent spectacle they almost forgot their troubles.

"Is there anything to report ?" Peschino asked of the stalwart sentinel who stood on the apex of the cliff.

"Nothing, *kapitán*," replied the man, hesitatingly; "that is—nothing of importance."

"What does that mean, you dog ?"

"I thought I saw something at early dawn, down *there*," pointing to a narrow opening among the stunted trees below.

"What was it ?"

"I thought"—deprecatingly—"perhaps it might be the—"

"Out with it, stupid !"

"The—the *Anthropodaímon*" (man-devil).

Peschino's swarthy face turned livid. "Listen !" he said to the cowering sentinel. "If I ever hear that fool's-word again, I will order the tongue that dares to utter it torn out by the roots ! Do you hear me ?"

The fellow glanced shamefacedly at the strangers, and muttered a sullen affirmative.

"These superstitious idiots," said Peschino, turning to Tsáras, "have a child's terror of a certain being that is said to haunt these regions. They think he is something more than mortal, bears a charmed life, kills with a glance from his eye, and all that preposterous, cursed nonsense. But I'll cure them of it, if I have to hang every man of them by his thumbs !"

"Have you ever seen this mysterious being?" Tsáras asked, eagerly.

"He is *not* a mysterious being," answered Peschino, with ineffable disgust. "He is nothing but a man like you or me. It was only three years ago that his father—just such another *Anthropodaimon* —was caught and disposed of as he deserved. But that's nothing to these numskulls! Seen him? Yes; and once I nearly captured him. *O Thĕĕ́ mou!* if I had been one minute quicker! But never mind, I'll track him to his den yet."

"Has he any other name than *Anthropodaimon?*"

"Of course he has—Hector Vyr."

"I knew it! I knew it!" cried Tsáras, in uncontrollable delight. "I have heard of him before."

"Well, and what then? Do you think he can help you to cheat me out of the game you have brought me?—How intently they are listening! Can they understand a word of what we are saying?"

"No; but they will expect me to translate it all to them when we are alone."

"Which you will, of course, do," significantly.

"I shall use *discretion.* But remember, Peschino, no *bodily* harm is to come to them, whatever else happens."

"I haven't promised that yet. Why didn't you make your bargain before you delivered me the goods?"

Let not Tsáras hoodwink the innocent reader as he has already partially succeeded in doing with the brigand chief. His crafty brain has devised a scheme which promises absolute safety to himself—perhaps even more—and at least life to the unfortunate foreigners whom his recklessness, not his treachery, has betrayed.

"Let us talk of this at another time," he said, uneasily. "My brain is not fertile enough to invent a translation for so much emphasis. What of this Hector Vyr?"

"Oh, he's a good fighter, that's all. He's a *sly* devil, though, and shoots little steel arrows from a noiseless, smokeless rifle, instead of bullets; so it is hard to see where he hides himself. My fellows are urging me to leave these snug quarters; but I am going to stay here, if for no other reason than to show them how foolish is their terror. Perhaps I shall catch him yet, who knows?"

"Well, well!" interposed Major Paul, losing his patience at last, "if you have finished your private confab with this bloody cutthroat, Tsáras, perhaps you will condescend to give *us* a little of your attention."

"Certainlee, Monsieur Paul. He was explaüin to me the little difficúltee which he have with the sentinél. I shall tell him to you when it is your wishes. It is all about the wond'ful Hector Vyr, Monsieur Paul. Aah, you shall faind those stoaries which I have tell to you is the truth."

"Oh, no doubt, no doubt," answered the major, indifferently. In Madeline's heart, however, there sprang up a sudden wild hope which even her sensible, practical reasoning the next moment could not entirely dispel.

Peschino now handed his field-glass to Major Paul, directing his attention to a wide-open space apparently only a few rods distant. "Do you recognize that place?" he asked.

"The flume?"

"Right. It is a kilométre off as the crow flies. Any one coming to us must pass that point, and cannot escape the vigilant eye of our sentry. We should have ample warning, therefore, to prepare for a defence, or, if we thought best, to withdraw to one of our other retreats. We have others, your brilliancy, nearly as good as this."

"What are those stones for?" asked Miss Wellington, pointing to two rows of bowlders arranged with such regularity as to indicate design.

"Let us go and look at them," anwered Peschino.

The bowlders were poised upon the very edges of the fissure through which the captives had passed the day before. Peschino asked Miss Wellington to try her strength upon one of them. She did so, and was astonished at the ease with which she sent it crashing down the precipice.

"Imagine a file of soldiers trying to make their way down there!" said Peschino, with a smile that sent shudders of horror through his listeners.

In the course of the forenoon Major Paul and Tsáras were summoned to the brigand chieftain's "office" for a "business interview." Hitherto the tension of the major's wrath had been so relieved by frequent liftings of the escape-valve that he had almost got to looking upon himself as the "guest" his captor called him. This summons, however, was like pouring a can of turpentine upon a smouldering fire. He obeyed with set teeth, flashing eye, and a tremendous boiling within.

At a rude table half covered with papers sat the irresponsible mountain despot, supported by two of his swarthy satellites. He motioned his prisoners to seats, and immediately began a grandiloquent panegyric on his "profession." This finished, he proceeded, with all the stateliness of a judicial magnate, to the inquisition.

The major, when asked if he were willing to be sworn, answered with an explosive

"NO!!"

"Very well, then," smiled the inquisitor, "we will dismiss you temporarily and summon the young *kurá.*"

This brought the father to terms.

When he had sullenly given his full name, residence, and occupation, he was required to state the total value of his estate, real and personal.

"What reason have you for supposing that I shall state it correctly?"

"Because you are a gentleman, and are on your oath," placidly replied the brigand-judge.

"Hear, then, the answer of a gentleman on his oath. I solemnly swear to you, Peschino, that I do not look upon you as entitled to the truth, even under oath! I believe that I should be justified, in the eyes of God and man, in using any means within my

power—even the commission of perjury—to thwart
your diabolical villany, and I should violate neither
my conscience nor my sense of honor in doing so!
With this understanding, do you still insist on my
giving you an inventory of my property?"

This was what Major Paul actually said; as rendered by Tsáras it became—

"Hear the answer of a gentleman on his oath. 'I
belong to a peculiar religious sect, Peschino, which,
among other progressive tenets, does not recognize
the sanctity of an oath. We look upon all swearing
as blasphemy, and, even if it were not so, I regret to
say that my financial affairs are in such an unsettled
state that I am utterly unable to give you the information you require. Under these circumstances, will
you be so unjust as to insist upon an impossibility?'"

"That is not *all* he said," said Peschino, glaring
threateningly at poor Tsáras.

"It is *substantially*, upon my honor," protested
the interpreter, with convincing earnestness. "I have
omitted only certain angry exclamations that do not
essentially modify the ideas."

"Why, then," said Peschino, continuing the examination, "is your nobility here, wasting your time?
Why are you not at home arranging your affairs?"

"He ask," interpreted Tsáras, "'Why you put
youself into sooch a perilous situaätion? Why have
you not thwart his "diabolical villany" by staying at
home?'"

"Because I thought a citizen of a friendly power
could trust himself in a country that professed to be

civilized. I thought Greece was a civilized country, sir. I didn't know it was a province of hell."

Translation: "'I left my affairs in good hands, and came away to recuperate my exhausted energies. I trusted that Greece would welcome a citizen of a friendly power as a guest, sir—I expected that you would treat him as such.'"

"We are wasting time," said Peschino, losing patience at last. "Once for all, will you make the estimate, or shall I?"

"I decline to pronounce my own sentence. The power is in your hands. I suppose you will do as you please."

The brigand ground his teeth with rage for an instant; but immediately controlling himself, he said, calmly, "You are dismissed for the present. Zoutzo, conduct him to his quarters, and bring the young man."

Griffin was detained but a few minutes. It would be futile to represent him as utterly unconcerned; he was mortal, and capable of suffering from financial ruin or a worse fate, when it came, as sensibly as others. But probably no one was ever less affected by the mere anticipation of evil than he. For him, amply sufficient unto the day was the evil thereof. He entered the dread presence with an air of gay indifference extremely annoying to the brigand chief, who at the same time felt it beneath his dignity to betray his irritation.

"What do you know of your friend's circumstances?" was asked, after the usual preliminaries.

"Major Paul has enjoyed the reputation of being one of the wealthiest merchants of Boston," was the unexpected answer.

"Ah, that is good." Eagerly—"Go on."

"But, alas! the war ruined him. The crash was tremendous. His great fortune floated away from him like the fragments of a shipwreck. He reserved nothing, and even then could only pay twelve *per centum*."

"A likely story, indeed! Why is he here, travelling with his family, like a prince of the blood?"

"You compel me, then, to reveal his disgrace? The unfortunate but really innocent man is simply hiding from his infuriated creditors."

"*O Diábolos!* You think me an imbecile! My time is too precious to waste on such a rattle-pate. If I did my duty I should wipe that shallow simper off your face with fifty lashes. Take him away, Zoutzo. I will see the elder of the women."

But he could make nothing of Miss Wellington. Ordinarily excitable, she had nerved herself up to preternatural coolness for the ordeal before her. She had thought better of her first resolution to be absolutely dumb, and had outlined a course of testimony which subjected her tender conscience to little or no strain. She was only a woman, she said, and could not be expected to know anything of business. She knew only that her brother-in-law had suffered losses during the war. On her oath she knew nothing definite of his financial condition.

"But you know his manner of living?"

"That is no criterion in America. Men often live recklessly to conceal their real poverty."

"They must have resources to do even that."

"Oh, people *trust* as recklessly as they spend. He may be living entirely on his credit, for all that I know."

"For all that you know? Do you *believe* he is doing that?"

"My belief can be of no value to you."

"Nevertheless, I desire to know your belief."

"I shall not answer you."

"I wish no better answer than that, *kurátza.* The young man says your brother's real poverty is no secret."

"I don't know, I don't know. I have never asked, and nobody has ever told me."

"What is to prevent my levying on his credit?"

"You would gain very little by doing so. Reckless as our people are, they know better than to trust a man in his unhappy situation."

"Surely they will risk something to release him from it?"

"I am afraid not. They will sympathize deeply, but when it comes to giving money they are like the rest of the world."

"*You* are the lady that knows nothing of business. How much would your brother and his friends be willing to pay to release you all from captivity—perhaps worse?"

"I cannot, and I *will* not answer."

"Four hundred thousand drachmas?"

Miss Wellington's lips shut tightly together.

"*Four hundred thousand?*"

The lips closed still more tightly.

"How much do you think you can endure before giving me an answer?"

"All that you can inflict."

"I may put you to the test. This is sufficient for the present, madame."

When Madeline's turn came she drew a deep breath to quiet her furiously leaping heart, and came before the brigand chief with outward composure. The starry light in her brown eyes, however, and the vivid flush on her cheek betrayed her inward agitation, while they greatly enhanced her marvellous beauty.

Peschino gazed upon her with undisguised admiration. He motioned his attendants to withdraw.

They scowled and muttered.

"I am the *Kapitán* Peschino," fiercely growled their chief. "You know both my honor and my discipline. Don't you see, your savage faces frighten the lady? She will say nothing while you are here. Leave me and this gentleman to deal with her. Go!"

. When they had gone, a look of intelligence was exchanged between the brigand chief and Tsáras which did not escape Madeline.

"Is it possible?" she murmured, as she gazed at the smooth-faced interpreter. Then a deathly faintness came over her.

"Have no fears, beautiful lady," Peschino said, in his softest tones; "I would cut my heart out rather than harm you. It is of your father that I wish to speak, and I do not wish those rough, greedy fellows to hear the generous terms I am about to propose. They have no sentiments of humanity in their breasts —they would never consent."

"Why do you not propose your terms to my father himself?" Madeline faltered.

"You must hear them first, *kopeloúda*. You are fond of adventure, of romance, are you not? Yours is a poetic soul; it is thrilled with the spectacle of heroic life among these glorious mountains. It is a wild life, but not a hard one, believe me. It is full of grand excitements, without discomforts that the noble soul feels. We know nothing of poverty. Peschino is a king, *kopeloúda*—a king that Georgias himself is afraid of. His willing subjects populate a hundred villages, and pour their treasures into his lap."

"Oh, then," cried Madeline, her voice coming forth in a flood of passionate entreaty, "if you are so rich and powerful let us go! Do not rob my poor father to add to your riches, which are already so great."

Peschino interrupted her with a gracious wave of his hand. "No, lovely girl; your father shall not lose a drachma. Peschino has no need of his treasures. He is a king, with a kingly heart which is not satisfied with riches and grandeur alone. It craves something more—*love*. Oh, beautiful *kurá*, be my queen."

Poor Madeline had known too well how his speech

would end; but when the last words fell on her ears
she seemed turned to marble. Her lips were open,
but no sound came from them. Suddenly her arms
flew up convulsively, and her voice returned to her
with a horrified, "Never! O, merciful Father in
heaven!"

The brigand's face flushed, then turned almost as
white as her own. He uttered some words in a low,
harsh voice, which were not repeated to Madeline.
Then he said, with comparative calmness, "I will
give you time to decide. Only one word more now.
If you love your father, you will breathe no word
of this matter. Say that you have been questioned
as the rest were—about your father's circumstances
—no more. In the mean time fear nothing from
this interview; you, as well as the rest, shall be treated as before."

An hour or two afterwards Major Paul was re-
called. Without preface or ceremony he was informed that the ransom for himself and family had
been fixed at four hundred thousand drachmas—a
sum equal to about seventy thousand dollars. Griffin
would be released on parole, and could be employed
as his agent. One month would be allowed for the
ransom to be collected and paid in. If it came safely, and no trouble followed, either from his own government or that of Greece, Major Paul and his party
would be immediately set at liberty, and escorted to
a place from which they could return to Athens in
perfect security.

The penalty of failure was death.

7

VIII.

THE "ANTHROPODAÍMON."

Now seventy thousand dollars may seem insignificant to you, the "unearned increment" of whose property on the Back Bay has been more than that amount within a year; but to Major Paul it was terribly large. *Entre nous,* Robert Griffin's testimony was not so absurd as it sounded to himself as well as to Peschino. It was true that while Major Paul had been risking life and limb on the field, his wealth had been rapidly diminishing at home. Not that his absence at the seat of war had aught to do with its diminution; on the contrary, it was probably one of the best things that could have happened both for his bleeding country and for his bleeding pocket. It was also true that he was now travelling with his family, not, indeed, to "escape from his infuriated creditors," but in obedience to the demands of his much-enduring partners, who had pledged themselves to redeem his fortunes if he would only consent to the status of *silent* partner for one year. As will be readily understood, the only possible way for him to fulfil such a condition was to be where neither his big voice could be heard nor his letters and telegrams especially troublesome.

Griffin, too, for reasons best known to himself, had been willing to be supposed far more forehanded than he actually was, and the fearful, naked truth was that, as matters stood, it was next to impossible for all the prisoners combined to raise the amount required for their ransom, save through disinterested benevolence—a forlorn resort, indeed!

But remonstrances, prayers, tears, threats to Peschino were like rain, snow, and hail to Gibraltar. Griffin set forth upon his well-nigh hopeless errand, bearing letters from his three companions to America, and another from Peschino to the Greek Government insolently demanding a decree of pardon and amnesty for life, with the most atrocious alternatives.

After Griffin's departure the brigands seemed to try in every possible way to make the remaining captives forget their captivity. They allowed them to wander almost at will on both sides of the pass, always, however, within sight of a strong guard; the slightest show of rudeness to them was promptly and severely punished; the best of everything obtainable was freely placed at their disposal; and had it not been for the dark, uncertain future, their life would have been far from unpleasant. The first day or two seemed an age. But terror, apprehension, indignation cannot last forever at extreme tension. Whatever might betide the captives, their consciences were unscathed, and gradually health of mind and body, sustained by the purest and most exhilarating of mountain air, and by a never-ceasing chain of novel experiences, brought back something like hope and cheerfulness.

As no attempt was made to escape, the vigilance of the brigands relaxed, and they made more persistent overtures towards comradeship. So far from apprehending efforts on the part of the Hellenic Government or of others to rescue the prisoners, they manifested only contempt for the combined force of all civilization against them. Even the superstitious fear of the terrible Hector Vyr which prevailed among the less intelligent of them, gradually died out as no new rumors of his exploits came to their ears. Whatever precautions they might take for their own safety when empty-handed, with such hostages as they held they felt perfectly secure. Every two or three days one or more of their number went to the neighboring villages, and on one occasion even to Athens, for necessaries and luxuries for themselves and their captives.

Incredible as it may appear, as time went on a curious kind of familiarity grew up between Major Paul and Peschino. True to his old habit, the major had expended the vitality of his indignation in a succession of terrific tirades, which at first had maddened the brigand chief, but afterwards only amused him. Less and less was said of the anomalous "business" relation between them; they played chess for hours together; they gave each other language lessons until they could converse, after a fashion, in both English and Greek; they went hunting together, and once, when a violent storm imprisoned them

over-night in a cave, they kept each other warm by
lying close together on their bed of thorn-bush, like
a pair of brothers!*

Much to her relief, Madeline was not annoyed by
a direct renewal of Peschino's love advances. No
rejected suitor in civilized life could have maintained
a more delicate or self-respecting reserve. He seemed bent on disarming her repugnance and winning
her gratitude by intruding himself upon her as little
as possible, at the same time that he displayed a
never-ceasing solicitude for her comfort and pleasure.
But she, of all the party, remained the most implaca-
ble. Peschino's artful policy was the more horrible
to her from its very subtlety. She witnessed the increasing communicativeness, if not friendliness, between her companions and the robbers, as she persistently styled them, with growing abhorrence.
Whatever may have been her feelings towards her
cousin, she now looked for his return as that of a
delivering angel.

At last he came, bringing with him an agent of the
Greek Government. A conference of several hours
was held at headquarters.

The letters which Griffin brought characterized
the ransom demanded as utterly beyond the bounds
of reason or possibility. After a stormy discussion
Peschino consented to reduce it to three hundred
thousand drachmas (about fifty thousand dollars)—a
sum which, Major Paul declared, was equally out of

---

* An actual occurrence.

the question; but not a drachma less would Peschino take—it must be that or death.

One of the letters, from a zealous young debtor of the major's, occasioned a gloomy sort of amusement, if such a thing were possible, among the prisoners. It threatened the vengeance of the whole American nation. A squadron of iron-clads would invest the peninsula, an army corps would scour the mountains and pursue the villains through Turkey to the deserts of Arabia, but they would avenge every drop of blood and reclaim every dollar of ransom with terrible interest—a great satisfaction to ears forever deaf to the thunder of iron-clads, and to eyes forever blind to the glitter of gold!

The negotiations with his Majesty's Government were, if possible, still more unsatisfactory. While, for the sake of the unfortunate captives, citizens of a powerful nation with whom the Hellenic Government was anxious to remain at peace, a most humiliating concession would be made, to wit: that neither the *Kapitán* Peschino nor his command would be molested on account of their present offence, provided the prisoners were set at liberty *on reasonable terms* —it was out of the power of the Government to grant pardon and an amnesty for life. By so doing they would bring down upon themselves the execration and hostility of the civilized world. It was believed that on reflection the *Kapitán* Peschino would recognize the unreasonableness of his demand, and substitute one that could be entertained.

But while the insignificant little tyrant was willing to make some concession to his prisoners, for whom he professed a strong personal regard, with his government he was scornfully inexorable. From his inaccessible mountain throne he issued a still more insolent and defiant decree, and the conference broke up.

Efforts were still to be made in America to raise the reduced sum demanded by Peschino, and as the time of grace was growing short, the result of the efforts was to be announced by the Atlantic cable. But the prisoners no longer indulged hope. From the moment the brigand chief declared his *ultimatum*, Major Paul looked upon himself and his companions as doomed. All comradeship with his enemies was forthwith dropped, and he sank into the gloom of despair. "Oh, my daughter!" he groaned, as his massive iron-gray head fell upon her shoulder, and his arms wound around her neck — "my great, grown - up, handsome daughter! Oh, my girl, my baby! If it were only I, but *Madeline!* Oh, what shall I do, what shall I *do!*"

"Don't cry, papa," sobbed Madeline, her own tears moistening his hair. "Thank Heaven I am with you! I'm not afraid, papa. I feel in my soul that we shall be saved. I have prayed to God, and I know he will not let them harm us. There, there, papa darling, *don't* cry so. I *know* the robbers will be satisfied; they will accept what we can give, rather than lose everything and have our blood upon their souls."

"Oh, you poor little kitten! you do not understand. The devils have their *rules;* they will not allow such a precedent. They believe I can pay the full ransom, and they will carry out their threats as a warning to future captives—contamination seize the poisonous cusses!"

"But the full ransom *will* be paid, if it must. Our friends will not let us *die* here for the sake of—"

"Who will pay it, my child?—who will pay it? Jobling & Hotchkiss wouldn't advance me ten thousand dollars beyond my credit to save us all from fire and brimstone. But that is not all; there's another demand which leaves no hope—not a red cent's worth of hope; may the black dragon scorch, roast, fry, broil, *fricasee* their filthy giblets to cinders!"

"Then," said Madeline, her tears suddenly ceasing and her face turning to marble, "we will meet our fate bravely—we will go hand-in-hand to *mother.*"

Thus the heroic girl tried to sustain her despairing father, who but for her would have been as brave as he had been on many a bloody field.

All at once his face lighted up. His own despairing question, "Who will pay it?" had suggested a thought which promised salvation, at least to his idolized daughter. If she could be persuaded that, by her superior tact and the pathos of a beautiful woman's appeal, she could best raise the ransom-money, she could not refuse to go back to America instead of Griffin. The prospect of her success would easily gain Peschino's consent. Then, *she* once safely out of their hands, the brigands might do their worst.

Perhaps Miss Wellington might be allowed to go, too, to hasten matters—who knew? With a torrent of eager argument and entreaty he told her of the plan. She listened in silence, and when he had finished she replied, in a low, calm voice,

"If they will let me, and if Robert and Aunt Eliza think as you do, I will go."

"That's my own good girl!" he cried, catching her in his arms.

"But, father, don't misunderstand me. Whether I succeed or not, *I shall come back*."

"Great Polyphemus! what *for?* Isn't it better that three should perish than *four?*"

"Dear papa, think for one moment. I should be on my parole, shouldn't I?—just as Robert was."

"Heh?" he asked, staring stupidly at her.

"Didn't Robert come back? Wouldn't *you?*"

"I?—but—but—you are a *woman*, you know."

"And therefore have no *honor*. No, no, papa; that will not do. If Robert should consent to such an act, what would you think of him? what would you say of him?"

"But," he faltered, piteously, "you are going, you know, because you can *do* so much better than he can; you can *persuade* them, you know, while he couldn't. That's reason enough, isn't it?"

"It's a reason, perhaps, why I should go and *try*, but not why I shouldn't come back."

"Madeline," he said, bravely, but with the hope gone from his face, "you heroine, you plucky little tiger, you are *right!*"

An hour later the four prisoners were seated on the flat rock on the outer side of the pass, talking over the plan which the major had proposed, and taking what comfort they could from it. A guard of four brigands were lying at full length on the grassless ground near them, while the sentinel on the cliff was lazily sitting *à la Turk*, his mind probably as little occupied with his duties as was his body. Within the pass Peschino, with several brigands, was in the valley, exhibiting his herds to the Government agent. The residue of his force were scattered here and there about camp, some with their muskets in pieces to be polished and oiled. If a government force could have surprised the guard at this time, they might have effected a rescue and capture without the least difficulty. Tsáras, who, since the examination of Madeline, had studiously avoided his fellow-prisoners, was swinging in a hammock within a clump of trees.

It was a perfect day; but the beautiful smile of Nature was to the prisoners a smile of bitter irony. The celestial blue seemed serenely taunting them with their dismal plight; the brooklets giggled gleefully at their misery; the careless *abandon* of the guard—kindly enough designed, no doubt—was an insult to their helplessness which stung the major to one of his sudden outbursts.

"See the lazy, basking reptiles! They'd spring up quick enough if Peschino should show himself. Perdition seize their insolence! don't they know the difference between a field-officer and a scrubby little

captain without a commission, except what the devil
has given him! I wish I had my sword for three
minutes!"

"I wish you had, papa," said his daughter, mourn-
fully.

"*I'd* prod the filthy camp scullions! I—I'd make
'em stand in the position of the soldier, if I had to
roast for it!"

"I wish you had not only your sword but the
whole —th regiment at your back!" added Madeline,
with gleaming eyes.

"*Ah-r-r-r!*" The major's growl was like that of
a mammoth terrier in the act of shaking the life out
of a rat. It even attracted the attention of one of the
victims of the imaginary charge, who opened one eye
in sleepy wonder, and immediately closed it again.

"Oh!" cried Madeline, clasping her hands, while
her bosom swelled with the agony of her prayer,
"why will not just and merciful Heaven send a le-
gion of angels to deliver us!"

"Don't call on Heaven," Griffin broke in, fiercely.
His gay light-heartedness had at last failed him.
"Heaven smiles only on robbers and murderers!
Heaven delights in martyrs! The smoke of their
torment arises as sweet incense to the pearly gates!"

"Hush!" said Madeline, terrified at his bitter
blasphemy, "or we shall deserve our fate!"

"Come, Robert," added her father, with unwonted
solemnity, "this is no time for such talk as that. No
sailor swears when his ship is sinking. You'd better
be saying your prayers, man."

A little while after this the party were startled by a wild shriek from the sentinel on the cliff, who, springing to his feet, fired his musket, and went hopping away on one leg. This aroused the guard of four, who frantically seized their pieces and aimed them down the path with shouts of "*Anthropodaimon! Anthropodaimon!*"

Looking in the direction in which the muskets were pointed, the prisoners saw a figure with bare head, shoulders, arms, and legs, darting from side to side with prodigious agility, at the same time that it advanced rapidly towards them.

The four brigands discharged their muskets almost simultaneously, and the next moment were frantically scrambling towards the pass, within which they disappeared with loud cries of terror, the last one barely escaping the grasp of the stranger. The latter, whose pursuit had been like that of a tiger leaping upon its prey, now turned towards the party at the rock, and burst into a long, loud peal of laughter. He held his sides, and bent forward and back like a huge rollicking school-boy. The deep, round, clear *ha! ha! ha!* rang out, echoing and re-echoing until all the majestic mountains around seemed to have lapsed into a Titanic frolic.

The captives forgot their captivity and their apparent sudden release in stupefied amazement. They could only gaze with open mouths and wide eyes at the marvellous spectacle.

In a few seconds the stranger's mirth ceased as abruptly as it had begun. He bounded towards the

rescued party before they could collect their senses,
and hustled them without ceremony into the path,
down which they found themselves the next moment
running with might and main. Miss Wellington's
pace not satisfying him, he caught her in his arms
as if she were an infant, and ran on with undimin-
ished speed, urging the rest before him with cries of
"*Grégora! grégora!*" (Hurry! hurry!)

His haste and solicitude were none too great. The
half-dozen brigands within call ran yelling to the top
of the cliff, and their bullets came *zipping* viciously
down the hill. No one of the fugitives was struck,
however, and presently they were hidden from their
enemies by the rocks and foliage.

They had descended perhaps a quarter of a mile
down the path when the rescuer shouted "*Alt!*"

They stopped running, and pantingly awaited further orders. They were motioned into a by-path
leading into a thicket, where they were brought to a
halt. To their increased astonishment and delight,
their mysterious deliverer now addressed them in
English, scarcely marred by an alien accent.

"They will soon rally their force and pursue after
us. I shall shoot one, two, three—the rest shall retreat away."

As he said this in a peculiarly deep, resonant
voice, he unslung a brass tube about a yard in length,
which turned out to be a spring-gun of enormous
power. Pressing down the spring with little apparent effort, he raised his hand to his shoulder, drew
one from a great number of slender, feathered steel

shafts, and dropped it into the bore. Then aiming at the tough, thick stem of a stunted tree at a considerable distance, he released the spring. There was a sharp *zip*, like that of a rifle-ball.

"Go and see," he said to Major Paul.

The tree had been pierced through; the shaft had passed beyond, and was not to be found.

"My *televodon* kills silently," the marksman said, in his wonderful, thrilling voice, "and it makes no smoking. They have no opportune to return my shoot. They cannot endure, and they soon retreat away, like it is from a malaria invisible, irresistible."

He had scarcely finished speaking when the report of a musket was heard. Aunt Eliza uttered a suppressed shriek. Madeline turned pale.

"Hide in these bush; be perfectly quiet," ordered the stranger, sternly. "I will soon return. The womans shall make no screams."

"Let us go with you," urged Major Paul, speaking for himself and Griffin.

"No. You have not arms. You shall only be obstacle. You shall draw their guns to me like to yourself."

"But if anything happened to you we could—"

"Have I not said NO?"

Before they could recover from the paralyzing effect of the word, the speaker had noiselessly disappeared in the thicket towards the pass.

"I'm going to follow him," said Griffin, recklessly. "Come along, uncle."

"No, sir! Always obey orders from a superior,

especially in active service. It's hard, I know, devilish hard, but we can't help it. Stay where you are."

They lay, as it seemed, for hours, listening with strained ears to every sound. At length there came the report of a musket—another—a volley. Then they heard loud voices, among which they thought they recognized that of Peschino. The noises gradually receded until they became inaudible.

"Well, I'll be consigned!" ejaculated the major, "if he hasn't driven the whole darned crowd into their old school-house again!"

"God bless him! God bless him!" cried Madeline, fervently, and the rest as fervently echoed the benediction—not excepting Griffin, whose eyes the next moment met those of Madeline fixed upon him with a look of pity mingled with awe.

"*Pray*," she said, in a scarcely audible voice—"pray for the forgiveness of the Heaven you so wickedly slandered — the Heaven that heard the prayer instead of the blasphemy!"

His eyes fell, and a dark flush covered his face.

"Madeline," said the major.

She turned to him.

"I heard what you two were saying just before—" He paused and looked up into the sky with a dazed expression. "Strange, wasn't it? You don't really believe that—that—"

"That God heard my prayer and answered it? Yes, papa, I *do*. How can any of us be so ungrateful as to doubt it? How can we *dare?*"

"It was a remarkable coincidence—wonderful. It

does seem as if— I have heard of such things happening; but then, after all, there's nothing so very mysterious in a mere coincidence. I can't really believe that—"

"Oh, papa!" she entreated, "don't say it. Who knows but there may be another coincidence?"

Her words struck him with a sudden awe. "Well," he said, presently, "I confess I shouldn't have the hardihood to say what Robert said."

At this moment their champion appeared boldly walking down the path. It is impossible to convey an adequate idea of the free, springing elasticity of his stride. It was as if he were the proud, unquestioned monarch of the mountains. As he came nearer, their attention was attracted to another and a very different matter—his left arm was bound with a ligature, and was covered with blood.

"Oh, sir, your arm!" cried Madeline, running to meet him; but her swift step was suddenly checked by his impatient answer:

"Make not fuss, young woman! It is a random gun. No bodies have saw me. It is in the flesh only, and the ball have gone out. You shall put a more better band on the arm."

All eagerly pressed forward with offers of assistance, tearing their handkerchiefs into strips. As Madeline readjusted the ligature and tenderly wiped away the blood, she was struck with admiration at the magnificently formed limb. While she is deftly performing her grateful office, let us look leisurely at her patient.

IX.

THE RETREAT.

THE prevailing impression the stranger makes is that of supreme virile power, an abounding vitality that pervades the whole man like an inward fire. A mighty soul looks out from large, dark eyes clear and luminous as those of a child. He is nearly seven feet in height, but formed with such symmetry that he seems tall only because he is standing beside others. Then, indeed, he seems colossal. His head is the ideal Caucasian ovoid, thickly covered with short, crisp brown curls. His massive shoulders, deep chest, and powerful limbs tell of ability for mighty achievement, while bright intellectual vigor, such as in all its freshness accompanies only the harmonious play of all the functions, is manifest in his countenance. In short, with a somewhat less pronounced muscular development, he would present in form and feature a model such as Phidias might have chosen for a Hermes. His dress consists of a sleeveless jacket, low in the neck and curiously embroidered, fustanelli of linen reaching only to the knee, and stout shoes of goat-skin. From a narrow leathern waist-belt is suspended a richly mounted dagger, while two cross-belts of the same material and width sustain the brazen spring-gun and the quiver of steel shafts which have served so good a purpose.

8

"Be quick, Madeline," said her father. "We must get away from here, or those wolves will be after us again."

"No," said the champion; "they will dare not to come if they shall not see us in the path. They are too afraid for the silent bullet which comes from the wind. We shall stay here a little more time."

"You are English peoples?" he asked, presently.

"No, your excellency," replied the major, with the greatest possible deference; "we are Americans."

"It is no difference. But you must not say to me 'your excellence.' I am not excellence."

"I beg your pardon. I won't again."

"Pardon! Why-fore? Have you commit some crimes?"

"No, your— Excuse me, I—"

"Excuse you! What do you mean? I do not understand."

"I mean, I ask your pardon for my mistake."

"Why-fore shall I pardon you for you make mistake? Is it some wickedness?"

The major colored up and began to flounder again, when Madeline came to his relief. "It is a custom with us," she said, with a smile, "to ask pardon for an innocent mistake as if it were a real offence."

He turned his great, inquiring eyes upon her. "Then what shall you say when you do the real offence? Shall you ask the pardon then, too?"

"Of course. There is all the more occasion for it then."

"But that what you say—it is no different?"

"Oh, we say it with a great deal more feeling—more *earnestness*, you know."

"Why-fore do you say I know? I do *not* know until you shall tell me."

At this they all indulged in a tenderly good-natured, highly respectful laugh. "We use a good many forms in our speech," Madeline explained, "which have no real meaning, but which serve to smooth and round out our sentences."

"I understand him now. How long time have you been at captivity?"

"Twenty-seven days," answered Major Paul, promptly.

"It is a long time. It was telled to me this morning. I came to you so quickly as I could come."

"You came in good time," replied Madeline, with deep feeling, and her father added,

"Heaven must have sent you, indeed, as my daughter says! I should be a cursed Judas to doubt it."

"Our poor thanks," continued Madeline, "are so utterly inadequate, that, indeed, we are almost ashamed to offer them. But we can at least pray God to shower his richest blessings on you."

"Allow me to say, general," put in the major, his face growing red and his breath coming noisily, "that you have done alone, and almost unarmed, what that infernal villain boasted the whole Greek Government couldn't do. You are a wonderful man, your excel— Beg pardon, sir. There isn't your equal in the world—no, sir, not by a thousand per cent.! You can be no other than the famous personage of

whom such wonderful stories are told.   I beg your
pard— Excuse me, I didn't mean—but—but isn't
your name Vyr—Hector Vyr?"

The stranger smiled, displaying two rows of teeth,
even, strong, and white as those of a savage.

"My name is Hector Vyr," he answered.   "Your
name is Mr. Powl?"

"Paul, sir; not Powl.   The young lady who is
dressing your arm is my daughter, Miss Madeline
Paul; this lady is my sister-in-law, Miss Eliza Wellington; this young gentleman is my nephew, Mr.
Robert L. Griffin; and we are all your grateful servants for life, Mr. Vyr."

"There," said Madeline, with a sigh of satisfaction,
"that is the best I can do for your arm until we can
find some water.   I hope I did not hurt you very
much, Mr. Vyr?"

"You *did* hurt me very much, Miss Paul; but I
did know you could not prevent it.   I did not think
of the pain.   I give to you thanks for your helps to
me."

"Oh," she cried, "I beg you not to speak of such
a trifle.   If there were only something a thousand
times greater we could do for you, we should all be
so glad to do it!   Is there not *something* more we
can do, Mr. Vyr?"

The amazing reply was:

"*Let me to see your teeths.*"

As soon as her friends had finished staring at one
another, and she was sure she had heard aright, she
uttered an embarrassed "Certainly," and at once ex-

hibited two sets of pearl as perfect as his own, though
on a very different scale.

"It is good," he said, as if to himself; "yet I
thinks you do eat the confection and drink the hot
teas and the coffees, like to your other peoples."

"Are you a—a *dentist?*" asked Aunt Eliza, timidly.

"What is 'dentist,' Miss Wellington? Ah, I know
that what it is: *dens, dentis.* Do you mean teeth-
doctor?"

Aunt Eliza bowed assent.

"Not more than I am all kinds of doctors. I
think I am that what you can name *health-monomaniac.* My father was one of those, and his father,
and *his* father—and away behind for great many of
generation. I asked Miss Paul that she shall show
to me her teeths, because she is so perfect in all other thing that I was inquisitive how she shall endure
the test so delicate." Turning to Madeline. "I
think you do breathe the *bacteria* in the cities, and
the dirt of the carpet, and you do dance all the nights
in the gas-lights like everybodies?"

"Indeed," rejoined Madeline, trying to cover her
confusion by laughing, "I am not nearly so dissi-
pated as you think me, Mr. Vyr. Have I not lived
a very sensible life, papa?"

"Oh yes; of course, of course—*some* of the time."

"Oh, you *traditore!* Well, at all events I've had
little enough chance for dissipation lately. I've
breathed nothing but mountain air, and haven't even
seen a gas-light for a month at least."

Vyr electrified the party again by turning abruptly to her father with, "Your daughter is the most
beautifulest young woman I have ever saw."

Poor Madeline blushed to the very roots of her
hair, Miss Wellington uttered an astounded "Why!"
Robert Griffin's lower jaw dropped, and the major
coughed an embarrassed, "H'm, h'm—*thank* you, sir
—a very great honor, I'm sure."

"Honor?" echoed Vyr, glancing curiously at each
face in turn. "No. Why-fore· is it honor? She
did not make herself to be beautiful like to the painted actress; she should not feel shame and be red because I say truth; she should say, 'Yes, I *am* beautiful like to the anemone, I am happy like to the
singing-bird, I am bright like to the sparkling cas-
cade, I am well and strong like to the young chamois
—yet, not like to all those, I am educate and cultivate like to the pale, ill lady of the cities;' and she
should fall down on her knees, and pray to the Great
One who gives all those good things, and say to him,
'I am only a little, little flower, infinitely below those
majestic mountains, those vast blue skies, those multitude of glorious stars—yet my little heart is full
with thank and adorations because for my beautiful-
ness and my sweet fragrance, and it is compassionate
for those peoples which are weak and ill and ugly.'"

That Hector Vyr has already made progress in the
use of English, even in the short time we have known
him, cannot, of course, have escaped our notice. It
appears less, however, in his words than in his improved modulation and diminished hesitancy. The

last long speech was delivered with scarcely a break, and with perfect self-possession. He seemed utterly unconscious of having expressed any but the most conventional of commonplaces. He quickly saw, however, the awkward constraint he had produced among his auditors, and went on, with the evident intention of restoring them to equanimity :

"You are not accustomed to words like those? You say truth of all things except yourselves and those peoples to which you speak? If I say truth of you, it is the flattery? if I say truth of myself, it is the vanity? Is it so as I say?" addressing Madeline.

"It is apt to be so regarded," she replied, fast re-gaining her self-poise.

"But why-fore?" he persisted, earnestly. "That mountain, is he not lofty and grand? and do I not say it? It is not flattery to the mountain. Do you not know you are beautiful, Miss Paul?"

The poor girl, suffused again with blushes, looked appealingly from him to her friends.

"*We* know it, if she doesn't!" Griffin answered for her. There was a certain metallic ring in his voice, and a hard, enduring look in his face, as he spoke.

"And Miss Paul knows it—she does not dare to say no. So it is not the flattery, which is only lies. Is not the vanity lies, too?—lies to himself? You know, for instance, that I am strong and brave, do not you?"

"We have had the most ample evidence of that," answered Madeline, with alacrity.

"Then, if I, too, know it, why-fore shall I not say

it? It would be boasts, it would be pomposity, egotism—would it?"

"An ordinary person might, perhaps, be open to those charges," said Madeline, her features now relaxing into an amused smile.

"But Mr. Vyr is *not* an ordinary person," interposed Miss Wellington, with decision. "I am sure it would be perfectly proper for *him* to say all this of himself, and much more, too, if he chose."

"Well, I should *say* so!" assented the major, with an emphatic blow of his open hand on his knee.

No one could say that Vyr frowned at this broad compliment. What right had he to express displeasure? Had he not himself been still more outspoken? Had he not invited the free expression of their inmost thoughts by his own example? There was not the slightest perceptible knitting of his brows; he did not assume a sudden air of offended dignity; his head was not a hair's-breadth more erect than before. He simply *looked* at the speakers an instant without replying. Nevertheless, Miss Wellington could not have blushed more painfully if she had unwittingly offended a monarch on his throne. Vyr perceived her uncalled for embarrassment, and immediately a gracious smile broke out over his face.

"I suppose I must grow red at Miss Wellington's words," he said, "like Madeline. Ah, you are offended, Miss Paul, because I speak your own name; your beautiful upward smile of amusement is change to a downward smile of proudness; you lift up your head like to a queen. Why-fore? I have broke the

law of etiquette? Well, all the laws have penalties.
Is it so as I say?"

As no one vouchsafed a ready answer, he went on:
" You will punish me—you will say to me, 'Mr. Vyr,
you have done to us a service, and for that we give
to you great thanks, and we will also do you a service
when we can; but you are a great savage, and we
must not associate.'"

"Thunder of great waters, no!" blurted out the
major. "We are not such ungrateful fools as that,
I hope. Call her or any of the rest of us what you
please. Madeline, why don't you speak?"

"Indeed, papa, I— We are all under too great obligations to Mr. Vyr to take offence at any little un-
conventionalities he may indulge in. He meant no
offence, I am sure, and I am not so silly as to take
offence."

"You make a mistake, Miss Paul; I *did* mean
offence."

Another general stare.

"Not *great* offence, my friends. I have heard
that in the civilized country it is more worse to
break the law of etiquette than to break the law of
the Government, and so I have make the little experiment. I wish to know if you will forget the
service which I have render to you because I am
rude a little. I wish to get to myself knowledge of
different kind of peoples. I respect the young woman and her friends, and I make to them honorable
apology because I speak her real name, and because I
say she is beautiful. Have I done that what is right?"

Madeline walked bravely up to him and extended her hand. "Please say no more about it, Mr. Vyr. You make us feel very insignificant. If it will give you amusement or information to try experiments upon us, I am sure we ought to submit with thankfulness that it is in our power to afford you any gratification whatever."

He took her firm little hand with evident pleasure. An indescribable sensation of vital warmth shot up her arm to her heart like an electric shock.

"No, Miss Paul," he returned. "You shall *tell* to me that what I wish to know of the custom and feeling in the polite society."

"Perhaps we can tell you something of the *customs*," she rejoined, with an "upward smile." "As to *feelings*, the more polite the society the less we know on that subject."

"And is it true that it is more worse to be ignorant of the polite customs than it is to commit some crimes? If it is true, Hector Vyr must be a terrible criminal in London and Boston. Would he be hang from his neck?"

"Rather a dangerous thing to try — *that* would be!" said Major Paul. "No, sir. You would be the greatest lion that ever condescended to favor those cities with his presence."

"Ah, put in the strong cage and exhibit with the tigers and the bears. It would be very good. I am a wild man of the mountains; I have never gone to the cities except two times to Athens."

"How, then, did you learn to speak English so

well?" asked Griffin, who had been remarkably reticent for him.

"My mother is an English lady, and a good many years ago she talked to me in her own language."

"Is she living now?"

"Yes, I thank God that she is living; but we have not talked English for long, long time. She loves my father's language better. But we have English books and magazine which I read. And last year I saved three captivated Englishmen from the klephts, like you, and they lived with us in our house three weeks. You will all come to my house, too, and stay a long time. You will teach me more English, and tell me such things that my books and papers do not say."

Major Paul accepted the invitation with the warmest thanks, but could not think of remaining more than a day or two at the longest.

"But have you not said that you would do all what you could for me?" asked Vyr, with a look of surprise. "You are not hastened; you have not great businesses to do; you are making a travel of observation and pleasure. I offer you much observation, and—is it egotism, Miss Paul?—I think I can offer you much pleasure also."

"There is no doubt of that, sir," replied the major. "It would ill become us to decline an invitation so generously and cordially given, especially by one whom we are so anxious to please."

"Why-fore did not you say that before?" Vyr asked, with simple frankness. "Did you think I did not *wish* that you should stay a long time at my house ?"

"I—I—" The great, clear, questioning eyes threw the major into a kind of stage fright. He turned appealingly to his daughter; but before she could speak, Aunt Eliza volunteered the explanation:

"My brother was afraid we should trespass too long upon your hospitality."

"Then why-fore did you think I asked you? Ah, I understand, it was one of the forms of your speech that Miss Paul told me to 'smooth and round out your sentences.'" He smiled again. "I am afraid that I shall not know when you say that what you mean."

"We must be very careful," said Madeline, "and be entirely frank when we are speaking to Mr. Vyr."

"Oh, I shall learn in a little time more. You shall be patient and teach me."

"Well," said Major Paul, rallying, "we will visit you as long as you want us to, I guess. And I hope that we may have an opportunity to reciprocate the favor in our own country."

"Yes, indeed!" added his daughter; "that is no mere 'form of speech,' I assure you. Papa and I, and all of us, mean exactly what he says."

Hector Vyr shook his head. "I must not do that. I seldom go far away from my own house. I like a few guests—not many of them, and not many times —but I wish not that I shall be the object of observation. I tell to you now, like as I tell to my other guests, that I have made the oath, like to my

father, and like to *his* father, to avoid all notorieties."

"You wish to know others, without being known
yourself," said Madeline. "Do you think that is
quite *fair*, Mr. Vyr?"

"Fair?"

"Do you think it is quite just to others?"

"Ah, just. No, Miss Paul; it is unjustice. It is
like to the detective which hides himself and looks
very slyly through the little holes in the walls. But
the world has no necessity for Hector Vyr, although
he has great necessity for the world. It is infinity
for me to see and know in the mountains, the trees,
the birds, the beasts, the little insects, the rocks, and
the uncultivate peoples which live here with me;
but I wish to know everythings. It is only a few
sides of me which grow here; I wish that all sides
of my heart and my intellects shall grow. I wish
not to tie up one little finger-joint in my body or
my heart or my intellects."

Here Griffin once more broke his moody silence:
"I should think the best way to accomplish your
purpose would be to go over the world and see for
yourself."

The formidable eyes rested for a moment on the
young man before the answer came: "Do you not
understand? Have not I told you? Why-fore do
not you listen, if you shall talk too? Shall I be ego-
tist, and say that peoples will not let me to be in
peace? They will run to look at me, like as I am a
big hippopotamus; they will importune to make me

to be generals and councillors and lecturers. I have swore not to be those things, and I like not so great troubles."

"But," said Madeline, " have you never considered how much good you might be the means of doing in the world? Don't you think you ought to give your fellow-men the benefit of your abilities?"

She and her friends eagerly listened for his answer.

" It is not good for me to talk to you; you do not listen to me. Forgive me—I am not gentle. I am not accustom to talk to peoples which live in the civilized country. But you shall teach me to be gentle. I have said to you that the world has not the necessity for Hector Vyr. They have too much already —too much generals, too much councillors, too much talkers, too much writers of books and magazine— too much to see, to hear, to read, to eat—too much everything. Why-fore shall they wish more of those things? No, my friends, men should not wish more outside, but more inside; not more to see, but better eyes; not more to hear, but better ears; not more to read, but better brains; not more to eat, but better bodies."

"Ah, Mr. Vyr," replied Madeline, "I fear you do not know the world very well yet. There are countless thousands who sadly need more to *eat*."

"The world is better, the race of men is better, that the feeble shall *not* eat."

This inhuman sentiment was received with unconcealed disapprobation.

"I am a monster," Vere continued, smiling. "I

have not a heart. Well, Nature is herself a monster, too. She has not a heart; she permits all the little, weak, sick lions to starve for million years, until it is none but great, mighty lions ; and if greater, mightier men do not kill them, the world would be full with great, mighty lions. To-day is not all the time, Miss Paul. I have heart for the million thousand men which will live million years hereafter, and I like them not to be the posterity from weak little peoples which must be fed like to the babies. I have heart for the whole race of men, in all the time, not only to-day. So I say to you, it is more better for mankind that those peoples which are not strong and skilful to get meat for themselves shall not eat."

"You forget that it is not the feeble only who suffer destitution," replied Madeline, her heart throbbing with mingled indignation and apprehension at the consciousness of having actually entered into an argument with him. "Many are unfortunate through no fault or deficiency of their own."

"Nature do not turn away from her great laws because of every little exceptions, Miss Paul," he answered, smiling indulgently.

"But *you* are not Nature, Mr. Vyr. You have a will of your own, which Nature has not."

"Do not you think that He which has made Nature, and which governs Nature, has a will of His own? Do you think that He wishes that the feeble and the undevelop shall be perpetuate to the future?"

"I—suppose not. But—but—I have no doubt it is His will that we—you as well as the rest, Mr. Vyr—

to whom He has given wills of our own, should do everything in our power to help the weak and the unfortunate, to feed the hungry, clothe the naked—"

"Yes, yes, Miss Paul," burst in Hector Vyr, "your heart is noble like as your face is beautiful! *I* wish, too, to feed the hungry and to clothe the naked which come in my path, because my heart has pity for them. I wish to rescue the unfortunate in every place which I find them, if it is my power."

This with a gentle significance impossible to misunderstand.

"Yes, indeed," Madeline replied, with sudden revulsion of feeling, "your acts have shown that you have a heart, in spite of what you say, Mr. Vyr."

"I have my mission, I think, like everybodies; but I think it is not that I shall go through the world to keep alive all the weak peoples which I can find, that they can transmit their feeble bodies and intellects to future generation."

"Madeline! Madeline!" ejaculated the major, "what are you talking about? Isn't it mission enough to stand guard over these mountain devils? Talk about keeping folks alive! Sun, moon, and stars! hasn't he kept *us* alive?"

"You speak too much of that what I have done, Mr. Paul," said Vyr, with the slightest possible shade of annoyance. "The young woman asks me why-fore I do not go out over the world and do some great things which she thinks I can do. I say to her that men do not have necessity to see great things; they see too much already. It is necessity that there shall be a more perfect race of men, not that there shall be more great things to make them open wide their eyes and their mouths."

"Well," said Griffin, "may I ask, Mr. Vyr, how you propose to bring it about?"

"I cannot bring it about, Mr. Griffin; but every one can make himself better and stronger if he shall choose, and that can help the generations which shall come."

This was the reply in words; but the magnificent figure drawn up to its full height, dwarfing the rest by comparison, the glorious countenance serene with conscious superiority, were a far more forcible and a sufficient answer.

"Now," said Vyr, a little later, "I know that the klephts are no more watching at us. They think that we have gone away. You shall creep through those bush. Go not near to the path till I shall tell. I will come after you behind."

X.

THE VYRS AT HOME.

TWILIGHT was just beginning to soften the nearer outlines of the landscape and to sharpen those more distant, when the rescued party and their rescuer came to a deep, wide chasm cutting directly across their path—one of the very pits, perhaps, into which

9

the old Spartans used to throw their criminals. Beyond arose a forest-covered mountain of very irregular outline.

"We have come near to my house, now," said Hector Vyr. "You can see it up there. It gleams whitely among the trees."

"But how in the world are we to get there?" asked Madeline, as she gazed shrinkingly into the fearful abyss.

"It will be very easy, Miss Paul," replied Vyr, "when I shall make my bridge across." He seized the long, branchless trunk of a fallen tree with his right hand, and holding down one end with his foot, raised it to a perpendicular, and allowed it to fall across the chasm. Then, after trying it to see that it did not roll, he said, "Now I will carry one across, and then I will come back and carry another. I could carry two at one time if my arm is not sore. Who shall go at the first?"

As no one responded, he walked over alone and returned, with as much apparent unconcern as if he were crossing London Bridge. "You see how that it is easy and safe. Will you go across alone by yourselves? It is no toll to pay."

Griffin walked about half-way across, often stopping to make sure of his balance, when, happening to glance downward, his head gave way, and he was obliged to finish the transit on all fours.

"Now, then, Eliza," said the major, "it's your turn next."

"Oh, I can't. I shall be dashed in pieces. I

wouldn't trust myself on that log for a thousand worlds."

"Shall I carry you?" asked Vyr, persuasively.

"Indeed I haven't the courage, Mr. Vyr. I'm afraid I should not only sacrifice my own life but yours also."

"I am not afraid, Miss Wellington. It is no danger if you shall keep yourself still on my arm."

After much more persuasion she consented, and was safely deposited on the other side, notwithstanding her feeble little clutches and small shrieks.

Madeline proposed to try to walk over if Mr. Vyr would go first, giving her his hand; but on being assured that such a method would involve the almost certain destruction of both, she followed Aunt Eliza's example. With closed eyes and suspended breath, seated on his powerful arm, her own clasped around his neck, she felt as if she were riding over in an iron chair.

Major Paul went last, hitching along astride, and helping himself with his hands, to the great merriment of the spectators.

"*Now*," said Vyr, as he pulled in his natural drawbridge, "all you are *my* prisoner!" His manner was that of menacing triumph.

They looked at one another with curiously different expressions on their faces. Miss Wellington's was pallid with alarm; Griffin set his teeth and scowled; the major lifted his brows and whistled; Madeline smiled in placid fearlessness.

"A faithful sentinel sees us now from yonder

thicket," continued Vyr. "My command is to him that he shall fire when one tries to go across without my permission."

Still Madeline only smiled.

Vyr looked upon her and upon the rest with keen scrutiny. Then his face softened, and in a tone of tender reproach he said, "Miss Paul has not fear. She trusts the wild man which has saved her from the klepht. Cannot you have trust, too? Do you so easily lose your faith in Hector Vyr because he plays a little with you, like a boy? Is a voice and a look from the eyes a greater thing to you than a deed? Is it a greater thing to you than this blood?" lifting his wounded arm.

For a moment there was a distressed silence. Then the major stepped boldly forward. "General," he said, "you must not be too hard on us. We haven't said anything, have we? You told us we were your prisoners, and that you had a sentinel posted with his gun cocked ready to fire on us. How did you expect us to take that from a man who had never condescended to joke with us before, especially after the experience *we've* had? Yet we never *yipped*. Excuse me, but *you* mustn't see too much in a 'look from the eyes,' either."

With undisturbed serenity Vyr replied, "It is right, what you have said, Mr. Paul. It was not generosity when I try to frighten you a little—it was not a just trial for your faith. You shall forgive me?"

The major seized his hand with delighted ardor.

"Say no more about it, general, say no more about it. We're all glad that we've had the chance to excuse something, even a trifling mistake like that."

"But it was not all a mistake, my friends," rejoined Vyr. "It was good, too, that you shall be a little frightened, because I show to you how that you are safe from your enemies. They do not know the path to my home, if no friend shall be traitor; but even if they shall find the path, they cannot come over this great gulf but one at a time, and my sentinel shall shoot them, and he shall call me and my followers to the defence."

"That's a fact!" the major exclaimed heartily. "It's a better stronghold than their own. You couldn't have taken a more effectual way than you did to impress us with its strength. And you may be sure of one thing, general, you can't scare us again, whatever you may say."

Vyr smiled. "Miss Paul was not scare?" he said, looking at her with pleased inquiry.

"Not in the least."

"I thank you from my whole heart." The look and tone with which he spoke thrilled her.

"You all shall be perfectly at your liberty," he went on. "You shall be my guests so long time as you shall have pleasure. Then, when you shall command me, I will carry you again over the little bridge—or you shall creep over it," laughingly to the major and Griffin; " or perhaps it is better that my servants shall bring down the great bridge which I keep under my house, and which they place over when the great marble stones and tables and divans must be carried across. You shall walk over on that, and I will lead you to Mikro-Maina, or even to Sparta, if it is your wishes."

While this talk had been going on, they had ascended a breakneck, stony path, and now, turning a sharp bend, they came into full sight of a white marble tower similar to those they had seen a month before, save that it was much taller. It surmounted an irregular building of large size, also of marble, at one side of which was a veranda with four Doric columns. Several enormous gables projected from the three visible sides of the building, consisting chiefly of long windows in slender casements of iron. On the veranda were rustic chairs, and a hammock which, Vyr informed his guests, was one of his favorite beds. Madeline asked if he always slept in the open air. He replied that he did not; he was not a rock, but rather a sort of hibernating animal. In the winter he went inside of his cave like other bears. And sucked his paws? Oh no; he made his paws work hard in the summer, so in the winter they rested. The major inquired if he and his friends were to sleep in the open air, like their host. Yes, if they preferred; or they might sleep inside the house, and breathe their own breath over and over again as many times as they liked. His guests always did exactly as they wished. They might eat and drink and *smoke* all the civilized poisons he could obtain for them. They might even turn the night into day and the day into night, as they had the reputation of do-

ing at their own homes. They could not make noise
enough to disturb either his mother's rest or his own.
Rubbing his hands with anticipation, the major declared him the prince of hosts; he and Griffin had
had nothing to smoke for a month but the brigand's
nasty nargiles.

As they approached the steps leading to the veranda, a handsome white face, crowned with abundant gray hair, appeared at the window, and the next
moment its owner, a tall, finely-formed woman, clad
in a gray jacket embroidered with silver, and a black
petticoat, stood curiously watching them from the
entrance. Vyr ran up the steps, and throwing his
unwounded arm around her matronly figure, he im-
printed a hearty kiss upon each cheek. She received
his embrace impassively, as the Americans thought,
her only response being to place her hand on his
bandaged arm and look inquiringly in his face. He
spoke a few short sentences in Greek, turned, and
bade his companions come up and be introduced to
his mother.

"They are English peoples, *mannáka*" (dear mam-
ma), he said, eagerly; "*English*, do you not understand?"

"Oh, they are English, are they?" she replied, with
something like interest; for her eyes, which had sur-
veyed them with stony apathy, or at most an idle curiosity, grew a few degrees brighter. "Well, I am
sure I am very glad to see them."

"I suppose we are the same as English to you,
ma'am," said the major, with a low bow, "as we are

to your son; but we are really Americans, from Boston, Massachusetts."

"Oh, *thank* you," replied the poor woman, with a blank smile. "It is a very pleasant evening, is it not?" Then suddenly she sprang forward, crying angrily, "Americans, are you? *And what have you been doing to my boy?*"

Vyr went to her and gently led her to a seat. "They did not do it—some peoples have shot me a little; but—"

"The *klephts!*" she almost shrieked, her pale face distorted with terror; " *O Thĕĕ mou!*"

"It is nothing, nothing," he answered, soothingly, kissing her again. "Do not you see that I am safe and well? Is not my step firm? is not my cheek red? is not my voice loud? These peoples have been very kind to me, and you must be very kind to them again. Miss Paul was a little doctor to me; she has bound my arm, and she has watered it when we have come to the little brooks. It will soon be strong again, like to the other."

"But we were the *cause*," exclaimed Madeline, pressing forward in her eagerness. "Oh, madam, when you know how much we owe to your son— how brave, how heroic he has been—"

"Yes," interrupted her father, impetuously stepping before her; "we have a great story to tell you, Mrs. Vyr—a most astonishing story of your son's—"

"You must not tell it now," interposed Vyr, authoritatively; "you must wait until my mother is more calmer. She is not well.—You must not tell

it to her at any time.—I will tell it to you to-morrow, *mannáka*. Now we shall go in, and we shall
show to our guests how that we live in these wild
mountains."

Madame Vyr tried to speak, but her son prevented
her with another kiss and a playful remark, and taking her hand, he led her unresistingly to the open
door. As they were entering he said, in a low voice,
to the major, "I will explain it all to you when we
shall be alone together."

With a natural dignity and grace that the most
hospitable nobleman might have envied, he conducted
his guests through the different apartments of his
unique dwelling. These were in strange contrast to
their wild environments; they might have been the
home of a wealthy gentleman of eccentric tastes in
the heart of a populous city. The walls and ceilings
were panelled and painted in Pompeian style with
old gold and dead colors and with elaborate friezes.
Heavy carved chairs, couches, and tables of Western
manufacture, and Oriental rugs and divans, statues,
and other ornaments of bronze or marble, paintings,
engravings, chandeliers and candelabra, articles of
vertu from every clime and of every age, books and
musical instruments, scattered about without the
slightest regard to general effect, all betokened a
luxuriant if uneducated taste. It must be understood that the craze for furnishings and decorations
of this sort had not then spread over the civilized
world, as it has since; so the four Americans beheld in silent amazement the discordant amalgama-

tion of art, ancient and modern, barbaric and European.

Their host smiled again and again at their looks of wonder and doubtful admiration as they proceeded from room to room. At length he said,

"Your tongues are paralyze, but your faces speak enough. You do not wonder only, but you are critics. You say you do not love the *tout ensemble*—it is very bad—it is not harmony—it is vinegar upon nitre—it is not order, it is chaos. Now, my friends, listen to me. I do not have care for the *tout ensemble*, it will be good for one only look; but I and my mother, we live here all the time; we have more than one only look. We enjoy each thing here by itself, like as we enjoy each book and magazine in our library, without its relations and its harmonies with the other books. The English gentleman and the American gentleman furnishes and adorns his house that he shall please his friends and his visitors. If he shall make mistakes, it is ignorance, and he feels the shame. My father, he furnished and adorned this house that he may please himself, and my mother she was please, too, because *he* was please. I have done the same like as my father did. He lived in the mountains; he did not expect guests—it was accident that he received them, like as it is accident now that we receive you; it was not that he shall please others, but that he shall satisfy himself and my mother. To him beauty was beauty; it was no difference between old and new things; his ancestors were of many nations; he was not Greek, not

Roman, not English, not Turk; to him there was not
Europe, not Asia, not America, not Africa. My mother she loves everythings which my father loved, and
so I do. For us all beautiful things are harmony,
both those wild things which no man sees except ourselves and the other peoples of these mountains, and
also the exquisite things which the artist makes in
Paris."

Madeline took advantage of the pause which now
occurred to say, "Indeed, Mr. Vyr, you have misin-
terpreted our wondering looks altogether. It is such
a delightful surprise to find here so many beautiful
things which we usually see only where men are
thickly congregated together, and where they are
impelled by ambition—love of approbation—to sur-
round themselves with costly adornments."

"That they shall make other men to envy them
and to hate them, is it?" asked Vyr, smiling.

"Oh no, not always, I hope. It is not impossible
that they may like to confer pleasure upon their
friends and visitors. You, it seems, are impelled by
love of beauty, pure and simple."

"Yes, Miss Paul; I love all beauty with a great
passion. My eyes are almost fill with tears when I
look upon the sweet anemones on the sides of the
hills, and my heart it thrills when I behold the beautiful face or the beautiful form of a man, a woman,
or a child. It is a passion which God has create, like
as he has create the sharp desire for food and for water. The undevelop man only is dead to beauty, like
as the dyspeptic man has not the hunger. I enjoy

to show to you these things which I love; but not to please *you* they were brought here; they would be here if no peoples in the world shall see them except my mother and myself."

He ushered them into a bedroom on the second floor, extending outward from the main building like a huge bay-window. Three sides were almost entirely of glass panels, which could be pushed down in grooves out of sight, leaving a wide, open balcony. Mosquito nettings then took the place of the glazing.

"You asked me if I always sleep in the open air," said Vyr. "I told you, when it is winter I come in my cave like to the other bears. This is my cave. I shut it up close, except one little window, and the bright sun shines in all around me and makes me to be warm. In the summer, when it is too much flies and gnats to sleep in the hammock at the veranda, I sleep out-of-door here."

"I suppose," said Major Paul, "you make it a point never to breathe anything but the purest of air, day or night, summer or winter."

"If I can breathe pure air, is it not foolishness to breathe that what is not pure?" Vyr returned, as if what he asked were the most obvious thing in the world. "You and your friends may sleep in rooms the same like this, if it is your wishes; but you can shut them up close, too, if it is your wishes."

Adjoining the bedroom was a commodious bathroom, into which water was conducted by a pipe from a mountain spring.

"I think you should not enjoy to plunge into my

frigidarium in winter, when you must break the ice," said Vyr.

"Ugh!" shuddered Aunt Eliza and Madeline together.

"I assure you," said Griffin, "we should be able to deny ourselves the luxury without repining."

"It is luxury," rejoined Vyr. "The water is so cold as I love only when it is cover over with the ice. Then it makes me to feel red and warm when I come out, and I am light in my feet and in my heart. In the summer it is not so luxury.

"Now we shall go up in the tower, and you shall see the beautiful things of nature, which belong to you, like as they belong to me and my mother. I wish that you shall see them sleeping in the moonlight; then to-morrow you shall see them awake in the sunlight."

Madame Vyr had scarcely spoken since they left the veranda. Nevertheless she had shown unmistakable signs of satisfaction at the frequent exclamations of pleasure and surprise in which the Americans indulged. She declined to climb the winding stairs with them, saying abruptly that she must go down and order supper.

"My mother thinks you are hungry for that what is more nutriment than the mountains and the valleys," said her son, as they began the ascent.

The last glimmer of the short Grecian twilight had disappeared, but the full moon shining into the narrow windows of the tower sufficiently lighted their way. The darkness above and below, the hol-

low reverberation of their voices in the cylinder of the
tower, the strange events that had preceded, the consciousness of their isolation from their fellow-men,
in the midst of a mountainous wilderness, and more
than all else, the character of their mysterious guide,
filled Madeline with a sense of romantic awe that almost made her shudder. "What if he were a Mer-
cury," she thought, "sent to transport us to Olympus!"

On reaching the summit of the tower they beheld
another of the glorious views seen only among the
Morean mountains. Snowy peaks arose against the
star-dotted sky, like giant billows crested with gleaming silver, while the black troughs of the valleys sank
into immeasurable depths between. Here and there
naked slopes reflecting the full moonlight seemed
like vast spirit-forms rising from amid the waves.
Far beyond lay the smooth, dark pavement of the
Ægean.

After gazing a while in silence, Major Paul began
pointing out the peaks and islands whose names he
had learned, and asked the names of others.

"Oh, papa!" protested Madeline, "let us not mind
their names. They seem to dwindle both in magni-
tude and number when we can name and count them."

"I think the same like you, Miss Paul," said Vyr.
"It is like when we know the names and the number of the stars in the heaven—they are no more a
great multitude, but they are a catalogue."

"I like to feel," Madeline rejoined, "when I look
upon a scene like this, as if I had alighted upon some

unknown planet. I can imagine myself wondering
where in the wide universe I am, what sort of inhabitants I am about to meet, and what strange things
lie beyond the horizon."

"I can give you the desired information," put in
Robert Griffin, lapsing into his old habit for almost
the first time since the rescue. "You are upon the
earth, which is round like an apple or an orange, except that it is flattened a little at the poles. Out in
that direction lies a little village known among the
natives as Boston, Massachusetts."

Hector Vyr looked at the speaker as if wondering
whether he were a lunatic or a fool. "Why-fore do
you say that?" he asked, gravely. "Do you think
she does not know?"

"Don't mind him, Mr. Vyr," answered Madeline,
feeling as never before the unspeakable smallness of
the conventional jest. "He is only trying to be jo-
cose."

Vyr nodded his head, smiled pityingly, and said,
"It is sometimes my own amusement, when I am
alone, to lie here and let my soul to fly up into the
sky. I can see the little earth below me, and myself
a speck upon it, occupied with things which are
smaller than myself. Then I say, 'What is it matter if I am greater or smaller than the other men,
because we are all so little? It is like to the little
worm which is longer than other worms at the
breadth of a hair, or perhaps he is shorter.' I am
glad, Miss Paul, because your imagination loves to
play, too!"

"Oh yes, Mr. Vyr, you will find us fully as poetic as yourself," said Aunt Eliza, who had conceived a sudden small pique, for some reason or other; whether because so little of the talk had been thus far addressed to her, or because she thought her nephew had been somewhat ungraciously suppressed, I cannot tell. "Like all other Orientals, I suppose you thought we Americans cared for nothing but dollars and jokes."

Although she said this laughingly, she was conscious of greater *brusquerie* than she had intended, and she shrank in confusion from the mild, penetrating look with which, even in the obscure light, she saw Vyr was studying her. They had all, in turn, shrunk from that look, innocent and mild as it was.

"Miss Wellington," he replied, "I have heard that your peoples have not imagination; but I have read much of your books of poetry, and I find in them sometimes very great imagination. They hear voices to speak in the winds and in the waves, and they tell the words which those voices say to them, which is the same like the old divinities of the Greeks. They feel the souls that live in the mountains and in the rivers—the mountain frowns angrily, the river thinks silently upon his own deep secrets, and the brook laughs with his shallow joy. But I find, too, much that what seems to me to be disease, like the fever, or like peoples with nerves and brains but no belly."

·This made the Americans laugh. It was an opportunity which Griffin could not forego. Placing his hands upon the part last mentioned, he said, with a comical grimace,

"*We* are not that kind of people, Mr. Vyr."

. The host was pleased with this sally.

"Forgive," he said; "I am starving you. We shall go down now."

XI.

JEALOUSY.

THE dining-room into which they were now introduced was one of the most ornate apartments of the house. An Ionic door-way opened into it; the floor was inlaid with Doric marble and other stones of different colors, forming one huge figure of kaleidoscopic symmetry within a wide Greek border; a dado and a frieze with human and animal figures in bass-relief harmonized admirably with the floor and with the panel-work of the walls and ceiling; in the corners were volutes relieved by gilding; here and there in niches were statuettes of marble and bronze; an elaborate bronze chandelier, with lamps of ancient pattern, hung directly over the centre of the dining-table, on which was spread an array of edibles in whimsical contrast with the vessels containing them. Boiled eggs in cups of delicate silver filigree, coarse but good bread on trays of rare porcelain, coffee of burnt barley in a richly embossed silver urn, sweet, fresh milk, and an abundance of fruit in vessels of similar pattern, constituted the meal.

10

"Sit, my friends," said the host, with the voice and gesture of a gracious king, "and give honor to me and to my mother by breaking our bread. You will not be feast like as you are feast at your own homes; but you have lived a month in the mountains, and you will enjoy our simple eating, perhaps, more better than you have enjoyed the richer feast before."

Protesting that there could be nothing better, Major Paul set his companions the example by accepting the invitation with an alacrity more creditable to his appetite than to his courtliness.

Hector Vyr drank nothing, but ate heartily, with vigorous, animal relish, of the coarse bread and of the fruits. Griffin inquired, with an apology for his inquisitiveness, but with a sidelong glance at Madeline, whether Vyr's system of dieting excluded all the delicacies of art.

"I do not think that I use a 'system of dieting,'" was the reply. "I do not think much of that what I eat. I take that what I like. I do not like meat much. I like the oranges and the figs and the apples best of all the other. What is 'delicacies of art?' Is it spices and confections? Those things are not to me delicacies. I do not like those, like as a horse does not like them. I think I am good deal like to a horse," he added, with his inimitable wholesome smile.

"Do you—" began Aunt Eliza. Then, abashed at her thoughtless presumption, she stopped abruptly, and her eyes fell.

"Why-fore do you not go on?" asked Vyr, graciously. "I like that you shall ask me questions of myself. I have told some things to you, and it is right they make you inquisitive of more."

"Thank you. I was going to ask if you never *drank* at your meals," she said.

"I do not know. I never think if I do or if I do not. I drink always when I feel the thirst. I do not think that I am thirst when I am eating. You think I am like to a feeble old woman which is dyspeptic?"—with another smile—"that I shall always think of that what I eat and drink?"

"We did not know," returned Aunt Eliza. "You said something about being a 'health-monomaniac,' and we supposed that—"

"Ah yes, Miss Wellington. I said that to you. But I think my health shall be better if I eat that what I like. I think my belly— Why-fore do you laugh, Mr. Griffin? Have I said wrong, *mannáka?*"

"You should say *stomach*, Hector, not belly," answered Madame Vyr.

"I shall learn to speak English in a few days more, if you will talk to me. Those three Englishmen which I saved from the klephts did not talk much. They said to me that they were afraid at me. I have tried that you shall not be afraid. Have I not succeed? I do not scare you, do I?"

"No, indeed, Mr. Vyr," answered Madeline, to whom his question was more directly addressed. "I assure you that your kind, genial treatment has placed us all entirely at our ease."

"I am very glad at what you say. I did not wish that those other should be afraid; but I have learned a little lesson. I will say now what I wished to say: I think that my stomach knows better what is right that I shall eat than my head knows it."

"I suppose that is very well for a perfectly healthy stomach, as yours must be," said the major; "but it would be a very unsafe rule for people in general to follow. And I suppose your guide determines the quantity as well as the quality of what you shall eat."

"I eat so long as I have hunger; then I stop. I enjoy great pleasure while I have hunger, and when I have not, then I do not like. You think I am an animal? Yes; if I am a poet on my tower and in the fields and on the mountains, I am a great animal at my table."

After supper, Vyr invited the two gentlemen to return to the veranda, promising them what he supposed would be a great treat to them. When they were comfortably seated in the brilliant moonlight, a servant appeared with a little vase containing half a dozen cigars. "Now," said the entertainer, "you shall be happy, like as you would be if you are at Boston. You may sit here and poison yourselves, and I will look upon the sacrifice."

"Ah," sighed the major, with unutterable satisfaction, as he took one of the little brown rolls; "this alone was wanting to complete our bliss."

"I have been longing for Boston, or at least Athens," chimed in Griffin, "with all due respect and gratitude for your princely hospitality, Mr. Vyr;

but now I am perfectly content. I don't care for
Boston, or Athens, or the whole civilized world."

"You are all alike the same," replied Vyr, surveying them with curiosity. "The three Englishmen
said almost those words when my servant returned
which I sent to buy for them those cigars."

"But are you not going to join us?" the major
asked.

"No, Mr. Paul. For what reason shall I smoke
tobacco? Does it give satisfaction to hunger or to
thirst? does it give health to the body or to the intellects?"

"I thought you didn't trouble yourself to think
whether a thing is good for the health or not," said
Griffin, rolling out with intense enjoyment a volume
of smoke, milky white in the moonlight.

"*I* may not trouble, but my *stomach* troubles," replied Vyr, laughing.

"Smoking would give you a great pleasure that
you know nothing of," said the major.

"My life is already full with pleasures. I have
no necessity for another, that I shall pay for it with
a part of myself."

"I cannot see how it could possibly harm so strong
a man as you are," said Griffin.

"Not harm? Yes, a little. The general which
has an army of thousand hundred soldiers must not
sacrifice one soldier without the necessity. A miser
which has thousand hundreds of gold and silver does
not throw away one little drachma if he can prevent.
Hector Vyr is a miser. He has swore that he shall

not throw away one little atom from his manhood of his body or his mind. If my father drinked whiskey, or smoked tobacco, or hurted himself in any little thing, he would hurt me too. When your English and American strong men shall fight for the prize, they do not drink whiskey, they do not lie lazy in their bed, they do not smoke tobacco. They '*train*,' as you say it. I train always, all my life. When the great artist shall make a statue from marble, you say it will not harm much if he shall make one little wrong cut with the chisel. Ah, it *shall* hurt. I am an artist—my statue is Hector Vyr."

"You have indeed reduced self-culture to a fine art," remarked Griffin.

"Yes, Mr. Griffin. Your father shall give you a noble horse. You are very full of thanks, and you take very great care. You do not wish that your gift shall be hurted in any little thing. God he gave to me this body. I am very full of thanks, because I think it is a very precious gift; and I cultivate it and I develop it to the best perfection which I can. God he also gave me a mind and a heart. I receive those with very much greater thanks, and I am very much more careful."

"Then," said Griffin, "in spite of what you have said, I can't understand why your thoughts are not always on what is good and what is not good for you, and I should think you would defeat your own object by such excessive care. *We* think the very way to be ailing is to be always on our guard against ailments."

Vyr laughed in his characteristic way. "You cannot understand how that it is my *habit*. I do not think about my habit. You do not always think, 'I must not cut myself with a knife, I must not shoot myself with a gun, I must not drink the poisonous cup, I must not sleep out-of-door in the snow.' You avoid all those things without think; the same like that I avoid all the little things that hurt without much think. I suppose it is the *instinct* in me, like as it is in the wild animal — the chamois, does he smoke tobacco or drink whiskey?"

"Well," rejoined Griffin, throwing himself back luxuriously in his chair, "you are, at least, very kind and hospitable to give *us* cigars to poison ourselves with."

"I am your host, not your master," retorted Vyr, without offence, but with an unconscious dignity that brought his two auditors up erect, and made them for the moment forget their pleasurable indulgence. "You are my guests, not my children. You ask me for cigars; that is your foolishness. I give them to you; that is my hospitality. I say to you, 'They are not good, they will poison you;' that is my friendship. You smoke them; that is your liberty. You are not slaves, except of yourselves. I can set you free from the klephts, but you must set yourselves free from yourselves."

When they had finished and thrown away their cigars, he said, "My friends, it is very late for me, and I am full of sleep. I shall go to my bed now, when I have said to the womans *Kalé nýkta.*"

The apartments assigned to the guests consisted of a capacious drawing-room opening into two sleeping-rooms that jutted out from the main building like the one they had already seen. All were luxuriously fitted up in European style; for which, the host informed them, they were indebted to the wishes of his mother.

"Here," he said, "you can think that you are in Boston; and you can dance till the sun shall shine again, if it is your wishes."

"Thank you," said Madeline; "but we don't dance all the time, even in Boston. For myself, I am tired enough to go to bed at once."

"Tired!" exclaimed Vyr. "I did not think that you can be tired, with that cheek like the rose and that bright eye."

"Indeed I am, and very often. You must remember we are not children of nature, like yourself. I suppose you haven't the least idea what the word 'tired' means."

"I do not think I know perfectly. I do not remember that I was ever tired. Is it a pain? an ache, like that I feel in this arm?"

"Oh," cried Madeline, "forgive me for my neglect. You have made so little of your wound, and I have been so dazed with the strangeness of everything, that, to tell the truth, I almost forgot it. Will you not have it dressed again before you retire?"

"I give you thanks, Miss Paul. I have a faithful servant which is a very good doctor of wounds, and he will do for me what it is necessary. Then I shall sleep. Is it 'tired' to be full of sleep? If it is that, I love to be tired—it is a sense full of delightness. *Kalé nýkta*, my friends. I wish that your sleep shall be like the baby on the bosom of his mother."

His good wishes were heartily returned, and he withdrew.

The moment the door closed, Madeline rushed into her father's arms.

"Thank God, my child!" he cried, gathering her to his broad breast. "Yes, thank God for answering your prayer!"

"And our brave, noble, godlike deliverer!" she murmured, as her long-restrained tears of joy and gratitude poured forth.

Griffin uttered no word, but he walked to the window and scowled fiercely at the moon.

"But what a singular—what a very extraordinary person Mr. Vyr is!" exclaimed Aunt Eliza, after the mutual congratulations and rejoicings had somewhat abated.

"Extraordinary? well, I should *say* so," answered the major. "Constellations of the zodiac! He is a prodigy—a miracle. I never even imagined such a character. It is a combination of the freshness of a child, the strength of a giant, and the wisdom of a sage."

"What strange eyes he has," said Madeline, musingly; "and what shining, satiny skin—for all the world like a huge, strapping baby."

"I've seen *that* matched more than once," said Griffin. "You never saw John Heenan 'peel;' I have. His skin was as rosy and glossy as your demigod's."

"No," replied Madeline; "I've not been in the habit of frequenting the prize-ring."

"Well, you needn't annihilate me with your scorn. I've never been there but twice in my life, and that was when I was a sophomore. I didn't go alone, either, I want you to understand; some of the best fellows in college went with me."

"*Best!*"

"Yes, *best*—such men as Harry Le Court, for instance, and Tom Richmond. You wouldn't curl your pretty lip at *them*, I fancy. Oh, well, you may sniff and sneer as much as you please; I've seen your poetic soul in raptures over the statue of some old Greek pugilist. How much better was he than John Heenan, may I ask? Wasn't the *pancration* a prize-ring, my sweet jewel of consistency?"

"If you've been through college, and see no difference between a high-born athlete winning his olive-crown in the presence of the noblest citizens of ancient Greece, in the presence of applauding statesmen, artists, poets, philosophers, and a brutal bully pounding another brutal bully for a thousand dollars, in the midst of a drunken mob of gamblers and thieves ready to scamper at the first sight of a policeman's billy—"

"Oh, for dear pity's sake," burst in Aunt Eliza, in her shrillest tones, "don't you two get to quarrelling."

"I hadn't the least idea of quarrelling, aunty," protested Madeline. "I was full of only joy and wonder and gratitude till Robert compared *him* to a vulgar prize-fighter; the very idea was so revolting, so utterly intolerable, that I couldn't help answering him as he deserved."

"I should never think of comparing Mr. Vyr to a prize-fighter," said Aunt Eliza. "He reminds me more of one of the sons of God the Bible tells of—"

"That loved the daughters of men." The humorous glance with which her father finished Miss Wellington's sentence, was entirely lost upon Madeline, who was busy with her hair at the mirror.

Griffin sprang up from the divan where he had been lying, in a rage which he tried to conceal under a show of petty impatience. "I didn't compare him to a prize-fighter," he snarled. "I only said Heenan had as good a skin as he had. I should think the rest of you had glorified him enough to make up for that. I'll grant you he's a wonderful savage, and has done us a devilish good turn; but for Heaven's sake"—choking under his increasing passion—"one would think he had said enough *himself* to cover all the points. What between his self-deification and your abject homage, I must confess I'm beginning to be—a trifle disgusted—and should be"—with an oath—"if he were an archangel, which you all seem to think him—especially Madeline."

"When you get over your senseless fury," returned Madeline, turning almost as white as he, "you'll see how wicked and ungrateful you have been. Go, Robert; lay the head which the 'wonderful savage' has saved on the savage's pillow. Good-night. Good-night, papa. Come, Aunt Eliza."

With this she sailed into her room and closed the door.

"Well," shrilled Aunt Eliza, "this is a fine time for such a scene, isn't it? Who would suppose it was only a few hours since we were all trembling for our lives? And here we are as safe as if we were in Boston."

"Good-night," said Griffin.

"Oh, good-night. I sincerely hope you will sleep off your disgust. Good-night, Warren." And the good lady sailed out of sight as proudly as her niece had done.

Griffin remained just as Madeline had left him.

"Oh, come, come, Robert," remonstrated Major Paul; "as your aunt says, this is a fine time to quarrel. What does it matter what Madge says?"

"It matters a great deal to *me*, as you well know," sinking into a chair. "What do *I* care for the life he has saved if he is going to rob me of what I value more than my life? She has already fallen in love with this 'great, brave, noble, godlike deliverer'— those were her very words! How can she help it? how could *any* woman help it—particularly under the circumstances?"

"Folly of the children of Israel! I'd as soon think of her falling in love with the Olympian Jupiter!"

"But she *has*, I tell you. Her face follows him like a sunflower. I have *eyes*, if they are not 'clear and bright as those of an infant.' There's another of her adoring phrases," he added, with intense bitterness.

"She *wonders* at him, of course, as we all do, but that does not necessarily imply love. Come, come, I'm older than you are, and I know more about these things than you do, Robert. A woman's heart doesn't always go with her eyes. A cat may look at a king, but she may not want to jump into his lap, for all that."

"She never cared a pin for me—and what chance have I now? I am more insignificant than ever in her eyes. Curse the day we started on this fools' errand!"

"I tell you, Robert, you are wrong. No woman ever cares for a man, whatever he may be or whatever he may have done for her, till he loves her first."

"Who says he *hasn't* loved her first?"

"Bosh! you corybantic ninny!—he thinks no more of her than if she were a kitten."

"I wish I could believe you, Uncle Warren. But you are blind; you are not in love yourself, and you are as blind as a stone."

"They say it is love that is blind."

"Proverbs are always lies, and that's the stupidest lie of all. No man has eyes like the lover; he sees everything. Haven't I seen this god, as everybody calls him, drinking in her charms with those glaring eyes of his, ever since he first set them on her? Don't you remember how he began his inventory by looking at her teeth? Great Heaven! as if she were a blooded mare! I wish she had made him *feel* them! He evidently knows he'll never find another like her, and you can bet your life he'll not let her slip if he can help it."

"Nonsense. He's a *scientist*, man; he wanted to see her teeth out of pure scientific curiosity. He doesn't often have such an opportunity for studying the civilized woman."

"Scientific humbug!" ejaculated Griffin, jerking his head from side to side in his impatience; "as if she were a beetle! That's worse than treating her like a horse!"

"I never knew before that beetles *had* teeth," retorted the major, thinking he would try the effect of a little humor.

"Oh, no doubt you regard it as a stupendous joke; but, I assure you, it's no joke to me."

"No, my poor boy; I do not regard it as a joke, by any means. I'm really sorry for your trouble. I like you, and have always liked you. To be sure, there are some things that— You know Madge complains of a few little points which you can easily correct, Robert, you can easily correct—and I have hoped with all my heart that she would like you a thousand times better than I do. Still, as I have told you, I cannot undertake to coerce her. It would do no good if I should—you know her well enough for that. I really think, however, that your suspicions are groundless. In the first place, I've no idea that this Hector Vyr would marry an American girl.

I've a notion he's on the lookout for all sorts of physical perfections in the woman he is to marry. He's a man with a theory and a mission, and our American girls have no great reputation for physical stamina, you know. But even if our Madge came up to his standard, I'm positive she would never consent to imprison herself in this wilderness; no, not if the finest god of Greek mythology should come to life out of the marble and offer himself to her. At all events, you may rest assured I should do and say all in my power to prevent it."

"Well," sighed Griffin, after a gloomy pause, "I hope Madge has taught him a thing or two besides her dental formula. Among the fine traits he is so anxious to develop he'd better include common decency. I'm thinking it will take a good many generations to evolute this wonderful race into gentlemen."

"Hippogriffins of Bagdad! but you *are* bitter, aren't you?"

"Do you wonder at it? By heavens! if he makes her any sign I'll fight him, big and smart as he is."

"There, there; go to bed—that's a good fellow. You are only killing yourself with this excitement."

"I say, Uncle Warren, how long do you intend to stay here? Can't we get away in the morning?"

"Perhaps so. We'll have to get away soon to get some clothes. We didn't bring our trunks, and I doubt very much whether our last landlords will send them."

"Confound it! I heard his half-crazy mother tell

Aunt Eliza that their head-servant Ghiánnes would go to Athens for anything we needed. But we needn't accept. We *can't* stay, possibly, can we?"

"We'll talk about it in the morning. Will you come to bed now? I'm going."

. Griffin threw his arms out on the table, and dropped his head on them. His uncle spoke a few consolatory words, and left him. He had been alone but a few minutes when a door opened, a light footstep tripped across the floor, and a hand was laid on his shoulder. He looked up eagerly. There stood Madeline, dressed as she was when he had last seen her.

"Forgive me, Robert."

"Oh, Madeline, you do not love this great—prodigious—savage, do you?"

She started back as if he had struck her. "Robert Griffin! what are you saying? I came to make my peace with you, and you have— Never *dare* to speak to me in this way again!"

Before he could reply she was gone.

XII.

THE TRADITIONAL OATH.

MADELINE arose the next morning with a delicious
sense of rest, of terrible peril past and perfect safety
present, of keen interest in the singular and romantic
situation in which she and her friends were placed,
and of a certain unreasoning happiness besides which
made her join the birds in their morning songs.
Then there came up like a cloud over the bright sky
the recollection of her last scene with Robert. Poor
Robert, why could he not be satisfied with her warm,
cousinly affection? Why must he spoil all, making
her as well as himself unhappy by his hopeless
persistency? Why, above all, must he arouse her
indignation by his obstinate ingratitude and injustice
to their brave benefactor? Did he not know that
he was taking the surest means of alienating even
her friendship? Had he not always shown a low
estimate of her mind and character by supposing
that she could tolerate the debased opinions and
tastes he took no pains to conceal from her? Should
she not be serving him right to show him that she
even felt insulted by his supposing it possible for
her to love a man with such ideas and habits as he
openly avowed? Why should she feel such tender
pity for him? He loved her; yes, poor, poor boy,

11

he *did* love her. But why, then, did he not try to please her? why did he not try to elevate himself to her standard? Until he showed some disposition to do that, what claim had he even on her compassion? Certainly none. Before aspiring to her love, let him show at least that he thought it worth making an effort to deserve. With this definite conclusion, she strove to banish the painful subject from her thoughts.

Descending to the drawing-room, she found Madame Vyr placidly entertaining Miss Wellington with a gossipy description of the few people she sometimes met. Rude and unlettered as they were, in general, they were vivacious and kind-hearted, and she had even found some of a better class at Mikro-Maina whose society gave her much comfort. To Madeline's inquiry whether she did not often sigh for old England, she replied that until her husband's death such a feeling had scarcely entered her mind. Since then her anomalous life had lost very much of its charm. No one, not even a son like his, could fill his place in her mind. As she went on, her eyes dilated, her face became chalky white, as it had been when they first saw her, and her words became more and more incoherent. With delicate tact Madeline gradually succeeded in drawing her thoughts to her native land. She told of her childhood and youth in an old mansion on the Thames; of the avenue of grand old trees under which she used to run races with her brother; of her school life in London, and, finally, of her leaving home with her father and

brother to make the tour which had sealed her fate.
Madeline quickly asked if she had never visited England since. Yes, she had made one long, delightful
visit, and was intending some day to make another.
Her son continually urged her to go; but he could
not be persuaded to go with her, and she would not
leave him with only the servants for companions.
Some day, perhaps, there would be one to take her
place; *then* she would go. She was very glad to
meet people who spoke her native tongue. She had
not seemed very hospitable the evening before, but
she was suffering from one of her ill turns, and they
must not regard it. Hector was always so tender,
never ashamed of her, whatever she might say or
do, although she knew she had mortified him terribly more than once. She could never make them
understand what a son he was to her, always so
thoughtful and loving, so obedient and deferential,
notwithstanding he was so great and strong and wise,
and she so weak and foolish. But she had not always been so; she had been considered even remarkable for her robustness of both body and mind until
—until the terrible event which—

Here Madeline gently interrupted her, to ask
whether she did not often speak English with her
son, who understood it so well. She used to, sometimes, when he was a child, but not of late; she had
become so accustomed to the language of the country in which she had spent so many years of her life,
that she found it much easier to her than her own.
It was surprising, however, how it all came back to

her, now that she was talking with English people, or, what was the same thing, Americans.

At this point Major Paul came in, accompanied by his host, the latter dressed in ordinary Greek costume, that is to say, with his brawny neck, arms, and legs covered, as they had not been the previous day.

Vyr's face glowed with something more than exuberant health, and his voice swelled with rich resonance, as he said, "*Kale-mĕra.* That is our way of saying good-morning. Miss Paul, your face shows to me that you know to sleep, although you have come from the country where it says sleep is a lost art."

"Why?" Madeline asked, with a laugh. "Do I look as if I were asleep?"

"Ah, that is the way that you play with me. Do those birds sing like as they are asleep? But we know from their happy noise how that they have sleeped most sweetly."

"Oh, I am noisy?"

"You are mischief. Your father shall whip you. You will be noisy then, I think. *Mannáka,* is the breakfast prepared? Mr. Paul and I are prepared for it."

"We are waiting only for you and Mr. Griffin."

"I beg you not to wait for him," said the major. "If Robert prefers walking to breakfast, let him have his preference."

"It is right," answered Vyr. "We must not all do the wrong because one does it."

They sat down to a meal which, though simple

as their supper had been, their keen appetites made
sumptuous. Vyr ate almost voraciously, but princi-
pally of fruit.

"Do tell me, Mr. Vyr," said Miss Wellington, in a
sort of mild desperation, "whether you really wouldn't
like a greater variety in your food, if you didn't think
it would—*hurt* you."

At this they all laughed, the host loudest of all.

"You think it is a strange thing," he said, "that a
lusty animal like me shall be so full of care, like an
invalid which is in the charge of the doctor. But I
have telled you that I do not have care: I eat what
I most like, because I know that is the best for my—
stomach. It is a strange thing to me, too, that your
peoples confuse in your food so many differing sa-
vors. Would you like those things if they are all
together mixed in one dish?—bread, oil, bullock,
wine, soup, fruit, fishes, nuts, birds, coffee, tea, garlic,
pepper, confection, mustard, butter, salt, vegetable,
vinegar, cigars? Do you like such *olla podrida?*
Yet is it not all then in your stomach, when you
rise from the table?"

"No," said the major, promptly. "I deny the
cigars."

"Yes, my friend; if you die—and it is wonder
why-fore you do not die—and if the doctor shall
make the autopsy, he will find the cigar, too."

A lively, half-playful discussion followed, which
Vyr seemed to enjoy hugely.

After breakfast the entertainer took Major Paul
to an eminence at a short distance from the man-

sion, whence were visible the wheat-fields, orchards, and pastures populous with herds, of the Vyr estate. Their extent and flourishing condition explained in part, at least, the opulence of their owner's home, in a country where the finest marble is cheaper than granite. Finding a natural bench of stone, they seated themselves with their backs resting against a rocky wall, which shaded them from the warm morning sun.

"Now," said Major Paul, with good-humored sarcasm, "can you point to something which does *not* belong to the Vyr estate?"

"Yes, Mr. Paul; we do not own the sky, not the mountain-tops, not the sea. I think, too, we do not own the ground, although the laws of Greece have given it to us for many generations. I think we own that what my knowledge and labor and the labor of my servants make from the ground. I have more than two hundreds of Albanian servants, and we together make very much to grow from the ground. I do not prevent that other peoples shall make from my ground, too, if it is their wishes, and if they do not rob like the klephts; but they must pay to me a little, because I and my fathers have made the ground to be better for them. It is justice."

"Most certainly it is justice," replied the major, emphatically. "By-the-way, I am curious to know what sort of arrangement you make with your servants."

"I pay to them that what their labor has value. It is enough, and they are content. I know very much more than they do know, and my knowledge makes their labor to be much more value, which I do not give to them. I hold the greater value to myself—it is justice. I also give good deal to the Government. That is justice, too; because I think that the ground is really their ground, and because they give to me much protection, and they make it that I can sell my herds and my harvests, and that I can buy all things that I wish from all the world. The Government also gives to me much money, because I have drived away the klephts many times from the country. It is all justice."

"Well, Mr. Vyr," said Major Paul, relieving the strain of the attention with which he had listened by a deep, long breath, "I do not see but that you understand the philosophy of trade and taxation as well as if you lived in Boston—and apply it, too, excepting that you are much more liberal than men usually are."

"I pay good deal to the poor peoples also, which I find—"

"Pay?" with a puzzled look.

"Yes, Mr. Paul. I pay to them, because I think it is justice. God has placed them here, and they own some of the ground like as all the children own the ground of their father. But I do not go all over the world to find them. Other rich men must pay to their own poor peoples in the places where they live together."

"H'm; you conduct your affairs on a very unusual basis, sir. I don't see how you prosper as you seem to on that principle."

"I have enough, Mr. Paul, to do all my wishes, and very much more."

"Do you go to Athens yourself to transact your business with the Government?"

"No; the agent comes to me."

"But how have you been able to gather so many choice books, ornaments, and other things as you have in your house, if you go abroad so little?"

"That is very easily explain. My old Ghiánnes goes away very much. He is wise and cultivate—he was once a teacher in Athens—he knows the things what I love, he sends to me description and pictures, and I send to him that he shall buy them for me. He brought for my mother the English tables and chairs and other things which you have seen."

"So you have never been to Athens yourself?"

"You do not remember, Mr. Paul. Have I not said to you that I have been there two times? One time was when I was a little boy, with my father; the other time was three years ago."

"You must have attracted a great deal of attention."

"Yes, a little; not much, because we put on the dress like the other peoples. Everybody stared at us a little, because we were so red in our cheeks, I suppose, and because we walked so strangely; but no one knew us who we were."

"You have mentioned your father several times. Are you willing to tell me more about him?"

A majestic sadness settled over Vyr's face. For a few moments he was silent; then he began: "My

father was killed by the klephts three years ago. It
was then that I went to Athens the second time, Mr.
Paul. I told you that I would explain to you of
my mother. It was the lightning-bolt from the sky
to her; she has never recovered herself from it.
Nothing has been left to her as it was, except that to
me, her son, she is the same. And I too—for long
time my heart was the furnace trying to consume
my big body. But nature is kind, and I was younger and stronger than my poor mother."

"Go on," said Major Paul, his broad face glowing with interest and sympathy; "that is, if you
are—"

"I will go on, because you ask it."

"Not by any means, Mr. Vyr, if it pains you."

"I do not wish to escape from that pain. I wish
that I shall never cease to offer to my dead father
the incense of my sorrow. In his body he was like
to me: in his character—it is my most highest ambition to be like to him. When he was older than I
am now a little, he tried to rescue a family from the
captivity of the klephts. It was an English family
of rank. He could not save them, only the daughter, and *she was my mother*. Oh, Mr. Paul, you have
never seen my mother. She was proud and strong
and beautiful; her talking was full of diamonds like
to the lights in her eyes. It is to *me* only that she
has not changed."

"She is very beautiful still," said Major Paul, in a
low, tender voice.

"To you, too?" replied Hector Vyr, his face lighting up with joy. "I am very glad for that. I had fear that— But I will tell to you the story: when I was a little child my father protected me against all the things which he thought can make feeble in any little way my body and my mind. He taught to me the habits and the thoughts which you have seen. Like to the father of Hannibal, he made me to say an oath. It was that I shall never relax those severe *regime* which he taught to me; that I shall never accept offices from the Government or from the peoples; that I shall always live in a home isolate from civilized men; that I shall avoid all notorieties; that I shall marry myself with none of those faults of the mind and body which are so great curses to the race of man; and, at the last, that I shall make my son which shall take my place to swear the same. Not until the fourteenth generation are the Vyrs to be released from this oath."

"A most remarkable oath," said his listener, half to himself.

"Yes. It is not like to any other, I suppose, that men have ever sworn."

"Do you not consider it rather—a—*oppressive?* Do you think a father has a *right* to impose such an obligation, or that his children are morally bound to obey it?"

"I said my father *made* me to swear: it is better that I say he *persuaded* me. But he persuaded so strongly, so irresistibly, his reasons which he spoke were so cogent, and the thing at which he purposed was so noble, and it so allured to me, that it was the same like he compelled me. It seems to me like as it was a command to me from Heaven."

"The object, if I have rightly understood you, is nothing more nor less than the highest possible degree of self-development."

"Yes, that is right. You do not see the nobleness of such object? It is like to selfishness? Ah, Mr. Paul, one man is only one little link in a long chain. He is a fountain, and it is to flow from him a river through all the ages that shall come, to the great ocean of Eternity. You do not think of all the ages that shall come—you think alone of to-day."

"Oh yes, I understand you perfectly, Mr. Vyr. But I must confess the thoughts you suggest are too —the issues you speak of are too comprehensive, they involve too much, for me to take them all in at one breath. One thing occurs to me, however: I do not see why even self-development would not be best effected by free mingling in society, by vigorous action with and upon men. And, Mr. Vyr, when I reflect what grand results you might accomplish with your wonderfully developed powers, how you might influence men by your example to imitate, in some degree at least, your methods, I cannot but feel that your asceticism is a great wrong both to yourself and to your race."

"You cannot separate your thoughts from here and now," answered Vyr, a little impatiently. "When the fulness of time shall be come, some of our lineage will go out from solitude, and do our mission in the world. But it is not the time yet. We do not pluck the fruit from the tree until it is ripe. We are not yet ripe; we are only in the seventh generation; we have not yet risen to the high *possibility*."

"But what possible objection can there be to going forth *now?* Instead of interfering with your self-development, I should think the very activity of life in the world of busy men would help it on."

"Mr. Paul," returned Vyr, with slow, emphatic utterance, "that day which takes me away from my solitude here shall be the doomday to the great purpose, that what the representatives of seven generations of our family have devote themselves like to a religion. That what you wish me to do, it has been tested. I have not yet explain to you one thing: our families have been few—most always it has been only one child. But sometimes it was more; then all except *one* were not bound by the oath. All the others they can go away where they wish to go. Some have made great reputation. You would be astonished if I shall tell to you their name. But it was the end. Their children have been swallowed up in the great ocean of men without name. That would be the same with me if I should do as you say to me. This is why-fore I have sworn to stay here as my fathers."

"And you really believe that want of intercourse with your fellow-men, of the stimulus to activity which they would be to you, is not a great loss?"

"I have the intercourse, all which I can spare the time. Do you forget I have many servants which I must teach and command? I see many times the agents and the men which do business with me. And I have enough activity. I labor every day with the greatest activity of all the powers of my mind and my body. You think I and my fathers have not write books?"

"Indeed I had no idea of such a thing. Did they publish over their own names?"

"They have *not* published. They write books for ourselves, not for the world."

"But why do you not give them to the world? That certainly could do you no harm, and it might be of vast benefit to others."

"Have I not said to you that the world has not necessity for more books? It has enough already, and much more than enough. No man can drink except a few little cups from the sea of books. I say to you again, because you do not remember, men have not necessity for more to read, but for better brains to read that what is already write."

"Then why do you write books at all even for yourselves?" asked the major, becoming more and more perplexed. "The libraries of the world are as accessible to you as to any one else, I believe you have said."

"We write because of the benefit to ourselves of writing. It is very great development of the intellects, like hard labor is to the body. It is very little good to me to look at you when you lift the great stone. I must lift it by myself, that I shall grow strong. Like that, it is more good to me to write a book by myself than to read that book which other men have write. But I must do the both, too. I must eat with the mouth of my brain, and labor with the hands of my brain. I must do the two things both."

"I hope," said the major, deferentially, "you will allow me the pleasure of reading some of the works of which you speak, especially those from your own pen—though I suppose, of course, I shall have to get some one to translate them for me."

"Not any one can read them except myself," replied Vyr, smiling; "they are all here," touching his forehead with his finger. "I write them when I walk, when I labor in the fields; it is too much of time to write them with paper. But you shall see the things which I and my fathers have discovered in our laboratory — chemistry, mineralogy, botany, zoology."

"You surprise me more and more. Have you made many *new* discoveries?"

"I do not know. I have not read all the books which men have write; but it is indifference to me if they are new or old. It is enough if I discover by myself. When you give to your little boy some questions of mathematic, he must answer them for himself; it is not good that other peoples shall answer them for him. Like that, Nature gives to us great questions, and it is better that we shall answer them by ourselves, not that we shall read those answers of other men."

"Even in your studies you think nothing of the benefit you might be to others—only of yourself," exclaimed Major Paul, with feeling. Then he reddened, and began to stammer an apology.

Vyr smiled again. "Do not you think offence, Mr. Paul," he said. "I am glad that you have learn to say to me your thoughts. I wish that you shall not hide them from me. Say some more."

Thus encouraged, the major went on: "I should think you would be afraid that so much thought about yourself, so much energy expended upon yourself, and so little upon your fellow-men, of the present generation at least, would develop a trait in your character that even you will acknowledge is neither admirable nor desirable."

"You mean the selfishness, egotism?" with a good-natured smile.

The major nodded.

"I shall show you different. If I think only of myself, it would be the climax of egotism; but do not you understand what that would make me to do? What do the selfish men, the egotists, try to do? What do they burn up their hearts and their souls to do? Is not it that they shall get to themselves fame, glory, the isolate name which shall sound loud among all the peoples of the world, and shall go down with great echoes to the posterity? I am content—yes, Mr. Paul, I *wish*—that the fame of Hector Vyr shall never go away from these mountains. Who is Hector Vyr? One man. Who is one man? He is nothing — except the preserver and the transmitter of a *Type*. It is my aspiration that I shall be one little step, one little round stick without name, in the ladder which shall elevate one family, at least, to the ideal manhood. I wish that the little stick shall be strong, that it shall not break. Is it selfishness, Mr. Paul? is it egotism?"

Overpowered by the inspired eloquence of the strange enthusiast's face, voice, gestures, the major could only say, in a low, humble tone, "No, Mr. Vyr; I beg your pardon for my— It is the climax of self-sacrifice."

"Not self-sacrifice," returned Vyr, with unabated ardor, "for I am very happy. What is fame, glory, to me? It is nothing. It is the envy of your friends, and the homage of your strangers, which love you less as they are more distance away from you. You are not to them a man, you are nothing except a name. If I shall be famous, I shall still be isolate like as I am now. What is it matter if I am above my fellow-men, or if I am far away from them; I am not one *of* them if I shall be one or other. No, Mr. Paul; I have not thirst for glory, for my life is full without it. Except one black year, my life has been intense happiness. Everything is joy to me, even the knowledge that I live."

"I think I can understand that," replied the major, thoughtfully and admiringly surveying his companion's splendid physique. "I have heard perfect happiness defined as the perfectly harmonious operation of all the natural functions. I thank you for what you have said. I feel highly honored by the confidence you have placed in me, and the pains you have taken to enlighten me upon matters which you must hold sacred above all others."

"One thing," said Vyr, speaking in a lower tone and more slowly, "I have not explained. You do not understand how that I speak so much to you, when I have sworn that I shall avoid all notorieties?"

"Pardon me," answered Major Paul, quickly; "I see no difficulty there. You recognize in me a man of honor. You know perfectly well that nothing would tempt me to violate your confidence, even if you had not placed me and my friends under the greatest possible obligation."

"Yes, Mr. Paul; I know that you are a man of honor, but that alone shall never make me to be a gossip to you. You are the only man except myself which knows our family secret. I have a great reason why-fore I give it to you. I shall tell the reason to you before you go away. I, also, am a man of honor."

Had the speaker been any other than Hector Vyr, the major would have felt no uncertainty as to his meaning. He gazed into his eyes in an eager endeavor to extort from them the promised revelation, but they remained as placid and unfathomable as a cloudless sky.

After a while Vyr went on: "My father was fifty-eight years when he died—at the ripeness of his great manhood. No wrinkle was in his face, no white in his hair; his foot was light and swift in its step like my own; his arm was more strong than my arm."

12

"How, then, was it," asked Major Paul, with deep interest, "that he fell a victim to the villains whom you so easily manage?"

"'Manage?'"

"Yes—conquer, vanquish."

"Ah! He was wound by a bullet from a klepht which hided himself; he was so hurted that he could not walk; he was made a captive—and *he was killed by the torture.*"

"Horrible!" exclaimed Major Paul, springing up from his seat. "Fiends as they are, I never thought they were such hellish fiends as that!"

Vyr answered, calmly, "They hate the Vyrs with the great hatred. We have been their enemies with the greatest success of all from many generations. If I shall be captive to them, they will do the same things to me like those which they did to my father."

"Is not your hate equal to theirs?" asked the major, in great excitement. "I should think the first great object of your life would be to avenge your father. Damn the wretches! I wouldn't rest till I had swept the whole race from the face of the earth!"

For some moments Vyr made no answer. He seemed altogether to forget the existence of his companion, while his great dark eyes were fixed with an inscrutable expression on vacancy. Suddenly he aroused from his reverie, and said, in a quieter tone than usual, "No, Mr. Paul; I have not revenge in my heart. The klephts are the victim of nature and of fortune. They have inherit from their fathers, like as I have inherit from my fathers. If there shall be a country like Greece, with the history like the history of Greece, it must be that there shall be such peoples in the mountains like the klephts, like as it must be that there shall be the reptiles in the marsh, and the bears in the caves of Arcadia. I know that it is necessity for mankind that they shall be exterminate, like to the other beasts of prey. It is one part of my business, my mission, that I shall hunt them and kill them like to other serpents. I sometimes go far from my home that I may do this thing, because they do not come near to me many times.

"Those Englishmen which were my guests before you, asked me if I do not have remorse when I have killed a klepht, if I do not see his spirit in my sleep. I say to them, 'If I shall do the wrong, I shall feel great remorse, God shall terribly punish me; but if I shall do the right, it is disease of the weak mind and of the weak nerves, it is not punishment, if I shall suffer. But I cannot prevent that I shall not feel great *compassion* in my heart.'"

Major Paul had indulged very sparingly in his characteristic ejaculations under the restraint of Hector Vyr's mighty personality; but here his growing astonishment entirely broke through his restraint. "Well, by the arrow-head on the tail of great King Diabolus!" he cried, "if that isn't the meekest, coldest-blooded philosophy I ever listened to!"

Vyr smiled, but there was no trace of mirth or of offence in his smile. "You did not think that I am meek or cold-blooded when you saw me at the first, Mr. Paul?"

"Not *much*, I didn't, general," answered the major, with a sudden and total change of manner. "And it's *actions* that tell, after all, not words. *My* energy goes mostly to words, they tell me. *Yours* doesn't."

"By-the-way," he added, after a short silence, "that reminds me of a question I have been wanting to ask for a long time."

"You may ask it."

"Suppose that bullet had gone through your *heart* instead of your arm—what would have become of the Great Object?"

"Ah, Mr. Paul," answered Vyr, looking solemnly upward, "my work would be finish. God's will would be done. *No stain of the coward must be transmitted to the Coming Type.*"

XIII.

THE REASON "WHY-FORE."

ROMANTIC as was their situation, our travellers were still in a world of numberless unromantic needs, for which no amount of poetry or sentiment can furnish a substitute. Great was their relief, therefore, when Ghiánnes returned from Athens, bringing with him sundry packages and big boxes, with a letter from the proprietor of the *Xenodocheïon tēs Agglias*

conveying his good wishes—most extravagantly expressed—and the hope that the various commissions
with which he and his wife had been charged, had
been satisfactorily executed. So, despite the entreaties and angry remonstrances of Griffin, and the vacil-
lation of the major—who, as usual, was tremendously
powerful in speech and correspondingly feeble in action—they remained day after day, until nearly three
weeks had passed.

During this time not the least wonderful among
the feats which their host was continually performing—with no thought on *his* part, however, of their
being feats—was the mastery he made of idiomatic
English. As is not unfrequently the case with men
of far weaker receptivity and grasp, he seemed to
achieve this mastery all at once. After continuing
for several days the various solecisms which we have
observed in his speech, he suddenly dropped them,
and thenceforth his English was scarcely less pure
than that of his American guests; indeed, so far as
the major's, at least, was concerned, it was generally
choicer, if not always so forcible. This was not, after all, the miracle it seemed. It was simply the feat
of a prodigious memory and of a no less prodigious
facility for catching the tricks of verbal expression.
He read a pocket dictionary and an English grammar as rapidly as most people would read a novel.
Once read, they were learned.

Late one afternoon host and guests were all seated
on the veranda. The sun had set, but not all his
glory. The distant waters slept peacefully under a

canopy of purple and gold, and the long, shadowed slopes of the mountains relieved their summits, still bright, and the velvety green of the nearer valleys.

"You are so accustomed to the beauties of mountain scenery, Mr. Vyr," said Miss Wellington, "that I suppose you hardly notice them, except when there are others to admire them with you."

"My thoughts are not directly upon them—often," replied Vyr, with an air of introspection. "Still, they have become a kind of necessity to me. I feel cramped and shut in, as if it were, when I am away, like a captive in prison or a bird in cage. When I am in Sparta or Athens, I feel as if I could not breathe."

"I think I know *one* reason why you go away so little," rejoined Miss Wellington, as if the thought had suddenly occurred to her.

"Well?" with his smile. "I am anxious to understand myself better."

"You are afraid the klephts will take advantage of your absence, and lay your house and fields in ruins."

"I think you are right, Miss Wellington; though it would be the same if there were no such beings as the klephts in existence. I should never go far away unless I were absolutely compelled."

"They *sometimes* venture into your vicinity, in spite of the terror of your name," remarked Griffin, who had developed a fondness for saying such things, particularly when Madeline was within hearing.

"Yes," answered Vyr, with the serene magnanimity which, instead of rebuking, had only encouraged the envious young man's covert insolence; "otherwise you would not have fallen into their clutches. But," addressing the rest, "it is not often that they come. They are not so safe in these mountains as they are in northern Greece from their other enemies—to say nothing of myself. There they can escape from one chain to another, while in the single chain of the Taygetus an energetic and well organized movement might cut off their retreat on both sides. I think they would never come south of the isthmus at all, if it were not for their hope of catching me at last. Notwithstanding their superstitious fear of the *Anthropodaimon* and his noiseless, smokeless *televodon*, a sort of fascination sometimes tempts them to their fate, as the flame of the lamp tempts the silly moth. They complain," he added, laughing, "that my warfare is not *fair* warfare. This last invasion of theirs, however, was probably entirely on your account. They heard of your intended visit, and came down purposely to meet you."

"No," said the major; "Peschino got his information from one of the Government messengers that was sent to announce our visit."

"He might have done that in the very heart of Athens," answered Vyr.

"How would that be possible?" asked Miss Wellington.

"Oh, these fellows venture everywhere. Peschino, in particular, is an adept at disguising himself. I have heard that he boasts of having danced with some of the finest ladies at the Royal Palace!"

"Don't you sometimes wish you were free to organize and head a grand movement to exterminate them altogether?" asked Madeline.

"I often wish there were many others to fight them in my own way; but your own adventure shows to you how useless ordinary troops would be against them. An army would be almost as helpless as a single man. Even if it were not so, many changes must be made before there could be the slightest use in such an attempt. First of all, the Ottoman Empire, the great refuge of the klephts, must be converted or subjugated. Then there must be internal changes—physical, social, and political: roadways must be constructed from coast to coast across the mountains; the *morale* of the whole nation must be raised; as it is, not only a certain part of the people, but some of the Government officials themselves are said to be the secret allies of the klephts. Do you not see they have nothing to lose by being so? If they displease the outlaws without destroying them, they are like the huntsman who but slightly wounds a dangerous animal. If they please the outlaws, they are only lightly taxed by them, and not otherwise disturbed. It is doubtless a fact that certain politicians depend for their principal support upon the brigand chiefs, who control the suffrages of the people they rob. If these politicians remain neutral, the suffrages of the people are given to their political rivals. No, Mr. Paul, I have no longing to organize and head any movement under a government made, in part, by its own outlaws. I

am content to go on fighting the wretches as my fathers did before me, and the Government is glad to
send their agents to compensate me, for, you must
understand, at *heart* the *real* government is right:
it is only a necessary policy that compels them to act
as they do. They are rejoiced if Hector Vyr or any
one else will fight the common enemy, if he will
only not throw the odium on *them*."

"The people seem to think a great deal of their
Government," observed Major Paul. "When I was
at Athens I heard little else talked about."

"Yes," replied Vyr, with a smile of contempt;
"the ridiculous little squabbles of their politicians
afford them a never-ending theme for dispute. The
Boulé supports one ministry or another as it pleases,
and it is more changeable than the wind. There
have been as many as fifty revolutions within half as
many years. It is always M. Tricoupis *vs.* M. Cou-
mondouros, or M. Mpotzaros *vs.* M. Bikezetis — one
rival *vs.* another always. Politics, which in other
countries forms an important subject of thought and
talk, has degenerated in Greece to one of the most
trivial; it is scarcely more worthy the attention of a
sensible mind than the common gossip of a country
village—in truth, it is very much like it. Yet the
Greek politicians wonder why foreigners are not as
deeply interested in it as themselves. Knowing little of the ancient glory of their country, except as a
matter for empty boasting, they cannot understand
why the enthusiasm of tourists should be confined to
antiquities?"

Here was an opportunity for Major Paul, and he improved it. "Some of us at home have a similar difficulty," he said; "we cannot understand why the enthusiasm of our scholars and educators should be so largely confined to antiquities—as it *is*, Mr. Vyr, although America is the exact opposite of Greece in all the respects you have named. You will admit that American politics and European politics in general are something above the gossip of a country village; yet many of our schools and colleges seem to think nothing is worthy of their attention but antiquity. There are no orators, no authors to-day, and there have been none since the time of Virgil and Cicero. It is all Greek and Latin, Greek and Latin, until we practical men are sick with disgust. Mastodons and blue-bottles! as if the world had fallen into its dotage, like a broken-down old man who can think or speak of nothing but the great things he did when he was a boy! I believe we know more, can do more, think better, write better, speak better, and *fight* better to-day, Mr. Vyr, than any past generation that ever crawled on the face of the earth. *Crawled*, I say, sir, for we are the only generation that ever did anything else. Great George Washington! to think of puttering over a Greek accent when there are stars in the sky and living kingdoms and republics on earth!"

Now there were few things which amused Hector Vyr more than the vigor of the major's verbal expression. His highly developed intuition had almost instantly divined the portly, loud-voiced American's true character, with its wealth of warm-heartedness and impulsiveness, and its lack of real strength. He listened to the stormy tirades, which were gradually resumed as their acquaintance ripened into familiarity, with the keen enjoyment of a naturalist over a new specimen. Nevertheless, out of deference to the major's *amour propre*, he usually repressed his mirth, and answered with the respect he felt due to his guest's amiable traits and relations towards himself, but more especially to him as the father of a far stronger, though scarcely less impulsive, daughter. So now, with a kindly smile, he replied:

"You are both right and wrong, Mr. Paul, as I think. As a whole, the race of man has greatly improved since the days of antiquity. We must admit, however, that in language and art we have degenerated as a race almost as much as the Greek nation has degenerated in all respects from the standard of their ancestors."

"Your language is not very patriotic, sir," said Griffin, with a glance at Madeline.

"Why-fore is it not, Mr. Griffin? I speak in pure pity, not in censure. The Greek people have suffered from great calamities, for which they are not to be blamed. It is the ages of Turkish oppression that have reduced them to their present level. Now they are free, and I believe that in time they will rebound to a greater height than they have ever yet reached!* I am by birth a Greek, although my

---

* Hector Vyr's prophecy is proving true. The situation in

ancestors represent many different nations. I have
lived all my life in Greece, I am grateful for what I
have received, and, as I have told you, I try to make
myself of use.   If I were free from my oath, I
would do what one man could towards a political and
social reform.   But I am not only a Greek—I am
one of the race of mankind.   The world is more
than Greece; man is more than the Greeks; time is
more than to-day—more than the nineteenth century.   I am a zealot, a visionary.   So be it."

"You appear to have very definite ideas in regard to
the distant future," remarked Griffin.   "How do you
know the nineteenth century will not be the last?"

Although his words were innocent enough, there
was an ill-repressed bitterness in the tone and the
look which he threw at Madeline that could not
have escaped Vyr.   With his usual serenity, however, the latter replied:

Greece is better to-day than ever before since the Revolution.
The flight of Otho and the accession of Georgias were inestimable blessings.   The ancient blood is once more stirring, and everywhere energy and enterprise are showing themselves.   The
reclamation of the vast marshes of the Morea is fast advancing.
Hundreds of villages have already been rebuilt, and many roads
have been constructed since 1874.   Best of all for the honor of
Greece, she has practically wiped out the greatest blot on her es-
cutcheon—the brigand.   After the capture and murder of Lord
Muncaster's party at Oropos near Marathon, in 1870, aroused by
the condemnation of the civilized world, the Hellenic Government put forth its best efforts.   Directed by the energetic minister, Zaimas, the entire army went against the treacherous foe,
and since then scarcely a klepht has dared to show his head near
a centre of population.

"How do you know this day will not be your last? Yet you lay your plans for to-morrow and next year and years afterwards, precisely as if you were sure of them. I know no more of the future than you; but I see everywhere in the organisms around me the Creator's plan. Every living species is born, grows to maturity, declines, and dies: that is the history of an individual man, and I believe it will be the history of the race of man, which, as yet, is only in its early youth. Many thousand generations, I think, must come and go before it will reach a maturity it has never yet dreamed of. God will not cut the best tree in his garden down until it has borne its rich fruit. This, Mr. Griffin, is why-fore I do not believe the nineteenth century will be the last."

The last gray fringe of twilight had now died out above the Ægean; Orion and the Dogs had reached their maximum brilliancy in the moonless sky; and the mountains had become mere masses of unvarying blackness against the horizon. In the increasing crispness of the air the voices of the speakers had become more and more distinct and resonant. By a natural impulse Madeline began to sing softly to herself.

"Louder, Madge!" said her father, and all but Griffin warmly seconded the invitation. Without an instant's hesitation she began Leonora's little song in "Il Trovatore,"

> " *Tacea la notte placida,*
> *E bella in ciel sereno.*"

As her pure, sweet voice poured out into the night air, it seemed to intensify rather than to disturb the calmness and peace that reigned around, as if the silvery notes made harmony with the voiceless music of the stars. Even those of the party who were familiar with her singing listened entranced as they had rarely been before; what, then, must have been the effect upon Hector Vyr? He scarcely breathed, but sat, with face bent forward and lips apart, as if fearful of losing her lightest note. When the volume of exquisite sound swelled in

" *Quando suonar per l'aere,*"

he left his seat, unconsciously advanced, and stood directly before her. He uttered no word, however, until she had finished. Then he walked twice up and down the veranda, stopped abruptly, and said, in tones thrilling with suppressed emotion,

"My friends, I never before in my life heard a woman sing. My mother could play very sweetly upon instruments a few years ago, but she could not sing. I have often read of female voices, and I thought I could imagine what they were like; but my idea was no more like what I have just heard than a blind man's conception of light is like light itself. Miss Paul, I thank you from my heart. Would it be asking too much if I should ask you to—to—"

"Sing again?"

"Oh *yes! will* you, Miss Paul?"

She sang two more songs, and then laughingly re-

fused to gratify him further, lest the charm of nov-
elty should be too soon dispelled.

Through it all Griffin had not spoken a word.

The next time Vyr saw the major alone, he asked
what could be the trouble with Mr. Griffin. Was he
ill? Major Paul tried to put him off. Robert was
subject to occasional fits of depression; in fact, to
tell the truth, he suspected the poor boy was a trifle
homesick, etc.

"I am very sorry for him," Vyr replied, fixing his
frank, inquiring eye upon the major's averted face.
"He loves your daughter, does he not?"

"Ye—*yes*," said Major Paul, explosively. "Un-
lucky fellow, I believe he does."

"Do you not *know* that he does?"

"He has said as much to me."

"Why, then, did you say you simply *believed?*"

"I—I— Bless my soul, Mr. Vyr, I believe what I
know, don't I?" desperately.

"Ah yes. I shall learn English by-and-by. Does
your daughter love him too?"

"Who can tell? Women are a great mystery."

"She does not say whether she loves him or not?"

"Oh, she *says* she doesn't."

"Do you not believe your daughter's word, Mr.
Paul?"

The poor father quailed under the look and tone
with which this home-question was asked. He lit a
match and applied it to his cigar—although it was
still burning—and finally replied,

"You do not understand American girls, Mr. Vyr.

On this subject I do not think they understand themselves. At any rate, they do not always feel compelled to *reveal* their feelings—particularly to a third party."

"And so," rejoined Vyr, with an air of astonishment, "to avoid revealing their feelings, they sometimes tell lies?"

Major Paul laughed. "That is a very strong way of putting it," he said.

"What do you mean by 'strong way?' Is it not the true way? If I should put it in a *weak* way, would it not mean the same thing? I ask you again, Mr. Paul, do young women think it is right to tell lies to avoid revealing their feelings?"

We have all been pushed in precisely this way by bright, persistent children, whose honest, inquiring eyes have made us feel ashamed of our own want of frankness. Add to the simple-hearted persistence of a child the power of presence and the penetrating vision of the highly developed man at his prime, and we have some notion of the poor major's embarrassment.

"You follow me up very closely, sir," he said, his face growing hot. "I—I—perhaps they think third parties have no right to pry into their secret feelings."

"Ah! then they should *say* so. And if you do not wish to answer my questions, my friend, *you* should say so too."

"I have no objection to answering your questions. Perhaps you have a right to ask them, sir?" turning with unwonted boldness and spirit to the inquisitor. Had the latter been any other than Hector Vyr, the proud American would have roused himself long before. So complete had been his subjection to that prodigious force of character, that he had usually submitted, without resentment or conscious humiliation, to things which, from any other source, would have called forth his stormiest indignation. If he thought of them at all, he attributed them to the ascetic's phenomenal simplicity of character and his ignorance of the world. In this he was partially right; for with rare exceptions no one could be more innocent of intentional offence than Hector Vyr. But, as we have seen, the major did occasionally bustle up. "Perhaps you have a right to ask these questions of me, sir?" he repeated. "I presume that is a proper question for *me* to ask."

"Have I not the right to ask any question I wish, since I do not compel you to answer unless you wish?" Vyr returned, opening wide his great eyes. With all his reading and study, with all his delicate receptivity, he had utterly failed thus far to understand some of the most obvious rules of human intercourse. His unflawed honesty of soul was his great stumbling-block in the acquisition of this most desirable accomplishment. Receiving no answer, he went on, presently: "Mr. Paul, I do not believe your daughter tells lies. If she has said she does not love this young man, I *know* that she does not love him." Then he added, calmly, "Is it your wish that she should, Mr. Paul?"

13

"Yes," answered the major, throwing his reserve to the winds, "that *has* been my hope. Griffin has a good many faults, it is true; he is not her equal, by any means, in mind or character, but he is devoted to her, and I have no doubt would make her happy if she only would think so. He is well thought of at home, occupies a good position, that is, in social and business circles, and will be amply able to give her any and every thing she can wish. To tell the truth, Mr. Vyr, that is the principal reason why I took them together on this tour."

· · The major's eyes had not been for an instant on his listener during the whole of this speech, else he could no longer have doubted the right or motive of Vyr's questioning.

"But your plan has failed," replied Vyr, with irrepressible eagerness. "She does *not* love him, she never *can*, he is too far, far beneath her. Mr. Paul,· I promised you that before you went from me I would explain to you the reason why-fore I told you so many things about myself and my fathers. The time has come—*I* love your daughter."

XIV.

MAJOR PAUL ASTONISHES HIMSELF.

ALTHOUGH almost constantly in Madeline's society, Griffin was not foolish nor weak enough to weary her with petty verbal importunity. He might as well, however, for he made no attempt to disguise his unhappiness; he indulged in frequent fits of ill-humor and moody abstraction, to which pity and sorrow made her charitable. She tried every means in her power to divert his thoughts and restore him to cheerfulness. At last her long-continued forbearance yielded, which, of course, was the surest way of bringing up the subject most constantly in his mind; for there is nothing like the effervescing wine of a good, sharp quarrel to loosen the tongue.

It was the very day after the scene recorded at the close of the last chapter. The major had thus far kept his own counsel; nevertheless something—a bird in the air—had made the unhappy lover still more fractious and despairing than ever. Madeline had been bantering him in her best-natured vein; she had sung to him, read to him, chatted to him, all without avail. "Come, Robert," she said, at length, "*do* throw off this everlasting gloom; it is getting utterly intolerable. You are worse than an immortal nightmare. You never seem to think of your good-fortune. Think where you were three weeks ago, and where you are *now*. Try to feel a little decent gratitude to Heaven and to—to—"

With jealous fury Griffin grasped at her momentary hesitation. "You *dare* not utter his name to me," he said, pointing his long finger and glaring at her from under his black brows. "You *dare* not utter his name—but your cheeks speak for you."

The glow which had suddenly risen in her face deepened to vivid scarlet.

"*Now*," he cried, pursuing the advantage he had gained in such unmanly fashion, "will you tell me you don't love him?"

In an instant her downcast eyes were lifted in fiery anger. He saw the fatal mistake he had made, fell on his knees, and besought her forgiveness.

She turned away scornfully.

"Oh, Madeline!—"

"Not a word till you are sane enough to stand on your feet at least."

This brought him to his senses for a moment. He rose, and began in a low, pathetic tone to bewail his fate. But soon his voice became louder and his utterance more rapid. Deaf to her replies, whether of anger or entreaty, he raved on: He loved her with the honest love of a natural man. Insignificant as she thought him, he claimed to be the peer of any *man*—he did not aspire to compete with gods or devils. No sensible woman with the flesh and blood of the nineteenth century could ask for more. He loved her, and would make her happy in a home among the children of men—in her own country and among her own kindred.

Overcome by her compassion for his hopeless love, her indignation at his merciless interpretation of her slight hesitation and her blushing—who *wouldn't* change color, so suddenly and cruelly arraigned?— her mortification at his repeated innuendoes—overcome by these conflicting emotions, she burst into a violent fit of weeping, hysterically lamenting that she had ever left her home in Boston. Nothing would have induced her to do so if she only could have foreseen. They had been such good friends for so many years, with nothing of this sort—and *now!* Oh, if she could only get away—anywhere from that place—home best of all.

Griffin eagerly caught at her last words. Get away? of course she could—that very day—that very hour. He knew the way to Mikro-Maina, whence they could return to Athens as they had come.

She was hardly prepared to be so promptly taken at her word. Her dilemma, with the tears she had shed, cleared her brain and restored her self-control. She would do nothing so foolishly heroic. She would talk with her father, and see what *he* said about their all going away together. With this promise Griffin was forced to be content, and they separated on better terms than had appeared possible an hour before.

While Madeline was waiting for an opportunity to redeem her promise, she became conscious of a growing burden upon her spirits, an undefined something that stilled her inclination to sing and laugh, and made her sigh instead. She tried to think it was pity for Robert, regret at their angry words, exhaustion from excitement, together with a perfectly natural reaction from the too great happiness of the past three weeks—the afternoon cloud which the too bright sun of the morning had brought.

As she thought more and more of going away, the weight upon her spirit grew heavier. She felt that she was under a spell too potent for her to break, a spell, she argued to herself, cast, not alone by a mere personality, but by the thrilling romance of past events and present environment, harbored with her dearest friends in a refuge so near the scene of their late mortal peril, and yet perfectly safe, among surroundings so wildly grand, whose master was an Intelligence so lofty, a host so benignant, a protector so powerful. Like the enthralled reader of a tale, she felt that she could not lay down the volume till the last page was read.

While she sat thus absorbed one morning at the window of her bedroom, her chin resting on her hand, her aunt entered.

"Oh, Madeline," Miss Wellington exclaimed, rapturously, "you ought to have come with me this morning. I have found the loveliest walk you ever saw in your life!"

"I know, aunty, everything is beautiful here. But do you think we ought to stay any longer?"

"Why—I don't know, I'm sure. Under any other circumstances, you know, my dear—Mr. Vyr and

his mother being total strangers before we came—
but they both seem so anxious that we *should* stay,
particularly Mr. Vyr—he looks so dejected, so utterly miserable whenever any one of us hints at going
—with those great soft eyes of his, that tell everything so plainly—that I really think, Madeline—
However, that is a matter for your father to decide,"
and she began to take off her hat and gloves.

"Of course," replied Madeline, oracularly. "But
you know how generous and democratic papa is. He
makes powerful speeches for the affirmative or negative, but he always *does* just as the majority vote."

Aunt Eliza thought.

"We are evidently conferring at least as much
pleasure. as we are receiving," she said, presently.
"It is not often, you know, that they have an opportunity to see and talk with civilized people. And he
is making such wonderful improvement in his man-
ners and speech—did you *ever* see any one learn so
fast as he is learning English?"

"It certainly is wonderful," assented Madeline.

"I really think, my dear, that it is *our duty* to
stay a little longer, and give them the benefit of our
society. It is little enough we can do, at best, to show
our gratitude. Think what we *owe* him, Madeline."

"Should we seem *ungrateful* if we refused to
stay?" Madeline asked, pensively. "I wouldn't do
anything ungrateful for the world; and yet I—I—
Robert is very anxious to go."

"Oh, he *is*, is he?" returned Aunt Eliza, with a
laugh. "Well, it is very easy to understand *that*."

"Has he — has he said anything to you?" a hot flush mounting to her brow.

"I should think he had. He thinks we are acting very improperly; that we are making ourselves ridiculous, to say the least, by making so long a visit to this hermit in this out-of-the-way place; that it is a poor way to return the favor he did us, to impose so long upon his hospitality. But that's all nonsense—*I* see what the real trouble is, if you or your father do not. He's afraid of Mr. Vyr's—*influence* over you, Madeline. In other words, the poor boy is *jealous*. There, there, you needn't look so terribly angry. I didn't mean any harm. I didn't say he had any real occasion, did I? To tell the truth, I'm afraid of Mr. Vyr's influence over *myself*, over us *all*. He's such a wonderful character, so overmastering, that I sometimes feel as if we should all become his *slaves* if we remained here long enough."

"Not *I*," retorted Madeline, raising her head proudly. "What right have you to say such things? No one could be more kind and considerate. He doesn't understand all our forms, but his occasional little rudenesses are the rudenesses of honesty — grand, manly honesty and power. He cannot handle such tender creatures as we are without sometimes hurting our delicate sensibilities — but he never *means* to hurt us, aunty."

"No, I suppose not—*you* least of all. Be careful, my dear. You are a strong little thing, the dear knows, but he is vastly stronger."

"Be careful of what?" burst forth Madeline, petulantly. "What have I done, what has *he* done, that I should be subjected to such humiliating looks and speeches? You and Robert and everybody seem bent on— I won't stay here another day. I promised Robert I would ask papa to go, and I am going to find him this minute."

"Perhaps that's the best thing you can do, my dear," returned Aunt Eliza, placidly. Then, as Madeline stood irresolutely playing with the door-knob, "You might as well wait until you are calmer. Don't be offended with me, at any rate; I only spoke as I did for your best good. I thought you praised Mr. Vyr rather warmly; and you talked as if you really *wanted* to stay here."

"That was because I am enjoying the place so much," replied Madeline, with pretty hesitation; "and — and — you said yourself that we should be ungrateful to leave—when he is so anxious that we should remain."

"Still," returned Miss Wellington, with decision, "I am afraid of Mr. Vyr's power over us. Don't you see how your papa yields to him, and follows him around like a child? If any one else should take such liberties with Major Paul as Mr. Vyr does — innocently enough, I'll admit—how do you suppose he would bear it? I confess, I cannot understand the secret of this man's power. He certainly makes no *effort* to control us."

"*I* understand it," said Madeline, her heart swelling with enthusiastic pride, for which the next moment she was covered with confusion. "It has been handed down to him from generation to generation, like his superb courage and—"

"If he were reserved and silently dignified," Aunt Eliza went on, without noticing Madeline's embarrassment, "I should understand it better; but he is so perfectly frank and unrestrained, he always speaks so freely of himself, one would suppose *that* would relax his power over others; it usually does. I *do* think he is the most remarkable example of what they call 'personal magnetism' I ever saw; don't you?"

"If we are all in such danger," replied Madeline, with a demure smile, "we'd better escape while we can. I'm calm enough now, you see, aunty, so I'm going to find papa, and beg him to flee at once from this moral and intellectual cuttle-fish."

She ran down to the veranda, where the major was usually to be found at that time of day engaged in reading or meditation. Not finding him there, she started for the cliff, another of his favorite resorts. She had just reached the base, when a voice fell on her ear which arrested her steps and sent a cloud of color to her cheek. It was at a considerable distance, but so clear and still was the air that she could hear every syllable with perfect distinctness—

> "*Tacea la notte placida,*
> *E bella in ciel sereno;*
> *La luna il riso argenteo*
> *Mostrava lieto a pieno!*"

Loud and clear as a clarion came the notes, yet mellow and full of tender sensibility. Only one chest

she knew of could send forth such sounds, so powerful, yet so sweet—

> " *Quando suonar per l'aere,*
> *Infino allor si muto,*
> *Dolci s'udiro e flebili,*
> *Gli accordi d'un liuto,*
> *E versi melanconici,*
> *Un trovator cantò.*"

Every word and note just as she had sung them
that night on the veranda!

She listened till the sounds died away, then she
slowly went up the ascent, her lips parted in a happy
smile.

"What a voice!" she thought—"and what a
memory! He said he never heard a woman sing
before. I suppose he never saw an American girl
before. I must be almost as great a curiosity to him
as he is to me. I wonder whether he altogether—
approves of me."

As she went on up the ascent, thinking upon this
profound problem, it must be confessed she was not
conscious of any very harassing doubts as to its
proper solution. At the top of the cliff she found
her father, to whom she immediately communicated
her errand. I suspect, however, that her pleading
lacked something of its wonted persuasiveness, for,
contrary to its usual result, it was fruitless. The
major, ordinarily so plastic, was for once actually
immovable.

Go away? what, when Vyr wanted him to *stay?*
Not if he knew it. In any other case he should un-

derstand, of course, that it was nothing but empty politeness; but when Hector Vyr said a thing, it was *so*—if it was only "Good-morning."

With a long face Madeline reported her defeat to Robert Griffin. He angrily accused her of purposely failing; she had not half tried; it was only necessary to get her father to scold a little more, and the thing was done. A little conscience-smitten, she received his reproaches meekly, and proposed that they should try the effect of their united powers of persuasion. But for some reason or other even these failed. Aunt Eliza was then induced to add the weight of her influence; still with no result. The major scolded enough to satisfy even Griffin, but, strange to say, his determination was not a whit undermined thereby. They might as well hold their tongues, he said, at last; not one of them knew what they were talking about. Then in a dogged way he muttered, "Griffin may go to-day if he wants to; the rest of us will follow when I think proper." With which he stalked away.

Griffin pursued him in a great heat. "Well, Uncle Warren, what am I to understand by *that?*"

"Hey? what? You're your own master, aren't you? If you want to go, *I* can't prevent you. But, by the Little Billy Peterson! I propose to be master in my own family for once, if I never was before!"

"You want to drive me off the field, do you?" said Griffin, growing white.

"Don't talk trash. You have a fair field. Go on

stay, as you please. If you want my advice, I'd advise you to *stay*." And he again turned his back.

Without more ado, Griffin returned to Madeline, whom he found alone. He told her that he had made up his mind to leave the next morning, and besought her again and again to accompany him. She persistently refused, at first with indignation, finally with tears.

"Well, then," said he, fiercely, "good-by, Madeline—and may God forgive you, for I never shall! But," he added, "*I shall return.*"

XV.

GRIFFIN RETURNS.

Miss WELLINGTON somewhat exaggerated both her own discomfort in the presence of her host and the major's subserviency. It remained true, nevertheless, that, although every effort was apparently made to put them at their ease, they were oppressed with an increasing sense of their own inferiority, and were, therefore, under a constant strain to appear at their best, which in time became very wearisome. At each observation made by one, the other furtively scanned Vyr's face for some little sign of disapproval or even contempt. Nothing of the kind ever appeared. On the contrary, he always listened with the most kindly interest, and replied with a fulness and a simplicity which should have precluded all suspicion of mental reservation. Perhaps it was this very unflagging attentiveness that made them feel as if they were being continually weighed in the balance—as if those luminous eyes were microscopic lenses, through which they were inspected with unsparing criticism.

Madeline alone felt no discomfort under this moral mastery. She rather gloried in it: to her there was an exquisite pleasure in the contemplation of a nature so lordly. She felt the loyal thrill of hero-worship which women so often feel in a lesser degree for men far beneath them in reality, but whom they have idealized—whose grossness they have taken for grandeur, whose brutality they have taken for power. In her mute homage she felt no sense of abasement. She pictured to herself a fitting mate for this natural monarch, a soul as queenly as his was kingly, a face and form as divinely beautiful as his were majestic, an ideal woman, the equal and complement of this ideal man.

In these reveries, if her thoughts ever reverted to herself, it was only to contrast herself with the peerless creation of her fancy, and to blush at the humiliation to which her friends had so inconsiderately or cruelly subjected her. More definitely than this she scarcely thought. If she had been conscious of a response within her heart to their accusations and innuendoes, though never so slight and timid, she would at once have crushed it back with terror. She could indulge for a while her wonder and admiration for this human prodigy, as she had basked in the glories of the Parthenon; and then — satisfied and ennobled—

return to America, where, perhaps, in due time she might mate with one of her own kind, to whom she would relate all her wonderful adventures. Poor Cousin Robert!

One afternoon, a few days after Griffin had taken his abrupt departure, she was swinging in a hammock among the trees at a little distance from the house. She had, of late, taken to wearing the picturesque Greek costume, partly, I suppose, because she thought it would please her entertainers, and partly because she liked to be herself in harmony with her surroundings: she liked to view herself objectively, as a part of the landscape. Upon her head she wore a fez with a long blue tassel, beneath which her abundant hair was twisted in a classical knot; a jacket of crimson velvet richly embroidered with gold fitted closely her superb figure; her petticoat was of lustrous golden silk, while her feet were encased in slippers of crimson velvet embroidered like her jacket.

She was alternately reading and thinking, when suddenly a shadow fell across her page. She looked up, and beheld Hector Vyr gravely contemplating her. His eyes did not fall nor waver, but remained fixed with an intentness which caused her to drop her own and uneasily to change her position, while the rosy cloud deepened on her cheek.

"I see I have been rude again," he said, smiling. "I did not know it. I am afraid I shall never learn to be like your American gentlemen. I was looking at you that I might read your thoughts in your eyes; I wished to know whether they were happy or sad—

whether they were upon what you have been reading, or upon yourself and your home so many miles away."

"And what is your decision, Mr. Vyr?" Madeline asked, recovering her equanimity.

"I do not think they are sad. They were very busy until I broke in upon them. If I had been a klepht I could have seized you and carried you off without your knowing it." And he laughed softly and musically.

"Not while Mr. Vyr was within hearing," retorted Madeline, looking among the trees with a little shudder.

"Ah, Madeline Paul, what joy it would be to save you!" he said, looking at her in a kind of rapture.

"Thank you," she replied, briskly; "*once* is quite enough to satisfy me. If you could read my thoughts correctly, Mr. Vyr, you would have seen that that was the very thing which was occupying them when you interrupted them."

"Then I am glad I interrupted them. You must not think so much upon the past, Madeline; you must think upon the present, as I do. It is a much pleasanter theme."

"It is very pleasant," assented Madeline; "but I like to think of the past, too, and contrast it with the present. By-gone dangers only enhance the happiness of present safety—

"'Rich the treasure,
Sweet the pleasure,
Sweet the pleasure after pain.'

I have been thinking how wonderfully and mysteriously your powerful succor came to us just after I had prayed for it. It seems certain that God heard my prayer and sent an immediate answer. Don't you believe it, Mr. Vyr?"

Vyr smiled. Then, after a thoughtful pause, he answered, "There is in my veins the blood of an imaginative race—fond of the supernatural. I inherit the tendency to see divinity in everything around me—events controlled by unseen hands. But I recognize the vastness of the universe, on whose throne sits the One Supreme, and the insignificance—nay, the utter nothingness—of our planet, with all it contains, in comparison."

"'Not a sparrow falls to the ground without His notice,'" said Madeline.

"Ah, that is woman's beautiful faith."

"It is not an unreasoning faith," she protested. "That which took place on that day *could not* have happened by mere accident. It must have been the act of a pitying, all-merciful Father, whose messenger you were. I can never believe otherwise. Simple gratitude would forbid, if nothing else."

"That does more credit to your heart than to your philosophy," replied Vyr, with another smile. "But who can say, after all, that you are wrong? Man's boasted philosophy is doubtless a far less stable structure than he thinks it. I wonder if He who knows all truth holds in derision the conclusions we so gravely form—our ascription of absolute supremacy,

14

for example, to what we call Natural Law, because we have never seen it superseded."

"But you and I have both seen it superseded, have we not?" asked Madeline, eagerly.

"Who knows? People in great distress or danger almost always pray for deliverance. Sometimes deliverance comes — sometimes not. Mere chance would bring it sometimes. Then, of course, it is but natural to attribute it to divine interposition."

Seeing the look of dismay which this cold philosophy cast over her face, he went on quickly:

"But, as I said, who knows? Men who think their reason infallible are often guilty of the grossest unreason. Only the absolute atheist can logically deny the possibility of divine intervention. He who writes of an 'unknowable' Source of all things writes absurdly when he says that He never can and never does perform special acts in the universe He has made. I questioned only our right to decide when and how those special acts are performed. The conception of the great First Cause as contemplating the merely automatic workings of his mechanism in utter *idleness* is monstrous!"

"Thank you for saying that, Mr. Vyr," responded Madeline, tremulously. "It would be a great blow to me if my faith in the care of a Heavenly Father were shaken. It is the sweetest thought in my recollections of the past."

Vyr seemed to be pondering upon her words. Presently he asked, as he seated himself upon the grass, "Do you not like to think of the future as well as of the past?"

"Yes," she replied, vaguely, "I love to dream—as, I suppose, every one does."

"People live more in the future than in the past or present, do they not?"

He questioned her with very much the same look and manner that a bright child might assume in questioning a much-beloved teacher.

"Some do: not all," the fair oracle answered.

"Who do not?"

"Well—those who have no future to look forward to—those who are perfectly hopeless."

"Are there any such people in the world? Did you ever see one who, you thought, was perfectly hopeless?"

"No; I never saw one, but I suppose there *are* such unhappy beings."

"In the Siberian mines, for instance?"

"Yes; poor wretches!" with a shudder. "There must be many such among them. I never can think of them without wondering how I or any one else can ever be happy, knowing that there is such utter misery in the world."

"But you *are* happy, are you not?"

He asked precisely as if he did not know, for the mere pleasure of hearing her say she was happy.

"Yes," penitently.

"Ah, you have a good heart, Madeline. I suppose you wouldn't be happy if you could prevent it; but Nature is kinder to you than you would be to yourself. She will not let you think forever of human suffering. You are never very unhappy, are you?"

"No; when I think of it, I am ashamed to acknowledge that I am not—that is—"

"Why-fore ashamed? You cannot help being happy, any more than you can help being young and healthy, and beautiful and good. You cannot make yourself to be miserable because others are, just as you cannot make yourself to be old or ill or ugly or bad because others are. Why-fore do you grow so rosy red? Is it because I said you were beautiful? or is it because I said you were young and healthy and good?"

"You do not know how good I am," returned Madeline, mischievously. "I may be very wicked, for all you know."

"Oh no; that is *impossible.*"

"But how do you *know?* Some wicked people appear very good indeed, Mr. Vyr."

"Not like *you.* Ha, ha! you may play with me, but you cannot blind my eyes. They can look through yours down into the pure little heaven of your heart, as they see the blue heaven at the bottom of that lake." Then, pitying her confusion, he added, more calmly and argumentatively, "If you were wicked, Miss Paul, you could not be happy."

"Why not?" she asked, quickly, still blushing and with downcast eyes. "Did you not say that happiness was unreasoning, like health and youth?"

"No, no!" with an energetic shake of his head.

"Wickedness is a disease that destroys happiness, just as consumption destroys health and beauty."

Madeline's whole frame was still thrilling with pleasure at his praises; but she retained coolness enough to think of various peccadilloes she had committed at one time and another during her nineteen years of existence, and she cordially assented to his last proposition. "But I do not agree with you," she said, after a little pause, "that happiness is such a negative thing. It may be with birds and little children, but with grown-up people it is very different."

"You think hope has much to do with it, as well as memory?"

"Yes; particularly hope. Did you ever read Pope's 'Essay on Man?'"

"No; I have never heard of it."

"Why, Mr. Vyr!" exclaimed Madeline, in great surprise, "I thought you were a great reader."

A little impatient frown crossed his brow. He never forgot anything himself, and he could not understand why others should forget. "I told you long ago," he said, "that I had only a few English books and magazines. Is this book you name written by Pius IX.?"

"Oh no," replied Madeline, a trifle coldly. "Pope is the author's name, not his title. One of his most famous lines is,

"'Man never is, but always to be, blest.'"

"It is not a good line," said Vyr, shaking his head. "He does not say what he means."

"Why, what *does* he mean?" Madeline asked, curiously.

"He means that man *thinks* he is never blest."

"Oh, that is *implied*, of course."

"It should not be implied; it should be said."

"Surely, Mr. Vyr," she cried, sitting bolt-upright in the hammock, "you would not *change* the line—you would ruin it utterly."

Vyr answered, gravely, "Men think more of what they call beauty, wit, force, epigram, than they think of truth."

"But there is no lack of truth here," persisted Madeline, more and more astonished. "Everybody understands exactly what it means."

"No, not quite, perhaps," he replied, thoughtfully. "The *spirit* of the line is not good, not beneficent; it is cruel; it does not help man to feel that he is *wrong* in thinking that he is never blest—it rather makes him feel that it is inevitable. It sounds like an oracle of Fate—which is *not* the truth, Madeline; there is no such fate pronounced upon man. He may be blessed to-day as well as in the future, if he will. What does To-morrow owe him more than To-day? Will the sun be brighter? the sky bluer? the fields and forests greener? If his heart shall be stouter, will it not also be heavier? If his head shall be wiser, will it not also be more gray? If his limbs shall be stronger, will they not also be less nimble?"

"But," returned Madeline, hesitatingly, "he hopes for *more* than all this, Mr. Vyr. He looks for—well, greater power, fame—and—and—"

"When he shall have attained all these, what then?"

"Why, then he looks for still greater power and fame."

Vyr shook his head again.

"If happiness depends on such things as these, your poet's line ought surely to be changed," he said.

"How?"

"'Man never is, *and never shall be*, blest.' If happiness depends on the things you have named, *I* wish never to be happy, Miss Paul. I wish never to be more renowned or more powerful, as men usually reckon power, than I am now. I would like to be even less widely known than I am. But it is not true. I have been, I believe, one of the happiest of men. I live, like a child or a bird, in To-day—in every moment as it passes. Every sense, every faculty is a channel through which enjoyment is ever flowing in upon me. I love to walk, to run, even to *fight*," laughing. "I love to read, write, sing, talk, listen, sleep, wake, and—animal that I am—to eat and drink. I love to walk forth upon the mountains and feast my eyes on the paradise which God has given us; to stand on some lofty peak and feel the proud consciousness of sovereignty over this luxuriant nature; to feel in my body and mind God's master workmanship. I love to look at *you*, as you sit there in your surpassing beauty, and think of you as the crowning work of all. Nay, Madeline, do not turn away from me. I have said that I live in the present, that I do not depend for happiness on the hopes which other men indulge. I *do* live in the present. These days are the most glorious I have ever lived; this moment is to me the central point of time—an existence in itself. But I live in the future, too. Did I say hope was nothing to me? Ah, it is everything. All the hopes which other men cherish are as nothing compared with the blissful hope that has sprung up in my soul. I have told you of things I love to do. Best of all, I love to love. Best of all things I love—above them all, more deeply than all —I love *you*, Madeline Paul!"

He had risen from the ground, and now towered over her, gazing upon her as if he would devour her with his eyes. It is impossible to describe the intensity of passion with which his last words were uttered. His tones vibrated like those of some mighty organ, his face seemed transfigured, while his powerful frame was shaken as by some great agony.

Madeline had also risen, and now stood looking at him, as it seemed to her, through a mist. His figure became more and more shadowy, but his burning gaze seemed to pierce deeper and deeper into her inmost soul. Her lips opened, but her tongue uttered no words.

All at once she became conscious of another presence. With a great struggle she threw off the spell, and beheld the face of Robert Griffin glaring upon her!

It was not an idle freak of nature that had given his features their forbidding form and color. The jester's mask was gone—utterly consumed, as it were, by the scorching heat of those demoniac eyes.

He was standing in the path not twenty feet distant. Madeline uttered a cry and fled towards the house.

XVI.

IN THE STARLIGHT.

Hector Vyr turned, and saw the intruder.

"*Gourouni!*" he roared, "it was *you* that frightened her away! I will tear you to atoms!"

He sprang towards him like an enraged lion.

Griffin sprang too, and before his antagonist could recover himself for another bound, he had deliberately aimed a pistol at his heart.

Vyr neither spoke nor moved. Marius disarmed an assassin by the mesmerism of his gaze. Griffin stood a few seconds looking into those terrible eyes. Then his arm slowly sunk to his side.

"I did not intend to frighten her," he said, with utterance abnormally distinct, from the very effort to throw off the awe he felt creeping over him. "I did not know what was in progress. I came back to join my friends, and happened upon you by pure accident—at a very inopportune moment, it seems."

Vyr held out both hands, while a smile broke out over his face, like sudden sunshine through threatening clouds. "Forgive me; I was a madman."

But Griffin drew back haughtily. "I cannot take your hand, Mr. Vyr," he said.

"Why-fore not?" Vyr asked, with innocent surprise. "Are you afraid of it? I made a mistake. It will not hurt you now."

Griffin's only reply was a scornful smile and a significant little wave of his pistol.

As if by a stroke of lightning, the weapon was torn from his grasp and hurled far over the tree-tops, exploding as it fell.

"When I play with a serpent," said Vyr, into whose face a calmer, deeper wrath had come, "I first pluck out his sting."

Griffin stared blankly at his benumbed fingers, then at Vyr. "You are very quick," he said, at length; "you can overmatch me; but you cannot make peace with me. I love that lady, Mr. Vyr, as well as yourself."

"Does she love you?"

"I—I—have, at least, as good reason for hope as you, sir; and I have a prior claim. I have known her almost from a child, while it is only a few days since you knew that such a being existed."

"There is truth in that what you say. But this is a matter in which there is no prior claim. Miss Paul herself shall decide between you and me."

"She is in no respect suited to you," retorted Griffin, angrily. "You have no right to ask her to abandon her own country and kindred, the friends of her lifetime, the comforts and refinements of civilization, to share your savage life in this wilderness."

For a while Vyr did not answer. The rich, dark bloom faded from his check, and it was with a strange faltering in his voice that he finally said,

"I have, at least, the right to ask. She has the right to accept or refuse, as her own heart shall dictate."

"And so," cried Griffin, following up his advantage with merciless vindictiveness, "you would shamelessly accept the romantic fancy which the poor young creature may have conceived for your—your barbarous physical strength and prowess, and your still more barbarous habits of life, and call it *love!* You would take advantage of this silly fancy, I say, to allure her to a step she would bitterly regret when she came to her senses! You would really *marry* her, would you, Hector Vyr? *You*, a nondescript mountain hermit, and she a tender flower of civilization! Faugh!"

He saw with malicious joy that his bitter words were producing an effect, and the consciousness gave new fertility to his brain and fluency to his tongue. But the calm, white face did not reveal with *how* terrible a power his blows fell upon that great, simple heart. For a few moments Vyr remained silent, then his face lifted with a look of sublime resignation, as he said in low, humble tones,

"Mr. Griffin, I have done to you a very great wrong. I believed in my heart that you were only a shallow trifler, with no soul above your little jests. I knew that you loved Miss Paul; but I also knew that she did not return your love, and I believed you

were unsuited to her, as you say *I* am unsuited to
her. I find that I made a mistake. I find you a
man of thought and earnestness. Perhaps you are
even capable of—no, I cannot believe *that.* Tell me,
Robert Griffin, is it true that she would be unhappy
here? Are her home and her friends, the excitements of society, so necessary to her that nothing can
take their places? Tell me," he repeated, his whole
soul in his adjuration, "do you really believe this in
your secret heart?"

The incredible simplicity that would ask such a
question, at such a time, of *him,* brought a con-
temptuous smile upon Griffin's face. "Believe it?"
he replied, with the careless insolence he would have
assumed to an inferior whose anger he despised—
"why, of *course* I believe it."

But Robert Griffin judged from his ordinary experience in the world, where such simplicity is usually the result of mere obtuseness of intellect. He
could not understand that in this case it sprang from
a grandeur of soul that, for the moment, was willing
to accept even *him* as a peer. He was instantly un-
deceived.

"Go!" said Vyr, waving his hand with utter loathing. "Why-fore do I stoop to talk words with you?
I thought you were a *man.* You have the tongue of
a man, but the soul of a lizard!"

Without deigning another look at the dazed face
of him he thus spurned, he strode majestically away.

Griffin had seen the best tragedians of his day, and
had himself no mean skill at tragic impersonation,

for which his peculiar physiognomy admirably fitted him; but never in his life before had he conceived of the wonderful capabilities of the human voice and countenance. He knew well that much of his own short-lived power over his rival had been due to his excellent elocution; he knew also that in one unguarded moment he had betrayed himself, that in that moment his rival had seen through his flimsy heroics. He felt that the tremendous outburst of scorn which had followed the discovery was *genuine*— that the man, powerful and mature as he was, was as incapable of mere acting as a child; and this consciousness left him gazing, like one paralyzed, at the tall retreating figure, whose very back seemed to dart upon him arrows of contempt.

When Vyr had vanished behind the trees, Griffin shook himself, drew in a long breath, and expelled it again in a series of blasphemous ejaculations expressive of wonder, self-reproach, and hatred for his formidable rival. He then went to look for his revolver, which he found at a marvellous distance from the spot whence it had been thrown. It had fallen upon a rock, and was ruined past repair. Spurning it with another fierce oath, he walked straight to the door of the house, and haughtily demanded to see his relatives. His uncle greeted him cordially, and asked what in the name of the Old Black Coal-heaver he had gone away for, and where he had been. Deigning no reply to these questions, Griffin angrily inquired if his uncle was aware how far matters had advanced between Madeline and their host, and without a pause proceeded to a lurid description of the scene he had just witnessed.

The major listened patiently till he had finished; then, laying his hand on his nephew's arm, he said, with tender deliberation, "Robert, my poor boy, I have been expecting some such thing as this."

"Oh, you *have*, have you?" retorted Griffin, recoiling and growing white. "And I suppose you have been *hoping* for it, too?"

"No, not exactly that. I have simply felt that I could not prevent it."

"Prevent it!" with a passionate oath. "Of course you could prevent it if you had wanted to. Why the devil didn't you take her away, as I asked you to so many times?"

"What, against his wishes? You couldn't expect me to do that, Robert. Have you forgotten what obligations we are all under to him?"

"So, to pay the debt, you are willing to sacrifice your own daughter, whom you have pretended to love so tenderly!"

"What's that you say, you young—" began the major, blazing up. But he instantly calmed down again. "I'll stand anything in reason from you, Robert, because I pity you from my soul; but I want you to understand there's going to be no *sacrifice* of my Madeline to Vyr, or you, or anybody else. She's to be absolutely *free* to choose for herself. I've promised her that, and I'll be as good as my word. She's got a level head as well as a heart of gold.

She'll never be such a fool as to imprison herself among these howling mountain caves—I'll trust her for that. If she's influence enough over this Hector Vyr to draw him out of his hermitage and lead him captive to Boston, she may do it without any interference from me. If she *hasn't*, there'll be the end of it. Mark my words, Robert Griffin, she'd never bury herself *here* for Jupiter Ammon himself!—neither you nor I need fear any such result. In any event, I shall never forget my debt to this man, or Madeline's either; and if he really wants her for his wife, the very least he is entitled to is a fair chance to win her if he can. Don't you see that's only right, my dear fellow?" in a softer tone, again laying his hand on Griffin's arm. "You've as fair a chance as he, haven't you?"

Utterly beside himself with rage, Griffin snatched his arm away. "*You* talk, you old hypocrite! Didn't you try to get me out of the way, so that he might have the field to himself?"

Up flew the major's ready fist. His reckless nephew would have measured his length upon the floor if he had not adroitly slipped aside. Instant consciousness of his folly flashed into his brain. "I take it back, Uncle Warren, I take it back," he whined. "I did not know what I was saying."

"Yes, you did, you insulting puppy!" bellowed the major, furiously, "and you knew it was a villanous lie! I told you to go or stay, as you pleased, and I *advised* you to stay."

If this had been their first stormy quarrel, it would

without doubt have been irreparable; but mere words were too cheap with both to be fatal. Even if the major's anger had not been habitually short-lived, pity for his unhappy kinsman would soon have quenched it; and as for Griffin, his returning prudence had already supplanted his exceedingly impolitic rage.

A partial reconciliation took place, therefore, after which Griffin dashed away to find Madeline. From Miss Wellington, whose eager questions he contemptuously thrust aside, he learned that she had taken refuge in her room. He flew up-stairs, and listened at her door. No sound. He rapped gently. A labored breathing, and a rustle as of some one rising from the bed.

"Madeline," he said, in a tone but little above a whisper, "will you not see me?"

"Oh, Robert," came through the door, "please go away!"

"If I do," in a louder tone, "it will be forever."

"But I—I *can't* come now; I am utterly exhausted."

"Good-by, then. Remember, it is *forever*." ·

"No, no! I will come." The door was unlocked, and she stepped forth, her cheeks burning, her hair unbound and enveloping her shoulders and waist like a brown mantle. "Why are you so cruel?" she asked. "Could you not wait till—"

"Till you were lost to me forever?" he burst forth —"till you had bound yourself like a slave to this monstrous—"

She threw up her hands as if to ward off a blow. "I can never be more lost to you than now," she cried, passionately. "No one could treat me more like a slave than you; no one could be more unjust, more insulting to—to—one who merits only your life-long gratitude. He has done you no harm, Robert; I have never changed my mind for a moment, and I never shall. I cannot tell you how sorry I am for you—but go away now; wait till we are both calmer, at least."

"And give you up?—leave you to drag out your days in this solitude with that mountain demon?"

"Don't insult him any more to *me!*" she retorted, her hot cheek growing suddenly cold and white. "Go to *him* if you dare. He could strike you dead with one sweep of his hand; but he wouldn't—no, he wouldn't stoop to harm you. He is not a mountain demon, he is a mountain god!"

"Yes, you poor, silly, romantic child, I know you think so. And you think you *love* him, do you? A fashionable young lady of Boston, only a little while out of boarding-school, daughter of a Yankee storekeeper, in love with a *god!*" Words cannot describe the stinging sarcasm with which he flung this at her.

But she was impervious. "Yes," she replied, drawing up her tall, slight figure; "imperfect and weak as I am, I *love* him!"

"Then listen to me, Madeline Paul. You say he could strike me dead. Imperfect and weak as I am, and god as he is, I'll strike *him* dead!"

15

With this menace on his lips, he vanished from before her horror-stricken eyes.

For a long minute she stood motionless as he had left her. Then, without knowing how, she was at the bottom of the stairs and in the path in swift pursuit.

"You need not follow me!" he shouted back. "I shall bide my time!"

She knew the sentinel on guard had orders to allow any of Major Paul's party to cross and recross the narrow bridge at pleasure. She called to him, but before he could understand the meaning of her frantic words and gestures, Griffin was safely over the chasm and out of sight. She darted back to the house, and tried to find her father. He, too, had disappeared. No one was there but Madame Vyr. Knowing, even in her terror, that it would be worse than useless to·alarm her, she ran with might and main towards a field where she had sometimes seen Vyr at work with his men. He was nowhere to be seen. Gradually she became calmer. Robert had only meant to frighten her. It was not possible that he really meant to carry out his murderous threat. At any rate, there was no immediate danger, and she would have ample time to warn her lover. Once on his guard, what had she to fear for *him* who had so long defied the combined skill and treachery of the klephts? She would not even distress her friends with the fearful tale; for if, as she became more and more convinced, Robert was only playing upon her fears, how glad she would always be that she had kept her own counsel.

The afternoon waned; the supper-hour came—but not the master of the table. His mother would not wait for him; for, she said, his meal-times were as regular as the rising and setting of the sun, and she knew he was at supper elsewhere. As the evening passed, and still he did not come, Madeline's terror by degrees returned in full power. She could not sit with the family, but went and paced to and fro upon the veranda. What if the threat had already been carried into execution? As the thought took full possession of her mind, blanching her cheeks and lips, she turned to fly, she knew not where—to her father, to implore him to go forth with her into the darkness and search for him—to Madame Vyr, to alarm the servants and the people in the valleys —somewhere, everywhere—to do something, everything, to prevent a catastrophe which seemed to her the destruction of the flower and glory of the world. But before she could act on any of her frenzied impulses, she heard quick, firm steps approaching, and in another moment Hector Vyr ran up the steps.

With an inarticulate cry she made a movement towards him, and sank trembling into a chair.

He knelt beside her, and seizing her hand, pressed it with his lips. "You have been waiting—watching for *me?*" he said in a low voice, that thrilled her through and through. "You have been waiting here to tell me that you return my love? My soul blesses you, bows in adoration before you. Until now I thought myself blest above my race; I thought my earth was fairer than other men's, my skies brighter;

but you have brought me a new heaven and a new earth. You have made my past life seem a waste of loneliness and selfishness, and have opened before me the gates of paradise."

"I—I have been watching for you," began Madeline, in weak, tremulous tones; "because I was afraid that— Oh," with a sudden outburst of joy and love —"oh, thank Heaven, you are alive—*alive* and unharmed! He said he would strike you dead!"

Vyr clasped both her hands, and laughed in an ecstasy of mingled tenderness and amusement. "Let not your woman's heart be troubled," he said. "Shall I fear the threatenings of a jester, who, though he speaks terrible words, has not courage to use the weapons he bears? He is as shallow in his boasting as in his jesting. If I did not pity his hopeless love for you, my own beautiful one, I should only laugh at him."

"Ah, he is not jesting now," replied Madeline, raising her head and timidly touching with her hand one of the short curling locks on his temple. "He is terribly in earnest. Oh, I have been trembling for you—you were gone so long."

"*O Theós nā sě eulogěsē!*" * he exclaimed, fervently. "You shall tremble no more. Consider, my darling one—I am accustomed to far more dangerous enemies than he is, men not only more reckless but skilled—as he certainly is not—in hunting down their victims. Have no fear in your heart, Madeline—if

---

* God bless you!

he ventures to attack me, I will scare him away with a look."

"If he should attack you openly, I should not fear —at least for *you*. He is my cousin, poor Robert! I cannot believe he would be so vile a coward as to— But, then, that fearful threat! And when you go away, as you have done to-day, and are gone so long—"

"My eyes are always open wide when I walk. I know all the hiding-places here, as you know the dwelling-houses in the street where you live. My ears are trained to hear sounds when to you there would be unbroken silence. Shall I tell to you why-fore I was gone so long? I have been fighting— no," with a laugh, as she started up—"not with the klephts, nor with *him*, but with *myself*. I told you of my love too soon. It burst from my lips, because my heart could not keep it imprisoned. I have been punishing myself for my too great haste, for my self-ishness, in asking you to turn your back on the country of your birth, on your father, who has cherished you from your babyhood, your mother's grave, your friends who love you so well and whom you love, the pleasures and refinements to which you have all your life been accustomed— to turn your back on all these, and live with me in this solitude—grand, glorious, filled with things which satisfy my mother and me, but still a solitude. 'What right have I,' I asked myself, 'even if she were willing, to transplant this tender flower, that has grown and bloomed in a sheltered garden in the midst of palaces, to even a paradise of uncultivated nature?'

"Then I answered to myself, 'But I love her with a love immeasurably greater than the love of father and friends. I will reconcile her to the loss of other society by an affection which shall always absorb her whole heart and soul; I will make her to forget those pleasures she leaves, by filling all her moments with greater pleasures than she ever dreamed. For the home she abandons, she shall have one fashioned after her own wildest fancy. If my wealth is not great enough, cannot I increase it as I will? And it shall awake in me a sweet ambition I have never yet felt to enthrone my peerless queen in a palace of her own devising.'

"I thought, too, of my mother; how she had left home and kindred and position—all I should ask you to leave—for this same mountain home; and yet how she was supremely blest—until," lowering his voice, "that dark hour, Madeline, that I have told you of."

A sudden trembling seized her, and he felt, rather than saw, that her face had grown white in the bright starlight.

"I read your thought, my tender-hearted love," throwing his arm around her, as if to protect her from her own fancies. "I thought of this in my struggle with myself to-day. She is not accustomed, I said, to ever-present dangers, as I am. But she shall grow stronger; she shall learn to laugh at fears of evils that may never come, as she now laughs at old nurses' tales to children. Yes, my Madeline, I thought of everything, and I resolved to say to you no more of love until you had smiled upon the confession that came unbidden from my lips. You waited for me here; your sweet soul was torn with fears for my safety; you *love* me; and here I lay myself, my love, my hopes, my promises, at your feet."

Madeline uttered no word, but her eyes, in which the starlight seemed condensed to soft, liquid fire, remained fixed on his till he had finished speaking. For a while longer she continued silent, hearing only the throbbing in her own breast. At length she spoke:

"It seems to me like a wonderful dream. I feel as if I had been lifted from earth into a gorgeous cloud-land. Nothing is real to me but you, my happiness, and my love. Can it be only four short weeks since my friends and I were trembling for our lives? It seems as if I had known you for years."

"And loved me?"

"I think I must have loved you from the first, though I did not know it. I thought it was only gratitude, wonder, admiration for one who made all other men seem like pygmies. I thought no more of loving you than of loving the sun. What was poor little I to dream of such a thing? But my fancy created a being suited to you, a creature who should match your splendor with beauty more dazzling and nature more lovely than poet ever imagined. Ah, Mr. Vyr, what an enchanting idyl I have been weaving! Is it not a pity that it should be spoiled? that this resplendent creature of my fancy should be supplanted in your heart and by your side by a commonplace, fashionable Boston girl?"

She looked up with a half-doubting, half-roguish smile, and was going on in the same strain, reminding him of his oath, when he suddenly smothered her voluble self-depreciation with kisses, protesting in the intervals that she was the one above all others who would enable him most gloriously to fulfil his oath; that no creature of her fancy could equal herself; that he would listen to no more hyperbole in regard to himself; that he was no sun, nor god, nor demigod, nor anything of the sort, but only a *man* with a sound head, body, and heart, who had simply taken good honest care of himself, as his ancestors had done before him, and who, thank Heaven, had now one whom he loved far better than himself to care for.

Thus they communed together, till the old moon, rising above the black Ægean, seemed to glorify their love with her radiant benediction.

XVII.

THE LABORATORY.

In the morning Vyr and Madeline went up the cliff to see the sunrise. It was not the first time they had together witnessed the grand spectacle; but there was now an inward glory that shone forth and magnified the outer glories tenfold. The mists of night had not yet fled: each summit was crowned with a halo that gradually took on the cool blush of morning, while the deep valleys seemed to awake, one by one, refreshed and smiling from their dreamless sleep As the "silver-orbed chariot" leaped above the sea, turning the purple clouds to many-colored flames, Madeline clasped her hands in an ecstasy of admiration. But neither spoke until the pageant had somewhat faded. Then said Vyr,

"*Sic transit gloria mundi.*"

"Why must it be so?" responded Madeline. "Why must the greatest glory always be the most transient?"

"It passes away, but only to return."

"And will it be so *forever?* Will the last sunrise of all never come?"

"I suppose it will," answered Vyr, smiling—"neither sun nor earth is immortal."

"Is it not a terrible thought that all life and beauty must perish, that all the lights in the firmament must be put out, that the universe must at last be one vast sepulchre?"

"Nay, that will never be. The universe shall never die utterly. When the time comes of which you speak, One shall say, 'It is not dead, but sleepeth.' Then He shall stretch forth His hand—'I say unto thee, arise!' And from Him there shall proceed virtue. The streams of force and life that have sunk to their lowest level shall again be lifted to their sources; the great heart of nature that has expanded shall again contract: the night shall pass, and a new day shall dawn."

" Oh, what a glorious prophecy !" exclaimed Madeline, her face glowing anew.

"I cannot believe otherwise. 'In the beginning
God created the heavens and the earth;' but they
were not the *first* heavens nor the first earth; they
are but the last of an infinite series, as to-day has
come after millions of yesterdays. Neither shall they
be the last: there shall come endless to-morrows.
God never has been idle; he never will be idle; it
is Brahma, not God, who sleeps."

"Oh, if this were only science, instead of a beautiful speculation !" sighed Madeline.

"Stubborn science will not read all the pages nature has written. Look at that carob-tree. It was
once a little germ; it has grown to its maturity; it
will decline and die. Will there be no more trees?
Yes; it has sown its seed. One great law pervades
all nature: birth, growth, decline, death, *reproduc-
tion*. The law governs every organism, from the
monad to man—from man to the universe !"

As he stood erect, overlooking the vast amphitheatre, he seemed indeed a prophet reading to the
mountains, valleys, and seas their destiny.

After breakfast the lovers went forth to renew
their communion with nature and with each other.
They threaded labyrinths, explored caves, and crept
under cascades. No wonder the ancient Greeks were
an imaginative race. They could not but people their
mountains with oreads, their seas with tritons, their
woodlands with dryads, their caves with satyrs. Amid

those wild, poetic scenes, Hector Vyr was more than ever a god to Madeline; she to him more than ever a goddess.

Passing through a little clump of carob-trees, they found themselves in the midst of a blaze of rhododendrons. Beyond were the remains of an old Spartan wall, built in two courses of hewn stone, and filled in between with the fragments. It was in a good state of preservation, though nearly concealed by ivy and thorn-bush. From the parapet they looked down a precipitous descent, which even without the wall would have rendered the height well-nigh inaccessible.

"My home was one of the Lacedemonian fortresses," said Vyr. "History does not mention it, but I have no doubt if these walls could speak they could tell as stirring a tale as old Ithomé. You see how this side is protected. On the north and east are impassable ridges; on the south the only approach is by my log-bridge."

"It is fortunate for the country that you are intrenched here instead of the klephts," said Madeline.

They followed the wall until they overlooked a beautiful little valley with a stream running through it. By the side of the stream stood a low, nondescript building of stone surmounted by a tall chimney. Madeline asked what it could be.

"That," replied Vyr, "is my chemical laboratory."

"Oh yes. Papa told me of your scientific as well as literary labors: how you wrote books and made discoveries for your own private pleasure and benefit, without hope or desire of other reward, either in fame or fortune. But he told me that your books were written only in your head, and I didn't know but—but—"

"That my scientific experiments were performed there, too?" asked Vyr, laughing. "No, I should scarcely be as cool-headed as I try to be, if I should admit nitric acid and electric fire into *that* laboratory."

That Hector Vyr should condescend to be funny, as any one else would have been in like circumstances, seemed strange to Madeline, but no more strange than delightful. She laughed merrily, but protested that her idea was not so absurd after all. She thought, of course, that *he* could make discoveries without the slow and tedious labor of experimenting—that was what *other* men were obliged to do.

"My beloved," he replied, gravely, "I hope you are speaking only in jest."

"Not entirely," she said, looking up with ingenuous homage into his eyes; "I really did think something of the sort. You are not like other men, you know."

"Yes, Madeline, in all respects except that I have tried to obey the laws of my being as other men usually do not. It troubles me to hear you speak as if I were otherwise, even in play; to hear you speak, as you sometimes do, as if I were a sort of unnatural prodigy. *You* seem to me the perfection of nature —the very goal towards which I am striving—and it raises a barrier between us when you attribute to me qualities and degrees I do not possess. I am no *An-thropodaimon*, although it suits my purpose that my enemies should deceive themselves with that superstition. I wish you to look upon me, as I look upon you, as a part of what is to be a harmonious whole. Let there be no barrier between us, my loved one, nothing to prevent our mingling heart with heart in perfect unconstraint."

"There is no barrier between us, Hector," replied Madeline, laying both her hands in his, while her upturned face shone with the perfect love which casteth out fear.

After a while they returned to the subject of the laboratory. "There are few discoveries without experiment," said Vyr. "Nature does not reveal her mysteries except to the patient, persevering questioner. The ancient philosophers trusted to theory and conjecture, and so they drifted apart from pole to pole; but to-day we put our questions to Nature herself, and we do not let her rest until she says yea or nay.

"Will you go into the laboratory and see the wrecks which my failures have left?"

"Failures? do *you* ever fail?"

"A hundred times where I succeed once."

Madeline was astonished, but glad. An *Anthropodaimon* would never fail.

There were broken retorts and galvanic cells lined with many-colored incrustations, blow-pipes, cupels, dialyzers, meters of all kinds—all the paraphernalia of a chemist's workshop, which showed in what manner many, many hours of the recluse's life had been spent. At the base of the tall chimney was a large furnace of strange-looking material and elaborate construction.

"I suppose you have a very hot fire here sometimes," remarked Madeline.

"So hot that no unprotected eyes could endure its brilliancy."

"Pray how do you make it so hot? Oh, you needn't hesitate to explain it to me," she added, laughing; "I am a graduate of a Boston school, you know. A Boston school-girl is supposed to know all about protoplasm and differentiation, all about central forces, the possible utilization of one hundred per cent. of molecular energy, and all such matters."

He regarded her in amused astonishment. "Ah," he said, at length, "you are going to surprise me more than I have been able to surprise you."

"Oh no, I can only *talk*, which is very different from *doing*. Please go on; how do you make your fire so hot?"

"It is very easy. You have only to seize the oxygen at the instant of its evolution from a compound in which it is abundant, and cause it to combine at that instant with its exact equivalent of hydrogen in the same *nascent* state. In the ordinary oxhydrogen flame both elements have assumed their quiescent state before combustion, which, of course, immensely reduces the energy of re-combination."

"Yes; I understand perfectly. That is the ideal

heat-producing flame. Oh, you have no idea what a chemist I am—in theory."

"That is the flame I make in that furnace. As the heat grows more and more intense, of course the energy of combination is proportionately intensified, and so it goes on increasing its own power almost without limit. This device for continually and entirely removing the waste products of combustion is mine. The clay of which the fire-box is made only grows harder and harder. I know not how intense a heat would be required to fuse or vaporize it. This is the baker's cap I wear when I work here."

He took a kind of helmet from a hook, and drew it down over his head, face, and neck—the eyes being protected by thick, apparently opaque circles of glass.

"And what sort of cakes do you bake?" asked Madeline.

"A great many kinds," he replied, after removing the helmet; "some useful, some beautiful, some only curious, but the greater part absolutely worthless. I will show you the last—what do bakers say?"

"Batch?"

"Yes, batch. It is, as you will see, both curious and beautiful. Look at this fine black powder. I wished to see if it could be crystallized. I enclosed some of it in a crucible of that same fire-clay, and subjected it for ten hours to the most intense heat I could produce. On opening the crucible, I saw that the contents had fused, but had solidified again into a soft, spongy mass no more crystalline than at first.

I tried over and over again, modifying the experiment in every conceivable way. I found, at length, the trouble. I had allowed the liquid to *cool* too rapidly. It requires a much longer time to build up the delicate structure of this crystal than that of any other. I allowed my fire to cool only a few degrees a day. My servants relieved each other in watching it night and day for many long, anxious weeks. At last the supreme moment arrived—I broke the crucible! I will show you the result."

He unlocked the heavy iron door of a vault that stood in the centre of the room, displaying two rows of shelves covered with boxes, bottles, and indescribable objects in great variety. Taking out one of the boxes, he showed her a collection of crystals, large and small, whose peculiar brilliancy caused her to look at him in wondering inquiry.

"Yes," he smiled, in answer to her look.

"The black powder was—"

"Pure carbon."

"*And these are diamonds?*"

"Pure and without flaw."

"But—but—" she replied, breathlessly, "you said they were only curious and beautiful. Why—they are a fortune—an enormous fortune!"

"To sell? yes, I suppose so. But they will never be sold. If men would only admire and enjoy their beauty, I should be glad to let them go; but men would, in the first place, give for them millions of times their real value, and then they would perhaps lie, plot, fight, *murder* for them. Why-fore should

I sell these pretty pebbles or give them away?
Their practical usefulness is very slight. Their
beauty is great, it is true, but not great enough to
compensate for the mischief they would cause. I
will not sell them. I should be like the man of civilization who takes from the poor, simple savages
their ivory and their furs, and gives them only a few
glittering, worthless beads in return. Neither shall
I give them away; I will not open this Pandora's
box to the world. They shall remain for the present on my shelf, a shining trophy of my victory over
nature. When you are all my own, it will not be a
gift to you, it will be only conferring upon you your
right to place these and all else I have in your keeping. Ah, you are a woman!" he added, laughing, as
she clasped her hands together in uncontrollable delight. "Your eyes are brighter than these worthless
pebbles. But, remember, my beautiful one, *you* are
not to be Pandora!"

XVIII.

THE SERPENT HISSES.

IF we have forgotten poor Tsáras, his late companions in misfortune had not. Many were the
speculations as to his probable fate. Sometimes they
were inclined to the opinion that he had dealt treach-
erously with them. Several little circumstances, besides the suspicious exchange of glances between him

16

and Peschino which Madeline had observed during her " examination," seemed to point that way. Generally, however, they were disposed to believe that these circumstances were merely fortuitous and without significance, and they blamed themselves for ever harboring ungenerous doubts of his honor and fidelity. It must not be supposed that their solicitude or that of their host concerning him was manifest in mere speculations. Strange as it may appear to inhabitants of well-ordered America, there was little greater difficulty in communicating with the brigands than with the most law-abiding citizens of that anomalous country. Letters passed to and fro under a sort of postal system skilfully contrived to secure absolute safety to the outlaws. Offers were made to release the remaining prisoner upon terms which Vyr would not allow the major to accept. " I have made a vow," he said to him, on one occasion, " that, if I can prevent it, the klephts shall never receive a drachma of ransom. I will try again to rescue your friend ; but I really do not believe he is with them. My men, who, as you know, have been always on the watch near their den ever since you came here, have never seen such a person as you describe. They have either released him already, or they have taken him so far away that it is hopeless to try to rescue him by force. You may be assured that they will not harm him before the time they have appointed ; and that is far enough away at present. If, when that time comes, it is your choice to pay to them what they demand, why, I suppose I cannot prevent you. I suppose I should do the same if I were you, and in your situation. But," he added, resolutely, "it is this *final yielding* that does all the mischief. If the friends of the first captives had let them die rather than yield, brigandage would have been strangled in its birth, and those martyrs would have done Greece more good than Zaimis, with all his Greek and Bavarian troops."

At last all doubt and solicitude were set at rest in a very unexpected manner.

One day, shortly after dinner, the three Americans were seated by themselves on the veranda, when they saw a well-known figure climbing up the steep ascent, accompanied by one of the bridge guards.

"Constitution of the United States!" exclaimed the major, "it's old Tsáras himself!" and he ran down to meet him with out-stretched hands. "What —where in the name of Jupiter Jones did you come from? How did you get away from those hell-vomited rattlesnakes?"

The little professor's reception of this effusive greeting was remarkably cool, considering the circumstances. "Monsieur Paul," he said, with stately Greek politeness, "I am mos' happee that I mit you once more again as a free man. I will give to you the explanaätion of myself when I shall see my other friends, the companions of my captivitee. Ah, mesdames," as they came tripping and stumbling, but with beaming faces, down the slope, "permiss me that I shall congratulaäte you. You see," turning back to the major, "that I have not lead you into

those 'hell-of-scraäpe,' as you have say to me, after
all."

The unblushing impudence with which he thus
accredited himself with the results of Hector Vyr's
prowess somewhat cooled their enthusiasm. "Never
mind that now," the major replied, "tell us how you
fared after we left you ; how you managed to make
your escape, and all about it."

"After you lef' me — aah, Monsieur Paul, your
eyes did not tûrn back one little look for poor
Teáras !"

"Oh, come now, professor, you couldn't expect—
why weren't you *with* us, as you ought to have been ?
Why "—here his voice grew harsher, and his face
more red—" why had you been systematically cutting
us for a week at a time? *hey ?*"

" *O Thĕĕ mou !*" cried Tsáras, raising his hands in
indignant remonstrance, "that is one mos' horríble
slander ! I have never cût you one little scrratch !"

"Nonsense. I mean why did you avoid us—run
away from us ?"

"Oh, aah—not cût you with knaifes ?"

"Certainly not."

"But—what for did you have súspicion for me,
Monsieur Paul? eh ?"

"Who told you that ?" the major asked, sharply.

"Your *faäces* have tell me—your *eyes*, which look
at me ûnder the brow. I am not a *chorikós* of the
ground ; I am a man of educaätion with honorable
proudness, Monsieur Paul. I know ver' well what
you thing of me: you thing I was maïke *barrgain*

with Peschino. Aah, it was mos' horrible, ûnjûs' sûspicion !"

The proud, manly way in which the olive cheek flushed and the graceful little figure straightened up, extorted from the Americans a deeper respect than they had ever yet felt for their late guide.

Major Paul hastened to propitiate him : "I don't think, my dear sir, that we ever gave you any real occasion for—"

"Aah, *yeas.* The faäce spik more plain as the töngue. I shall tell to you the whole truth. I perreive that Peschino was fascinaäte with beautiful Miss Paul. If she shall *smaile* a little, she can maäke him one fool, and he shall let us all to go. So I spik to him privaäte a little encouragement."

"Then," said Madeline, with scornful, flashing eyes, "what did you mean by accusing us of unjust suspicion ?"

"Pardon, *kurátza*—you shall wait till I have finish. I say you can maäke him one gret *fool.* It is not dishonor when you shall cheat the klepht which try to rob you."

"Right, by Jupiter Johnson !" put in the major. "Give us your hand, old dragon "—his habitual short for dragoman. "Now go on with your story. How did you escape ?"

"I cannot tell the stoary to you. I have maäke one mos' saäcred promise that I— You know, my friends, when they loses the big fishes, they throw away the little fishes sometaime."

A quick glance shot from eye to eye among his auditors.

"Aah"—straightening up again—"you have sûspicion. I shall not talk to you. I have come to bring one mos' important commission to Monsieur Hector Vyr. Will you have the kaindhood to tell to me where I shall faind him?"

"Go up on the veranda, sir," replied the major, haughtily, "and take a seat there. Madeline, go and find Mr. Vyr."

When she had gone, Tsáras, with increasing dignity, took from his pocket a paper, and presented it to Major Paul. "Will you faävor it with examinaätion, Monsieur Paul?"

It was his account to date for services as guide and interpreter. The major gazed upon it and upon Tsáras for a moment in speechless amazement. "I should think, sir," he said, when he could recover his breath, "that you would, at least, have waited until you had conducted us safely back to Athens before you had the audacity to give me this."

"Pardon"—with a low bow—"it was the agreement that you shall pay to me every wik. It is now—"

"Why, contaminate your insolence, you bowing, scraping Greek harlequin! what do you mean? You lead us into the lions' den, and then bring in your *bill!*"

"You shall not forget that *I* fall in the laions' den too, also," retorted Tsáras.

The major was so choked by his disgust and choler

at this absurd rejoinder, that he could only grow more red in the face and wildly gesticulate.

But Miss Wellington spoke for him: "You deserve to stay there, sir, for attempting so dangerous an undertaking, knowing as you must your utter incompetence. If you were willing to risk your own life, you had no right to risk ours."

While Tsáras was replying in his characteristic way, his eyes fell upon a tall, majestic figure standing upon the veranda. "Aah!" he cried, suddenly breaking off his specious argument, "at las' I see the wond'ful Hector Vyr! Is not he what I have tell you? is not he prodigee? miráclé? Monsieur Paul, you shall make the introdûctions."

Tsáras was received with the forbidding dignity, almost rudeness, with which the singular ascetic treated all intruding strangers. The rebuff was intensely galling to the sensitive little Greek. He colored, bit his lips, shuffled from side to side, but presently plucked up spirit and ceremoniously presented a letter.

"I have intruded upon you," he said, in his own language, "not on my own account, but because I was sent to you by a person whom I believe you know. Will you do me the favor to read his letter, and give me your answer, in private?"

Without a word, Vyr led the way to a small room which served him as an office. There he broke the seal and read, while the messenger stood vainly trying to still his loudly beating heart:

"Sir,—A short time ago you rendered me, in common with my friends, a most signal service. I joined them in the expression of profound feeling which so gallant and beneficent an act naturally awakened.

"Since then, however, events have occurred which have released me from my obligation to you, and changed my sense of gratitude to one of bitter indignation. You are the cause of a disaster, sir, which to me is far greater than captivity among the klephts. From that I might have found other means of release than your intervention; but for the loss of the greatest treasure man can possess, a loss which, as you must be fully aware, you have inflicted upon me, there is only one atonement in my power to ask, or in yours to give. For this, therefore, as well as for the insulting and threatening language you saw fit to use at our last accidental meeting, I hereby demand the atonement which you, as a gentleman and a brave man, cannot refuse.

"My friend, Prof. Markos Tsáras, has kindly consented to make the necessary arrangements with any gentleman you may designate.

"I have the honor to be

"Your most obedient servant,

"ROBERT GRIFFIN.

"M. HECTOR VYR."

The look of indifference with which Vyr began the perusal of this letter changed to a smile of ineffable contempt as he read on, and to a peal of laughter as he finished.

"This poor angry fool," he said, raising his eyes to the wonder-struck Tsáras, "wishes to fight a duel with me!"

Tsáras bowed.

"He has talked with you about it?"

"He has."

"What is his purpose?—does he wish to kill me, or does he wish me to kill him?"

"That is a strange question, monsieur."

"Answer it"—authoritatively.

"Why, I suppose he hopes that the fortune of battle will favor *him*. It would be no more than natural."

"He assumes that I shall choose a weapon in the use of which his skill is equal if not superior to my own?"

"He knows that Monsieur Vyr is as generous as he is brave."

"Ah, then, of course he wishes to kill *me*. Why?"

Tsáras was writhing under the cool, penetrating eye and the overpowering presence of his questioner. "Will monsieur have the kindness to answer my friend's letter?" he asked, ruefully.

"Certainly not, until I understand it."

"Is it not a sufficient explanation in itself?"

"By no means. It does not reveal the writer's *motive*."

"Pardon; but is not that his own affair?"

"No more his than mine, if I am to *assist* him. He cannot fight this duel *alone*, my friend; and if I am to be his accomplice, I must know whether his motive be right or wrong. I ask you again, why does he wish to kill me?"

"Surely his letter explains the cause of offence."

"You imply that his motive is *revenge*. If so, I will not help him to gratify so base a passion. If I have done him any wrong, I will repair it in a manly, sensible way. You may say to him this: 'Mr. Griffin, in a moment of ungovernable passion, of which I am ashamed, I threatened to tear you to atoms. I explained to you, a few minutes afterwards, that this was the speech of a madman, and I asked your forgiveness. That is enough. I did not carry out my threat, and the breath I breathed out I breathed in again. Afterwards I told you that though you had the tongue of a man you had the soul of a reptile. These words were figurative, it is true, but their import was truth; so there can be no wrong in them, and hence no reparation is due.'"

"I suppose," interrupted Tsáras, now quite restored to equanimity by the quiet, argumentative tone which the conversation had assumed—"I suppose you will admit that to be a matter of opinion."

"Assuredly. I speak only my own opinions. I am not responsible for those of other men."

"But one man's opinion may be grossly insulting to another—at least its *expression* may be."

"No. If it is truth, it is no insult. If it is an error made in good faith, it is an injustice, which a just man will correct as soon as he is convinced. Let Mr. Griffin prove to me that I was in error, and I will hasten to acknowledge it."

"And so," cried Tsáras, pleased and astonished at his own boldness, and the "wond'ful" Hector Vyr's condescension—"and so any man is justified in saying any outrageous thing he chooses to another, provided *he* thinks it is the truth, although his judgment may be warped by anger, malice, prejudice, misinformation, jealousy, or stupidity!"

"Others may respect or despise his opinions as they see fit," replied Vyr. "Your friend Mr. Griffin has this freedom in respect to mine. If my contempt for him is the fault of my imperfect judgment, he may despise it as a thing of no significance."

"Suppose a man insults you by saying to you what he himself does not believe to be true?" suggested Tsáras.

"Such a man is but an idle babbler, not worthy of my notice. If Mr. Griffin thinks I have done so to him, he may regard me in that light."

Tsáras looked far from satisfied, but made no reply. Vyr went on:

"There is *one* respect in which I freely acknowledge that I have done Mr. Griffin injustice. I said to his cousin Miss Paul that he had not the courage to use the weapons he bears. I also said to her that I could scare him away with a look. I am convinced that this was an error."

"May I ask if these things were said in his hearing?" asked Tsáras, curiously.

"No. And it is this I most regret. You may say so to him, Monsieur Tsáras. And now I believe I have made full reparation for all the wrong I have done him."

"The things we have been speaking of are trifles," said Tsáras, as if the thought had just occurred to him. "You make no mention of the great grievance of all—the disaster which he says you have caused, far greater to him than the captivity from which you released him."

"I have not mentioned it, simply because there is no wrong to acknowledge nor difficulty to explain. Mr. Griffin needs no words from me to understand that, when he charges me with robbing him of the greatest treasure man can possess, he is what I have called an idle babbler, not worthy of notice. He says what he himself does not believe. Can a man lose what he has never possessed? What no man already possesses, is it not free to any man to win if he can? No wrong has been done here, and hence no reparation is called for. Why, then, I still ask, does he thirst for my blood? If it is to gratify an unreasoning revenge, I refuse to be his accomplice.

"But perhaps it is *hope.* Perhaps he imagines my death will give him the treasure of which he thinks my life deprives him. You may tell him, Monsieur Tsáras, first, that such a hope is futile, for the murderous deed would only drive that treasure farther than ever from his grasp; and, secondly, that such a motive is no better than that of the klepht, who also murders that he may gain. In such a business I shall never participate.

"There is only one other supposition possible: that he wishes me to kill *him.* This, of course, is extremely improbable; but even if it were the true one, I could not gratify him; unless, indeed, he should enroll himself among the klephts, and thus give me the sanction of the law."

"And this, Mr. Vyr, is your final answer?"

"It is my *only* answer."

"Would you not like"—hesitatingly—"to think of it for twenty-four hours?"

"No. Why should I? It is a very simple matter—there is nothing more to think of."

"Very well, then. Will you kindly write a line, that my friend may be in no doubt as to your decision?"

"He will not believe your word?" asked Vyr, with a smile.

"It is more business-like."

Vyr laughed outright. "You call it *business?* Well, I will humor you."

He took a scrap of paper, and dashed off, in a big, round, black hand,

"Mr. Griffin,—I have read your letter of to-day. My answer to your demand is no.

"Hector Vyr.

"*My house, Sept. 24, 18—.*"

"Thank you," said Tsáras, folding the paper carefully and putting it in his pocket. "I will now take my leave; but my friend may send me back."

"It would be a waste of time. However, you shall be admitted, as you were this morning."

In a few hours Tsáras returned with the following letter:

"SIR,—Your insultingly short reply to my letter of this morning has been handed me by my friend, Prof. Tsáras. In it you decline to give me the satisfaction I have an undoubted right to demand. In its stead you offer me, by word of mouth, only a specimen of that peculiar philosophy in which you evidently take so much pride. Permit me, therefore, to say that such conduct is no more in keeping with the character which you have hitherto maintained for courage, than your recent treatment of myself is in keeping with the honor and magnanimity of a gentleman. I shall lose no opportunity of setting you in your true light before the public, before which you have been so successfully posing as a prodigy of valor, and before my *personal friends*, upon whose good opinion you place so high a value.

"Permit me further to say that *you will not escape with this punishment alone.*

"I have the honor to be

"Your obedient servant,

"ROBERT GRIFFIN.

"M. HECTOR VYR."

The same changing expressions passed over Vyr's face, as he read through this ferocious epistle, that its predecessor had called forth.

"Take this back to your friend," he said, "and thank him for me for the amusement it has afforded me."

"You are a remarkable man, indeed!" muttered Tsáras, half to himself.

"Why? because I laugh? I suppose it is cruel.
I ought to feel only compassion. Your friend has
been unfortunate, and is very unhappy. I would
express my sympathy for him, but you know very
well it would only be rejected. I cannot feel frightened by his terrible words, so nothing remains but to
be amused by them."

"I was instructed," said Tsáras, with formality,
"to ask you, for the last time, will you give Mr. Griffin the satisfaction he demands?"

"Why is that asked again?" returned Vyr, with
the first sign of real intolerance he had yet shown.
"Have I not told him plainly? He has the satisfaction of having challenged me. He is therefore entitled to all the credit—whatever it may be—of an
actual encounter. It is no fault of his that I will
not descend to the idiotic barbarism of a prearranged
duel. He may enjoy the further satisfaction of
branding Hector Vyr as a coward, to say nothing
of the additional punishment he says he has in store
for him. What more can he ask? Come, my friend,
this interview has been sufficiently prolonged. It
is only the genuine sorrow I feel for Mr. Griffin
that has made me patient all this time. You may
go now."

And although Vyr made no movement, yet it almost seemed to Tsáras as if he were taken up bodily
and carried out by some invisible power.

XIX.

THE SERPENT STINGS.

AFTER Tsáras had finally gone, Major Paul and his friends anxiously waited for some intimation as to the nature of the business which their absent kinsman had to transact with Hector Vyr. The latter made no reply, however, to their inquiring looks, but, after a few commonplace remarks about the long-continued absence of rain, and the effect upon his crops—with scarcely a glance at Madeline—he started to return to his field. The major saw the startled, wounded look upon Madeline's pale face, and, springing up with sudden determination, followed him. Vyr saw him coming, and smilingly waited.

"Mr. Vyr," said the major, "is the matter between you and my nephew one that I have a right to know about?"

"You may know it if you wish, though it is not essential that you should. It affects neither your daughter nor yourself, and I do not wish the slightest hint of it to reach her. In reality, it affects only Mr. Griffin himself. He has sent me a challenge."

"Apotheosis of Blazing Idiots! I was afraid of that."

"Why-fore afraid, Mr. Paul?"—with a smile— "you paid a very poor compliment to my self-respect, intelligence, or humanity, if you supposed for one instant that I should *accept.* I should ill fulfil my mission if I consented to an act which belongs to an inferior stage in the development of civilized man, and beyond which, thank Heaven, he has already advanced. My mission is to go forward, not backward."

"Poor Robert! I don't suppose he really knew what he was about. He is in great trouble, Mr. Vyr."

"I know that; and I pity him from my heart; but I could not give to him what fate has refused him, even if I would.

"Mr. Paul"—stopping and speaking with slow, intensely earnest utterance—"until lately I had but one great object in existence. To that object I have sworn to devote my life and energies. I shall keep my oath, at least its letter: its spirit compels me to seek in marriage the most perfect example of womanhood fortune brings to my knowledge. With no direct thought of my oath, I found myself plunged into a love for your daughter which has swallowed up my soul as the ocean would ingulf my body. With unutterable joy I became convinced that my coolest judgment could not choose better than my heart had already chosen. We have spoken our love to each other, and you have not frowned upon us. But now my great object in life has sunk almost into insignificance in comparison with another — that of securing for my beloved the greatest possible degree of happiness of which she is capable. To this I feel as if I could sacrifice all others, except the preserva-

17

tion of honor. I have read of man's love for woman in poems and tales; but mine is not like that. That demands love for love, like the payment of a debt to the uttermost farthing. It demands possession at all hazards. It is *not* love; it is the greed of a devouring dragon. But mine demands above all other things the choicest blessings that Heaven can bestow upon her beloved head. My own happiness I could throw into the scale as a willing sacrifice, if it would enhance hers—that would *not* be sacrificing my happiness, it would be insuring it—I could yield possession of her, I mean, and live in contentment, if I knew that thereby she would be more blessed than with me. Mr. Paul, tell me from your heart of hearts, do you believe she would lead a happier life without me in her own country than with me in these wilds?"

This solemn appeal, delivered with an intensity of feeling the major had never before imagined, almost stopped his pulses. He knew not what to say. At length he stammered:

"But—but, if my darling Madeline is, as you say, the finest example of womanhood you expect to meet —how are you going to—what about your *oath*, Mr. Vyr?"

"Its language is simply negative; it does not compel me to marry, it only obliges me to avoid allying myself with mental, moral, or physical deficiency. And it is better that the lineage should end with Hector Vyr, than that he should transmit to posterity the smallest germ of the greedy, selfish passion which goes under the name of Love. If it is not love itself, pure, self-sacrificing, heavenly—preferring the welfare of its object to all other things, even a posterity that it would otherwise debase—far better that it should die!"

Major Paul looked at him with an admiration amounting to awe. "I cannot answer for Madeline," he replied, in a voice shaken by his emotions; "but, if she does not prefer such devotion from such a source to a thousand Bostons, she is unworthy of you. That's all I can say, Mr. Vyr." And he turned and marched away, as if he were on parade.

"Mr. Paul."

The major halted and faced about.

"Not a word of this to *her*."

"No, Mr. Vyr."

As Vyr went on his way alone, he mused:

"Poor dove! I have played upon her wonder and gratitude until she is in my toils, and cannot escape if she would. Does she not even now secretly regret that her love for me will exile her from her home, notwithstanding all I have promised her in return? *Will* all I can do compensate her for the sacrifice? That poor, foolish young man loves her well enough to throw away his life for her. He deserves a better fate, mean-spirited as I thought him. Can it be that her heart might have softened to him if she had never fallen in my way, and that she might have lifted him, if not to her own level, at least to one of harmony and mutual happiness? Would it be better for her, after all, if she could cease loving me? Could she cease loving me if she thought I had ceased loving her? Would it be cruel to put her to the test?"

Thus he renewed the battle with himself, till, iron-nerved as he was, the sweat stood in great drops on his brow.

When he returned at supper-time, his manner towards Madeline was that of a ceremonious host, nothing more. Throughout the short evening he maintained the same unlover-like reserve. He seemed to have entirely forgotten the tender scenes that had taken place between them. She, poor girl, besides being chilled to the heart by his changed manner, was devoured with anxiety in regard to the mysterious "commission" of Tsáras. But she would not speak —not she; she sat with proud indifference, occasionally chatting with her father and aunt, until she finally rose to say "good-night."

Vyr followed her to the foot of the stairs, but he offered her no embrace; there was no tenderness in his look, no lingering pressure of her hand, only a little tremor in his voice, as he said, "Good-night, Madeline. May your sleep be as sweet as your soul is pure."

"Thank you, Mr. Vyr. I *always* sleep sweetly. Good-night."

She walked up-stairs with a firm, steady step, and sat down at her window to—think.

And this was her hero, the *god* she had worshipped!. The change had immediately followed Tsáras's visit. Robert had in some way *frightened* him—*him* who was to scare the poor fellow away with a look! Oh,

what a fall was there—what a height, what a depth!
Oh, the scorn, the bitter self-scorn, that stung her for
her folly, her absolute inanity!

And yet, was it not this very god, this very pyg-
my, that had dashed up to the mouth of the lion's
den, and, single-handed, brought her and hers away in
safety? Had she sinned unpardonably against him
in her thought? If she had, could she ever look upon
his face again? could she ever dare to *think* of him
again?

Could it be that Robert had tried to poison his
mind in regard to her past history? No, no! Desperate, passionate, revengeful as he was, he was her
cousin, the son of her own mother's sister. But, if
it were possible, would Hector Vyr believe him?
Would he not repel the slanders with unutterable
contempt, or at least give *her* the opportunity of
doing so?

"May your sleep be as sweet as your soul is pure."
Were not these kind, beautiful words enough, from
lips that could utter falsehood no more than the
heavens could fall to earth?

No, he had repented his own impulsive haste; he
had seen his mistake; he had taken her for a divinity
worthy of himself, and had at last discovered that
she was no more than other women. And now he
was sternly, cruelly undoing his mistake. Soon he
would unsay the words that had lifted her soul to
paradise.

And she? Alas! she ought to have known, if *he*

did not. It was, as she had told him, all a gorgeous
dream. She was awaking, and she would banish it
like other dreams from her recollection.

One day more and she would return with her
friends to the solid earth beneath the clouds, and he
would never see nor hear of her again.

Would he think of her? would he feel sorry that
he had taken her up in his mighty hand, like a little
bird, only to dash her down again?

The livelong night brought her no sleep. In the
morning she stood before her mirror until she had
schooled her features to an expression of calm, even
gay unconcern, and then tripped down the staircase
with the same lively air upon her lips that had answered the birds upon her first morning there. Vyr
darted a keen glance at her as she entered the break-
fast-room, which was lost upon her no more than was
the momentary pallor on his own face, or his silent
preoccupation during the meal. She chatted briskly
about their return to Athens, and the wonderful stories they should have to relate to their friends in Boston. She even spoke of Robert as if nothing had
happened to disturb their cousinly friendship, wondered what comical mischief he had been concocting
during his absence, and whether he was not coming
to bid his entertainers good-by. She hoped that Madame Vyr and her son would, for once at least, break
in upon their ascetic habits, and accept a return of
their delightful hospitality. It was altogether a singular, one-sided conversation. Vyr looked and lis-

tened as if neither seeing nor hearing. The major scarcely uttered a word, but sat looking from one to another, wondering when the farce would be over and the real play begin, when he should be having something to say for himself. Madame Vyr's face wore a more anxious and bewildered look than ever. Aunt Eliza ventured upon a few non-committal observations, but Madeline alone seemed to be mistress of the situation.

Finally, as they were about rising from the table, Vyr roused himself. "Mr. Paul," he said, "while I was at the village yesterday I learned something that I think will interest you."

"I shall be most happy to be interested, sir," replied the major, a little stiffly. ·

"His Majesty's Government has at last listened to the demands of the American Minister in your behalf, and has sent a detachment of one hundred and fifty men to rescue you from the klephts."

"Indeed! I am under great obligations to his Majesty's Government. It was a handsome thing to do. I have said a great many hard things of that institution—I am happy to retract 'em all."

"They are now in the village," Vyr went on. "Their commander has expressed a very strong desire to meet you and your friends, and to extend to you his congratulations on your not needing his services. If he were not prevented by my well-known inhospitality to uninvited guests, he would doubtless have presented himself here before this. I happened to fall in with him—a very good-hearted, soldierly fellow—but I assure you I was glad to escape from his tongue. He could not understand by once telling that I would not accept any demonstrations in my honor, nor permit any to my guests at my house. I am a bear, and it is not only right but necessary that all who know of me at all should also know this of me."

"*We* discovered it long ago," remarked Miss Wellington, facetiously.

"I have not been a bear to you," replied Vyr, coldly, "because you have a perfect right to be here. I desired your society for my own purposes, and I invited you to visit me."

Soon after breakfast, of which Vyr scarcely tasted, he proposed a last ramble through the neighboring forest. Madeline assented with cheerful alacrity, and was running to call her father and aunt, when he prevented her by a decided "No."

She controlled the sudden throbbing in her breast, and simply replied, "My father, at least, would enjoy it as well as I."

"As well as you?" thought Vyr, giving her a long, wistful look. "Are you weaned from me so soon, so easily?" Then he said aloud, "I do not invite you for the sake of mere enjoyment to-day, Madeline. I have much to say to you alone."

"Say it *now! here!*" she answered, bravely. "I insist upon your telling me at once what is wrong or strange."

"There is nothing wrong or strange so far as *you*

are concerned. *I* am the only one in the wrong, and it remains for me to—do right."

"Then do right—*now!*"

"That is what I am trying to do," he said, with unutterable sadness. "Come with me, and I will tell you what the right is."

For a few moments she stood regarding him in proud defiance. He moved slowly away, with his great soft eye fixed steadily upon hers. Against her will her feet followed him.

They went silently down the narrow, stony path to the deep ravine which they had crossed at their first approach to his home.

"Not across *there*," she said, firmly.

"Yes, Madeline; I wish it. I have a good reason."

"Mr. Vyr, I will *not!*"

But she might as well have opposed Fate. As if he had not heard her last words, he gently approached and raised her unresisting form in his arms. The angry tears rushed to her eyes; she tried to speak, but her tongue was paralyzed. He stepped upon the perilous bridge. For an instant she looked down into the frightful abyss, and her arms flew around his neck. She felt convulsive tremors darting through his frame, and she clung more closely.

When he set her down on the other side, the tears still stood in her eyes. "You are a tyrant!" she cried, with a passionate outburst, "a cruel *tyrant!*"

"Am I?" he said, sorrowfully. "Forgive me. I did not mean to be. I did not think you would be so frightened. You were not before. There is no more danger now than then, Madeline. Are you angry because I brought you here against your will? I will carry you back again if you command me, and by-and-by I will tell you why-fore I brought you here."

She hesitated, looked again into the gulf, and recoiled. "No," she said, weakly; "not now. Let me rest a while."

"Poor, tender bird! I *have* been cruel. I am not fit to be with you. I shall never learn to be gentle. Here, darl—here, Madeline, rest under this fir. You are pale, you are trembling. I will not frighten you any more. I will obey you like your slave."

His penitence and submission soon reconciled her to her position, and she waited for him to begin his promised confession. But, intolerable as was her suspense, she was too proud to betray the least impatience. She even feigned interest in the natural objects around, asking him for their names and uses.

So perfect was her disguise that he was completely deceived. "Ah!" he said to himself, "how have I mistaken this beautiful, soulless creature! Her heavenly lips have spoken love which I thought was as deep as the sea, but which was only as the foam upon its surface! Will my heart ever recover from this bitter, bitter blight? There is nothing for me to say—the work is already done—*she has forgotten why we came here!*"

The poor unsophisticated soul even felt something akin to her own pride. He answered her questions with a clumsy attempt at her own indifference of manner. While thus engaged, his eye fell upon a solitary ant slowly dragging along the mutilated body of a beetle. He broke a dry twig in two, and carefully placed the pieces in its path, leaving a passage too narrow for its burden to pass through.

"What a little fool!" he exclaimed, after both had watched its unavailing efforts for a while. "Why doesn't she go around, where her path is clear? They say she knows almost as much with her atom of brain as we do with our three pounds, more or less. Let us see her prove it. Stupid! doesn't she see the beetle is too big to go through that little gate? She could have carried it around twenty times while she has been wasting her strength there."

"Here, you poor little simpleton," said Madeline, "let me help you." And she pushed away one of the sticks.

"You are no naturalist, Miss Paul," said Vyr, with a singular, desolate smile, "or you would have waited."

"No, Mr. Vyr, I have no heart to experiment— even on an insect."

In spite of her self-mastery there was something in her tone so unconsciously accusing, so appealing, that it penetrated to his very soul. Not all the eloquence of words could have equalled the pathetic reproach of that voice. He stood before her a while, regarding her in silence. Then he said, in a low, humble tone, "Your rebuke is just; I *have* been experimenting upon you!"

"And most cruelly!" she burst forth, all her self-restraint giving way. "Could you not *speak?* could you not *ask* me what you wished to know, as you promised to do?"

"I promised to ask what your lips could tell," he answered, without lifting his eyes. "But we do not always know our own hearts, Madeline. I know yours is true—Heaven forgive me for doubting it for one instant! I know you believe you could always be happy with me, even in the life-long exile I offer you. But 'always' is a long time; 'life-long' means throughout the heat of youth, throughout middle life, with its cooler weighing of blessings and privations, throughout frozen age. Love must be a chain as well as a garland. It may have the beauty and fragrance of flowers, but it must have also the strength of adamant. A chain that is to hold so long must be *tried*, Madeline. If a little strain can break it now, is it not better that it should be broken? Better for *you*, I mean," he added, with intense fervor—"it is of *you* only that I think!"

"Strains will come soon enough without our seeking for them," retorted Madeline, bitterly, yet with a gleam of tenderness in her reproach. "If your faith in my love is so weak that you cannot trust it without such cruel tests, you had better never have sought it. But are you quite sure it is *I*, after all, whom you are testing? Have you no misgiving lest you may have chosen wrongly? She whom you rescued from the klephts, and whom your first blind impulse exalted to your own level—have you, at last, discovered that she is only one of countless thousands, any one of whom might have filled her place in your fancy to-day, had fortune so willed it? Have you discovered that poor Madeline Paul is not the divinity you thought her?" Rising calm and cold before him—"And is *this* what you meant when you said you were in the wrong, and were going to—*do right?*"

Before Hector Vyr, gazing entranced into her eyes, could reply, the sound of a sudden rushing was heard —a loud shout—there was a heavy blow—and he sank unconscious at her side.

XX.

THE MAJOR'S RIDE.

That had taken place which, under any other circumstances, would have been impossible. Eye and ear, heart and soul completely enthralled, there was nothing to Hector Vyr either audible or visible beyond the shade of that fir-tree.

Peschino caught Madeline in his arms, while two other brigands pounced upon the prostrate form of her lover. Her piercing shrieks partially restored Vyr to consciousness, and a mighty spasm shot through his body, throwing one of his captors upon his back and the other to his knees. With a curse of rage and fear, Peschino dropped his burden and sprang to their assistance, fetching another blow upon the bleeding head of his victim..

As if in response to Madeline's agonized shrieks

for help, a man came running towards her from among the bushes.

It was Robert Griffin!

"Thank God!" she cried, springing to him with out-stretched arms. "Oh, Robert — *save him! save him!*"

At the same instant a loud report rang out among the trees on the other side of the ravine, and one of the brigands fell. The sentinel and two others were seen hurrying down the slope.

"*Fĕrĕtĕ tēn mădzi mas!*" (Bring her with us!) shouted Peschino, as he and his men made off with their inanimate prisoner.

Griffin replied by a shot from his revolver into the air. Then, seizing Madeline's hand, he dragged her towards the bridge.

"Save him, too! Let me go!" she cried, struggling to escape.

"Hush!" he hissed through his teeth; "the others will look out for *him*. Come along, I say! When you're safe in the house, we'll arouse the village."

In her frenzy she charged him with treachery—murder!

He turned upon her, his face white with fury. "Is this your gratitude, you viper! Are these the words you spoke to *him* when he did no more for you than I have done this day?"

Poor soul! notwithstanding that she shrank with loathing from his very sight and touch, uncertainty made her retract her terrible charges, and plead for his forbearance.

It was now she that urged him forward. He was obliged to strain every nerve to keep pace with her nimble feet. The bridge was lying, as Vyr had left it, over the ravine. Heedless of danger she crossed it, calling Griffin to follow. On she sped, up the path until the white tower came in sight. The sentinel's shot as well as her own shrieks had been heard, and her father, with two or three of the servants, was hastening to meet her.

"What is it, Madge?" puffed the major—"for Heaven's sake, what is it?"

"The brigands!—*Hector!*" she gasped, seizing him by his arms.

"What do you say?—the brigands have—got—*him!*—got *Hector Vyr?*"

"Yes! yes! Save him! oh, save him!"

Griffin now came up, and breathlessly told how, while on his way to join his friends and say farewell to the Vyrs, he had happened on the scene of action in the very nick of time.

The major blessed him with few but vigorous words. "We'll save *him*, too, Robert," he panted. "Run up with Madge—rouse everybody—meet me at the demarch's."

In an incredibly short space of time, Major Paul reached the little office of the demarch of Mikro-Maina. Bursting in without ceremony, he inquired whether the detachment of troops had left the village.

His month of language-lessons with Peschino now stood him in good stead.

The big, red-faced Mainote stared in open-mouthed wonder. "Yes," he managed to answer at length; "it left this morning."

"Where has it gone?"

"Back to Athens, to report to his Majesty's Government the complete success of the expedition. I congratulate you on your—"

"Where will it stop for the night?"

"Probably at Peschino-Chorio."

The name startled the major. "Does that place belong to the villain I'm after?" he asked.

"The klepht? No," smiled the demarch. "They have nothing to do with each other that I know of."

"How far is it from here?"

"About six hours' journey."

It was nearly three o'clock.

"Who has the swiftest horse in the village?"

The demarch reflected.

"Mikhális Panoûtso has one that is very fleet; Pétros Maurídes has another about as good; but, *Panaghía!* no one has an animal that can compare with my own 'Alogon."

"Will you let me have him?"

"Holy Virgin! no one could hire my 'Alogon for half his entire value."

"But I will *buy* him of you at double his value."

"*E eugenía sas*" (You are a prince). "He would be cheap at six hundred drachmas."

"Have him saddled immediately," ordered the major; "and, in the mean time, write me a letter of introduction to the commander of the detachment:

Major Warren Paul of Boston, U. S., late of the —th Regiment Massachusetts Volunteers, recently rescued from the klephts."

When his order had been executed, he said, "If Mr. Griffin calls here— You know him, I believe?"

The demarch nodded.

"Tell him to wait for me at the Kutchuk inn."

Mounted upon a large-framed, powerful creature, Major Paul rode for dear life, stopping only to inquire his way as he passed through one straggling village after another.

For dear life? He rode for one whose happiness was dearer to him than life—for the life of another worth to humanity a hundred of his own, a life which might even then be going out in lingering torture— he rode for sacred honor, for the payment of a debt that life to that other or death to himself only could repay!

Now dismounting to rest his panting horse while they climbed a steep, narrow, crooked path, now careering down the opposite incline, scouring over the valley, thundering across the rickety foot-bridge that spanned the stream in its midst, plunging into a forest, emerging on the other side—he at last, just as the sun was setting, dashed up to the barracks at Peschino-Chorio.

The officer of the guard was called, who took Major Paul's letter of introduction, and with elaborate politeness conducted him to headquarters. His reception there, while it necessarily pleased and en-

13

couraged him, wasted precious time. He impatiently interrupted it, therefore, with a statement of his
errand, which his broken Greek rendered forcible, if
not eloquent.

We will attempt a free translation of the conversation that ensued.

. "I have heard of this Hector Vyr," said the *lochagós* commanding, " even before the gallant act which
anticipated my own, and for which he so persistently
refuses all recognition, official or private. Until then,
however, I never believed the stories they tell of him.
He shall be reported in spite of himself; he cannot
help that. He must be a marvel indeed! How is
it possible the klephts ever caught him ?"

"But they *have* caught him!" fumed the major.
" And if he is to be rescued there is not a moment to
lose. We must march *instantly.*"

"My orders were—"

"Curse your orders! Go back to Athens without
striking a blow for the man that alone did your work
for you and your whole command—if you dare!"

"Certainly not. I will despatch a courier without
delay to—"

"But he'll be *dead*, I tell you! He's dead now,
for all I know. Come, my dear colonel, *I'll* take the
responsibility. You shall run no risk. I promise
you the influence of the whole United States Government to protect you. Lose another moment and
your head shall be covered with infamy, both at home
and abroad. Suppose you *are* disciplined—a thing
your minister will never disgrace himself by doing—

what then? You will have made a glorious record,
bagged a score of klephts, perhaps, to say nothing of
rescuing the man who is an army in himself. I
promise you success, colonel. I've been there, myself, and will show you the road to victory. We
needn't go by the Flume at all. Great King Devil!
what do you want? If it is money—"

"Sir! this is an insult."

"Never mind. We'll settle it afterwards. What
are you waiting for? Give the order this instant, I
say!"

"Well, well. Don't be so furious, my friend. I'll
venture it."

"*Now!* We must march at once, and fight all
night if necessary!"

But in spite of entreaties and threats the *lochagós*
refused to stir till morning. So, lest he might become so incensed that he would give up the undertaking altogether, the major finally submitted, though
he spent half the night in chafing and raging like a
caged animal.

XXI.

THE ORDEAL.

HECTOR VYR'S first returning consciousness was
that of a terrible throbbing pain in his temples,
the smell of brandy, a fiery, pungent taste in his
mouth and throat, and iron chains pressing tightly
into his arms, wrists, legs, and ankles.

He drew a deep, gasping breath and opened his eyes. He was lying on a pallet in a rude hut. The pillow was red with blood from his head. A dozen faces were glaring at him in savage exultation.

"Go!" he heard a loud voice say; "every man to his quarters."

Reluctantly the brigands withdrew, leaving their captain alone with his prisoner.

"So I have you at last!"

"Yes. You have my body."

"That's all I want. As for the rest of you, the devil may have it and be welcome—he'll soon get it," with a ferocious laugh.

"You are happy now, are you not?" asked Vyr. His voice was so changed by the first great physical shock he had ever suffered, that he almost wondered whether it was he that was speaking or some one else uttering his thoughts.

"Happy!" echoed Peschino. "I am in paradise! This is the grandest day of my life. It is joy enough for a hundred lives to see the *Anthropodaimon* lying like a helpless infant in my cabin!"

"Enjoy it while you can, Peschino," answered his victim, fixing his great mild eyes, languid with pain, upon him. "There is little enough you can enjoy, poor soul!"

"Ho, ho! Never you fear for me. I'll get enjoyment enough out of you before I have done with you!"

"Play with me, and then slay me. Then there is the rest of your life on earth—then eternity."

Vyr spoke more as if he were communing with himself than replying to Peschino. His eyes had turned away from his enemy, and now looked dreamily out through the little window at the foot of his pallet.

The brigand crossed himself. "I'll meet you in eternity, Hector Vyr," he retorted, with a fearful scowl, "with all my followers whom you have sent there."

"Yes. We shall all meet together before our Judge—and may He forgive us all!"

"You preach and pray!" growled Peschino. "You sing psalms and I—I'll *play the instruments!*"

But the terrible significance of this taunt extorted no sign of fear from the helpless prisoner, who asked quietly,

"Are these chains designed as a part of my punishment, or simply for security?"

"Will you swear to attempt no violence if I loosen them a little?"

"I shall attempt nothing that would be useless."

"Will you swear to make no effort to escape, or to harm any of us, if I take them off altogether?"

"No. Let them remain as they are."

Nevertheless, Peschino sounded a whistle, and while two brigands who answered the call stood covering the prisoner with their rifles, he unlocked the fetters, loosened and relocked them, one by one, affording inexpressible relief to the swollen, suffering limbs.

"I have no intention to 'punish' you," he explained, after the men had been again sent away, "until the proper time. I have a *proposition* to make to you first."

"You will doubtless waste your breath. Nevertheless, go on, and I will listen as well as I can with this thumping brain. You have lamed my thinking power somewhat with that bludgeon of yours, Peschino. If you wished to talk with me, you should not have struck so hard—twice, I think it was, was it not?"

"Ah, it was *Hector Vyr* that I struck!" laughed the brigand, exultingly. "Santa Maria bless the sweet bait that trapped him for us, the beautiful Madeline Paul! Without her help we could as well have trapped the moon!"

Two lurid flames seemed to leap from the eyes before so soft and mild. Peschino started back, expecting to see the chains snap under the tremendous struggles of his prisoner; but in a moment or two the latter sank panting back upon his pallet.

"Aha!" thought Peschino, "*there's* where the quick lies. *Now* we'll see what you'll say to my proposition.

"What," he asked, "if I should myself break those chains for you? What if I offer to you release—not merely from death, but *torture?*

"Yes, Hector Vyr, liberty is yours if you will accept it. I, the *Kapitán* Peschino, pronounce it upon the honor of a klepht. I will forget the many disappointments we have suffered at your hands, the terrors, wounds, and death you have inflicted upon my brave followers; you shall once more behold the face of your twice-bereaved mother, and clasp in your arms the beautiful daughter of the Frank — I, who loved her and swore that the very bed whereon you lie should be hers, will yield you even this—all upon one condition!"

"Become one of you?"

"Yes. *Will you do it?* We will make you our leader, our *king!* Heavens! what could we not do? We would make all Greece our pasture-land and vineyard! We would laugh at the world!"

"Even as I now laugh at you."

The eager solicitation of Peschino's face changed to a demoniac scowl. "You shall pay dearly for this!" he growled, and turned to the door, as if to call his men. But avarice once more mastered his rage and thirst for revenge. He hesitated, and turned slowly back.

"Well, hear one more condition, one that demands no sacrifice of honor—only simple justice."

"Go on."

"In the first place, you will not deny that you and your father before you have many times interfered with our business. You have lost us many hundred thousands of drachmas. The *Kapitán* Paul alone was to pay us three hundred thousand. It was not your affair. If he and I had been suffered to finish our transaction of business together, you would not have been accountable. Have we not a right to demand that you shall let us alone? that you shall attend to your own affairs, and let us attend to ours?"

"It is just. You attend to your affairs, and I will attend to mine."

"Make good to us, then, at least this last loss. Mark, Hector Vyr, I ask only what was already ours. You call us thieves—what have you and your ancestors been but the greatest thieves in Greece? Restore to us, I say, the last game that you stole from our snare; put the *Kapitán* Paul again in our way; swear to interfere with us no more, and you are free. Refuse this most reasonable, most generous condition, and I swear to you I will measure your fortitude, inch by inch, hour by hour, till I have reached its utmost limit! or, if that is equal to your power of life, till the last spark of life has faded out in slow agony! Think it well over, Hector Vyr. Remember your father, and from his fate be assured that the heart of a klepht never relents. Well, what do you say?"

"You have done well, Peschino," answered Vyr, with white, firm lips, "to speak of my father. If for one instant my heart should fail me, the thought of *him* would nerve me to the end. It is you that should remember him, and know, without another trial, what a Vyr can endure.

"If you indulge in this idle chatter because you think it torments me, continue it by all means—I am in your hands; but if you think it will cause one little tremor in my resolution, spare your breath. My brain is weary. I shall say no more."

With this he closed his eyes, and turned his face to the wall.

"Very well," said Peschino, drawing a long breath

between his teeth as he arose, "I will leave you now. I will give you till the sun again shines in at this window to make your final decision. Perhaps a night's thinking will make your brain clearer."

Within a half-hour after Peschino's departure the sentinel at the door of the hut reported the prisoner fast asleep!

There are some things too horrible to paint, though they are not too horrible to be. Art averts her face in high-bred disgust, or in compassion too keen for her fine sensibilities, from scenes which Nature tolerates without flinching, and history delineates in every horrifying detail. For four interminable hours Hector Vyr endured that of which no one shall suffer the pain even of reading a description. Suffice it that his tormentor was an adept in his fiendish art, that he knew too well the secret of prolonging agony—he knew that the breaking of bones, the direct injury of vital parts, even the free shedding of blood, was but a clumsy waste of the victim's vitality, and hence of his capacity for suffering.

Did Vyr suffer without a murmur or a groan? Before the ordeal began he said to Peschino, "I shall play no heroic folly for your admiration. I shall assist your executioner by no self-torturing repression. Do not, therefore, mistake my cries for prayers, or my wailings for signs of yielding. They are *anodynes* which I shall employ without stint. Begin when you please. I am ready."

*   *   *   *   *   *   *

At last a more effectual anodyne came—perfect unconsciousness.

"Quick!" shouted Peschino, "the brandy!"

They had partially released their victim, and were in the act of forcing the burning liquid down his throat, when a musket-shot was heard from the cliff, and the cry, "*Strătiótai! strătiótai!*" (the soldiers! the soldiers!) resounded through the camp.

Peschino had far underestimated the tremendous vitality of Hector Vyr. It was now that his reserve-power, the faithful husbandry of seven generations, triumphantly showed itself. As the terrified shouts of the brigands fell upon his reviving ear, the vital tide came pouring back into his veins. Back surged his giant strength into every nerve and muscle. A feeble invalid will sometimes put forth a maniacal force which will tax strong men to their utmost. What, then, must have been the might with which the long-tortured Hector Vyr arose at that electrifying sound? He shook off the remaining bonds that held him as if they had been wisps of straw, snatched a musket from the paralyzed hand of his nearest guard, darted forward, dashing down his enemies right and left, and disappeared in the pass before a shot had been fired!

With loud imprecations Peschino and three more started in pursuit. A few others sprang to the top of the cliff to shoot down the fugitive as he emerged. But none of their wild shots struck the half-naked figure that darted its zigzag way down the hill and quickly vanished in the thickets. Then, raising their eyes for the first time, they saw a line of muskets glittering along the open space below, and disappearing one by one among the tall bushes. Leaping back into their intrenchments and seeing nowhere their chieftain, they rushed into his hut, hurriedly overturning pallets, tables, etc., in their search for a certain strong box they knew of. Not finding it, they rushed out again with yells of "*Grégora! Grégora!*" ran down the valley, up into the mountain on the other side, where they were closely followed by their panic-stricken comrades.

Meantime Peschino and his three followers continued their pursuit until they reached the outer entrance of the pass. There, instead of their late prisoner, they beheld a swarm of soldiers just beginning to pour forth from the thickets, led by the well-known figure of Major Paul. They turned to retreat—but too late. There were rattling explosions, and Peschino fell with both knees shattered. His companions caught him up in their arms and hurried with him into the pass. The shouts came nearer—nearer—their burden grew heavier—it was too much for brigand courage and fealty; they laid him on the ground, and, heedless alike of his entreaties and his curses, they left to his fate their captain, in whose defence they had sworn to die!

A few minutes later he was surrounded by his chattering, huzzaing captors. The *lochagós* ordered two soldiers to take him in charge, and hastened on with the rest in hot pursuit of his faithless comrades. With renewed yells the troops poured through the pass, then scattered here and there, in and out of the huts, and down the valley. But Peschino's boast was true. In the mountain labyrinth beyond, all but the wounded chief and three or four stragglers were as safe as was the eagle looking down upon them from his aerial circuit.

Major Paul found Peschino lying on the pallet in his hut volubly cursing his two guards, who were baiting him as they would a wounded bear.

"Let him alone, you cowardly rascals!" he roared. They fell back respectfully to their places.

"Are you badly hurt?" he asked, kindly, bending over the pallet.

Peschino uttered an inarticulate growl, and tried to turn away, but the movement extorted from him a howl of pain.

"Oh, come, come! you're in for it now, and you may as well make the best of it. I'm not going to hurt you, man. I only want to make you as comfortable as I can. What did the surgeon say to you?"

"He say cut off. No; *die!*—no cut off.—Ough-o-o-o!"

The major tried to place the lacerated legs in a more comfortable position, but only brought down on his head a shower of mingled Greek and English curses, from which he was glad to beat a retreat.

"*You* bring them!" snarled the brigand, presently.

"I am proud to acknowledge the charge," replied the major, upon whom his ungracious reception was beginning to tell. "You showed me the way, and I improved the knowledge. *What have you been doing to Hector Vyr?*"

Peschino's lower jaw dropped, and his face, already pale, turned to the color of ashes.

"Well, well," said the major, startled by the effect of his question, "I will not trouble you any more now. I must go and help look after your subordinates."

Outside of the hut huddled an eager crowd striving to get a sight of the famous captive. The major drove them all away, threatening to report them to their commander and have them court-martialled if they did not keep their distance.

After an hour or two all further pursuit was abandoned, the spoils were collected, the huts fired, and with their prisoners the troops prepared to return.

On reaching the rescuing party, Hector Vyr had thrown his arms around Major Paul's neck, and then sunk once more into unconsciousness. Even he was at last exhausted.

Long before the victorious detachment came in sight of Mikro-Maina they were met by a throng of excited villagers in quest of news. A little apart from the crowd was a group consisting of the servants of the Vyr estate and two women, at sight of whom Major Paul rode forward on the full gallop. Dismounting, he embraced the younger of the two.

"Darling daughter, we've saved him!"

With a low, joyful cry she fainted in his arms.

"Where is he?" asked the mother, grasping his

arm and glaring at him with fierce, insane eyes; "where is he? Have they burned him to death with hot irons?"

"No, no!" he answered, eagerly. "He is safe! Can't you understand, my poor woman? he is *safe!* You will see him in a few minutes."

When they laid that majestic form before her, helpless but alive—the smooth forehead colorless as snow, save where the hair lay in thick curling masses stiff with blood, the eyelids closed like sculptured marble under the noble arches of the brow, and the deep, broad chest laboriously heaving and sinking under the blood-stained jacket—she uttered a loud, wailing note, and fell on her knees by his side.

The eyes slowly opened, their lustrous black contrasting vividly with the pallor of the face. "*Mánna!*—Madeline!" came in scarcely audible tones from the lips, and the eyes closed again.

He was tenderly conveyed to his home, where, for the present, we will leave him in the care of the surgeon of the detachment and others, whose loving, anxious ministrations were far more effectual than all the surgeon's skill.

The entry into Mikro-Maina was a triumph in miniature. Those of the villagers who had not already sated their curiosity and admiration, flocked to see the valiant warriors and their prisoners, as if the latter were some new and strange variety of wild animals, instead of men with whom some of them, at least, had talked as familiarly as with any others of their occasional visitors.

Among the crowd Major Paul recognized his nephew, whom he immediately asked to give an account of himself. Where had he been all this while?

Been? Where *should* he have been, but at the Kutchuk inn, where he had been told to wait until his uncle should call for him?

"What the devil are you *here* for, then?" retorted the major, disgusted at a mere civilian's obeying orders with such military precision.

"The campaign being over, I took it for granted that I was discharged from duty," replied the young man, with provoking coolness. "But I say, Uncle Warren, the next time you go klepht-hunting, I shall go with you, orders or no orders."

As one of Peschino's late prisoners, Griffin was of course allowed to speak with him.

"Well, captain," he said, with affected exultation, at the same time darting at him a significant glance, "circumstances have somewhat changed since I last had the pleasure of seeing you."

The brigand understood the glance, and replied with simulated scorn and defiance. Seizing his opportunity, Griffin said, in low, hurried tones, "Don't betray me. I'll do my best to help you out of this." Then aloud: "I suppose you are willing to reduce our ransom a little, under the circumstances, eh, captain?"

"Oh, come!" interposed Major Paul; "that's cowardly, Robert. Let the poor cuss alone, if you can't treat him civilly."

It was found impossible to save Peschino's legs; so, in spite of his opposition, they were both amputated, and he was left under good care until he should have sufficiently recovered to warrant his removal to Kalámas, where he was to undergo his trial.

XXII.

A NIGHT OF FEVER.

From the moment when Madeline found herself in the grasp of the brigand chief, and her lover lying stunned a few feet away, up to the time when he lay weak and only half conscious in his own house, her mind was so taken up with his terrible peril and her frantic desire to do something to extricate him, that she scarcely thought of the barrier that had arisen between him and herself. But, as by degrees her hope became firm that he was not going to die, but would sooner or later recover his full health and power, her proud resentment returned. So, when after a day and a night he awoke to a clear consciousness of the faces and forms around him, she simply congratulated him on his escape and assured recovery, and hurriedly left the room.

The sick man gazed at the closed door in consternation. "Why has she left me, *mannáka?*" he asked, querulously. "Call her back again."

"You must not excite yourself, Hector," replied his mother, in whose face the insanity of despair had given place to a calm, fixed happiness ; " you are very weak yet."

" Then call her back. I shall get dangerously excited if she doesn't come."

" Wait till you are a little stronger, *paidí mou*. The doctor says positively that you must be kept perfectly quiet."

" But I say I *cannot* be quiet unless she comes. Go and tell her that, *mannáka*."

" Oh," cried Madame Vyr, wringing her hands, " what shall I do? what will the doctor say? Will you promise not to talk ?"

" I *must* talk a little, but I promise to say no more than is absolutely necessary."

At that Madame Vyr left the room, still complaining to herself. In a few minutes Madeline re-entered. " You sent for me ?" she said, commanding her voice with a great effort, as she took the chair by his bedside.

" Sent for you ! Of course I sent for you. My life came back to me, but it seemed to leave me again when *you* left me. Madeline, did you think I had ceased to love you ?"

" You — said — you had done wrong, and were — going to — *do right*."

" What is right ?"

" Why—to unsay all you have said—isn't it ?"

" No, dearest one, that can never be. It is to say it all again, from the lowest depths of my heart—and much more. It is to tell you that I love you so well that I am willing to sacrifice all other things to your

19

best happiness. What have I to offer you in place of native land, friends, everything that has made your life a perpetual pleasure? Only a splendid solitude in exile, myself and my love. If these are enough for your joyous youth, how can I be assured that they will suffice for the long, long years of a lifetime? It is only a love longer than life, stronger than death, that will be satisfied with my offering. Such, my Madeline, is my love for you, and such must be your love for me if I accept the sacrifice that I have asked too soon."

"Oh," she exclaimed, rising and standing before him like a beautiful statue, "how little you know, Hector Vyr! with all your power, with all your wisdom, how little you know! You think that your lion heart has lower depths than a woman's — that your love is more enduring, more unselfish than hers! You think I prize a life of shallow pleasure above my very soul! and doubt whether the palace you offer me in the midst of this splendid solitude will compensate me for the loss of *society!* I say to you, I do not want your palace! Your love is enough for me, and will be till I die!"

As he heard these words, uttered with convincing fervency, a glow of rapture lighted up his pale features. "I believe you," he said. "Come to me, my own love!"

After a while she raised her face, dewy and radiant, from his bosom. "There will be no more experiments now?" she asked, with a lovely smile.

"Never again. And when I have shown you my perfect faith for a year, will you forgive me?"

"I have already forgiven you. You did not *know* —poor recluse, how *could* you?"

"No, I did not know. I was blind, and you did not open my eyes, Madeline; you only drew the veil more closely over them—so artfully did you feign indifference. *Now* shall I tell you why I insisted on carrying you over the log-bridge?"

"Ah, I called you a tyrant. And you *were*, Hector. I tried to defy you; but my will against yours was no more than my feeble arm would be against your strength. Yes, tell me—why did you insist on going, and carrying me with you—to your—*fate?*"

"It was indeed to my fate!" he said, his face answering the sudden paleness of her own. "Why could I not have looked into the future one short hour? I thought you as devoid of emotion as you seemed. I thought I must lose you forever—but, before the last tie was severed between us, I wanted to fold you again to my breast as I did on that first day —to feel your head again nestling upon my shoulder, your arms clinging around my neck. Was it not an artful stratagem?"

"I must leave you now," Madeline said, a little later, "or my visit will do you more harm than good."

"Yes; you may go now."

Late in the afternoon there were alarming symptoms of fever. Vyr's cheeks burned, and his eyes shone with a lustre that was almost frightful. His friends stood gazing in silent awe upon his countenance, transfigured by the fire of disease to a dazzling, unearthly beauty. The doctor summoned Major Paul to a private conference.

"We have a terrible night before us," he said. "If he becomes delirious no living man can hold him. Unless he is restrained by a power stronger than his own, he will tear himself and everything about him to pieces."

"What can be done?" asked the major.

"The first thing is to get rid of the women."

"I am afraid that is out of the question—at least so far as my daughter is concerned. She is under a great obligation to him, like the rest of us, and nothing could persuade her to desert her post."

"Well, she seems to be a strong, sensible young woman, and if she can stand it, she may be of some help. Sometimes these women are cooler than we are."

"They *generally* are, in dealing with the sick, are they not?"

"I don't know how it would be in such a case as this promises to be—it is going to take something more than coolness, you will find."

"I suppose we shall have to—strap him down."

"If we can find straps *strong* enough," replied the doctor.

"Poor Madeline!" thought the major.

As darkness approached, the patient rapidly grew worse. His chest labored painfully, and his pulses came like jets of hot quicksilver.

"I am afraid I am going mad," he said to the doctor. "A moment ago I thought you were Peschino, and I was on the point of seizing you by the throat. If this goes on, you will have to leave me by myself, or I shall do mischief."

"You certainly will do mischief if we *do*," answered the doctor.

"You must chain me down, so I can't. Give me some more water—I am on fire!"

During the ever-shortening intervals of reason which followed, Vyr tried to quiet his poor frenzied mother, and to soften the .deeper grief and terror which he saw in Madeline's calm white face; while, like Karl the Martyr, he helped to devise means of controlling the fury of the coming delirium.

———

He struggles with all his might, but he cannot move a muscle; for a demon, with eyes like molten metal and huge overshadowing wings, holds him in a horrid embrace.

"Will you betray him?" says the demon in his ear. It is the voice of Peschino.

"No."

"Then fall!"

He is in motion, slow at first, then faster, faster, down, down, swifter and still more swift, until, like a material body shattered by its own motion, the ties of conscious existence snap asunder.

Again he is in motion, inconceivably swift, up like a ray of light darting through the darkness of space. He looks upward. He is suspended, like a pendulum, by a thread of fire coming from a point far away in the immeasurable void. It is the upward swing of the pendulum. There seem to be hours of diminishing speed, until he stops and is again in the demon's embrace.

"Will you betray him?"

"No."

"Then fall!"

Once more the accelerating motion of descent ends in unconsciousness, to be followed by another awakening in the vast upward cycloid.

The slender thread of fire parts, and he falls down through the illimitable darkness into an oblivion from which it seems there can be no awakening.

But he awakes. He is lying chained upon a bed of solid rock, that stretches in all directions around him like a waveless ocean. Far, far above is a sky of leaden cloud of one unvarying hue. As he gazes, the distance above him shortens. The leaden sky is sinking. Erelong it will envelop him in its chilling folds. It comes nearer. Its surface takes on a more substantial appearance. It is not cloud—it is *solid granite!* In the distance, sky of rock and sea of rock meet in a soft blue horizon. Still the solid heavens sink. It will be hours, perhaps days, but they will surely reach him at last, and crush him to powder. And he cannot move a link of the iron chains that bind him.

Now the mistiness is all gone. He can see the little black and white specks and the glittering grains of mica. He makes a mighty effort, and frees his right arm. He reaches it up, and feels the rough, hard, cold surface.

"Will you betray him?" says the voice of Peschino.

"No."

"Then die!"

Again he awakes. The rocky incubus has arisen, and now smiles in a vast dome of blue crystal, with the bright sun in its midst. The granite plain has heaved into grassy hills and snow-capped mountains. In a valley carpeted with flowery verdure are sporting troops of maidens, each of surpassing beauty. The melody of their laughter falls upon his ear like silvery chimes. Among them, most beautiful of all, walks their queen. Her form and features are those of Madeline Paul.

He tries to throw his arms towards her and to call her name; but he is bound immovably, and his voice is smothered by a rude hand.

"Will you betray him?"

"No."

"Then die!"

White-hot irons are laid upon his flesh. The intolerable anguish rouses his giant strength to a supreme effort. He bursts his bonds, leaps towards his love, clasps her in his arms, and sinks with her into oblivion!

He is lying upon a bed of softest down. A cool breeze plays upon his brow. The sunlight filters through his closed eyelids. His chest rises and falls with slow, gentle motion. A sense of delicious languor weighs down his limbs. A voice that tingles to his fingers' ends utters a cry of delight. His heavy eyelids open. He sees Madeline Paul standing over him with a cup and a teaspoon in her hands.

XXIII.

ON THE VERANDA.

It was a fierce but short-lived invasion of disease. Not long could the enemy maintain his foothold within a citadel so strongly built and hitherto unshaken by his assaults. The forces of life rallied at every point. Day by day the work of reinstatement and reparation went on. In no other way, perhaps, could the exceptional vitality of Hector Vyr have asserted itself so strikingly as in his rapid rebound from a fall which must inevitably have destroyed the majority of men. The terrible blows he had received upon his head would alone, in ordinary cases, have entailed weeks, perhaps months of prostration, if not instant death. That his skull was not fractured, was due, under Providence, to the unequalled texture and elasticity of that helmet of nature; that his cords and sinews were not broken or permanently injured, and his nervous system shattered, in the excruciating ordeal which followed, was because they were of Nature's best handiwork, compacted to endure the severest tests that mortality can sustain.

But he was not a patient convalescent. Hours of torture he could have borne without a groan, had he so chosen; but day after day of enforced idleness, mental and physical, was an experience so foreign to his nature and life-long habit, that it is by no means certain he could have borne it without murmuring and chafing, even if he had tried, which he certainly did not do. Every member of the household, mistress, guests, and servants alike, had to bear his vigorous fault-finding and restless lamentations. Once Madeline actually lost her temper, and boldly asked if he were really the heroic Hector Vyr, or some commonplace invalid who had assumed his shape. At that, for the first time since his capture by the brigands, he burst into a fit of laughter.

"Impertinent!" he exclaimed. "If the klephts had not robbed me of my nails, I should scratch your eyes out with them! Make up your mind to endure my unruly tongue till I get well. It amuses me to scold you, and helps me to pass the endless days. Haven't I already borne enough, without being expected to play the martyr now? It is part of *your* share of the pain to tolerate my ill-humor, and I promise you I shall not spare you any more than the rest. But you may scold, too," he added, with another laugh; "if you can make me really angry, all the better—anything to spur on the leaden-footed hours."

"Forgive me," said Madeline, laughing, though the quick, penitent tears started to her eyes. "You may scold all you like, if it relieves you. It is little enough for our share of the pain —though, if you think it is *all* we have borne for you, you are most egregiously mistaken, sir!"

"I said it was a *part* of your share, mademoiselle."

"Well, we ought not to complain, but rather to rejoice," she rejoined, "for a bad temper is said to be one of the surest signs of returning health. But I am afraid my impatient giant would make but an indifferent hero in a dungeon."

"I am not a hero, Madeline; I am a philosopher. Many of the heroic things men are said to do are the sheerest folly. My standard is what is on the whole the greatest good and the least evil. If I were in a dungeon—which God forbid!—I should do my best to alleviate the tedium of my imprisonment, whatever my keepers might think of me. No doubt Peschino and his minions thought me anything but a hero when they were exercising their villanous ingenuity upon me. But what were their opinions to me?—my aim was so to occupy my mind with action as to leave the least possible scope for passive endurance, and I succeeded. A man is much less conscious of agony when he is struggling and yelling with all his might, not to speak of the quicker approach of exhaustion and unconsciousness. Ah!"

with tender regret and solicitude, "I should not have spoken of this."

For she had grown deathly pale, and was trembling from head to foot.

"Yes," she replied, with firm lips. "Go on. I know something of it, and I ought to know all. I should be but a poor wife for you if I had not the courage to hear what you had the fortitude to bear."

"But, my dearest, there is no need of your hearing it. It would be so much gratuitous suffering, which would be altogether contrary to my theory. The sympathy of my best beloved is sweet; but I have all I wish and more. If her sympathy is sweet her pain is not. I referred to that ordeal only to convince you that I made it less intolerable than you might have imagined. Pain can be endured, Madeline. We cannot be fully conscious of more than one great throe at a time. Happily for me, the klephts did not understand that. It would have required at least three distinct persons to realize what they did to me at one and the same instant. It does not seem to me, as I look back upon it, that I suffered so terribly, after all. A part of the time I was protected by a merciful numbness in every nerve. I can scarcely decide which I remember the most distinctly—the pain, my desperate struggles, or my ear-splitting shrieks and yells."

He accomplished his beneficent object. She listened with rapt attention, and when he had finished, heaved a long, deep sigh of relief.

After that he scolded less, and chatted more.

One morning he sat in an easy-chair on the veranda, breathing in great draughts of crisp air, while his eyes roved over the deep green of the valleys and the delicate pearl of the distant mountain-tops. A luxurious gown lined with white fur enveloped his large person, and a light fez concealed the bandage which he still wore upon his head. A bright color in his cheeks enriched their softened olive and the bronze of his hair. Madeline sat near him, her graceful figure clad in a morning-robe of soft orange-colored stuff lined with white and relieved at the throat by a cluster of blue and white anemones, which, added to the effect of the morning air and her restored happiness, rendered her eyes and complexion more beautiful than ever. She had been reading to him from a volume of English poetry, of which, in presence of the sublimer poetry of nature, they had both wearied. After a long silence she abruptly exclaimed,

"How wonderfully fast you are gaining, Hector! I can almost see the life-blood pouring into your body as I look at you."

"Like wine into a bottle," he answered, laughing.

"Don't you enjoy the process? Health and power will be all the more delightful to you now that you know what it is to be without them."

"It is one of the most delicious sensations I have ever felt," he replied, dreamily letting his eyes rest on the blue water in the distance. "I am becoming convinced that it is almost worth while to endure evil for the sake of the exquisite pleasure of relief, and the greater enjoyment of positive good that follows. The blacker the shadows, the brighter the lights. How the rocky grandeur of those mountains would be tamed if the dark mantles should be stripped from their sides! The Creator of beauty does as well when he dips his brush into the dyes of midnight as when his pencils are the beams of the morning sun."

"We shall some day understand the mystery of evil more clearly still, I suppose," returned Madeline, thoughtfully.

"To my mind evil is scarcely a mystery. It is like the shapeless rocks in those mountains, over which men must toil and sweat if they would change them into forms of beauty and usefulness."

"But there is so much that never can be moulded into good," protested Madeline.

"What is good? It is not only the squared and polished block of marble that is good and beautiful. All mankind could not carve these rugged crags and ledges into smoothness and regularity. But they are not evil: there is a beauty and a good, *kalòn k'agathòn*, in their very shapelessness, which, in its place, surpasses that of the most magnificent palaces of human workmanship."

"Oh," said Madeline, "we can enjoy mere picturesqueness and roughness, but we can take no pleasure in suffering, however picturesque. Or, if we *do* feel a sort of horrible fascination in contemplating it, we may be sure the sufferer feels nothing but pain. Prometheus's vulture was not a good to

himself, whatever it might be to poets and paint-
ers."

"On the contrary," said Vyr, smiling with pleasure at her zest and spirit, "it was the very incarna-
tion of good to him. It devoured nothing in him
but what was corrupt and vile. It was to him what
the furnace seven times heated is to gold. Your allusion, Madeline, gives us a key to a part, at least, of
the 'mystery.' Prometheus is man; the vulture is
what we call evil."

"And what shall we call that which the vulture
devours?"

"Ah, *that* is the only real evil. And the only
remedy for it is the so-called evil, pain."

"It is that real evil that puzzles me," persisted
Madeline. "Why need it have existed in the first
place, to require so fearful a remedy?"

"Who is man, that he should fathom the Infinite?"
returned Vyr, reverently. "If the beginning had
been perfection, there could have been no change but
to imperfection. Is it not better that imperfection
should be eternally employed in struggling towards
perfection?"

"No," answered Madeline, with decision. "There
was no necessity for change. Perfection might have
been eternal."

"Brahma's endless sleep," said Vyr. And though
the world-old problem was as far as ever from solution in her mind, Madeline made no reply.

Both remained for a while in thoughtful silence.
At length she said, with a sort of tender awe, "When

you were speaking as you did, of pain and its beneficence, it almost seemed to me as if you were Prometheus himself—especially when I thought of— Can you accept *that* as good?"

"Yes, Madeline—now that it is over, I can. It has enlarged my vision. It was a revelation to me, which will make the remainder of my existence deeper, broader, higher." Then, in a lower tone, "When I am a little stronger I shall visit Peschino. He is said to be growing worse every day."

"Can you trust yourself to look upon the wretch's face? How shall you be able to restrain your hands from tearing him limb from limb?"

"Not by the aid of such words as those from your lips!" he replied, knitting his brows.

She shut her lips tightly together, as if to prevent a retraction of her question. He went on more calmly:

"I should be restrained by the reflection that the wreaking of my vengeance would do no good, but very great harm. Even if he lives and escapes with a light punishment, or is acquitted altogether, which is not an impossibility—for he has wielded a great political power—he can do no more mischief. As a klepht chieftain he is forever disabled. All that is left him now is to learn the use of artificial limbs and try to live an honest life."

"And have you no desire for *retribution?*" asked Madeline, looking very much as if she would not refuse to be herself the minister of vengeance.

"*Desire!* Every nerve in my body thrills at the

thought of clutching his throat in my fingers—of feeling them cut through flesh, cords, and bones together! Ah, the *rapture* of that supreme moment!"

The paroxysm was appalling while it lasted. It continued but a few seconds, however. Then the lurid fire went out in his eyes, which now regarded her in mild, sorrowful reproach. " You see what an afrit you can evoke from the bottle into which you ' can see the life-blood pouring,'" he said.

" You surpass my ideal of nobleness and goodness, Hector. When I think of what you endured at Peschino's hands my whole soul rebels at the thought of impunity for him. I know it is terribly wicked, but I can't help wishing him to feel in his own vile body some of the agony he made you suffer. If the opportunity should come, I am afraid I should try to evoke the afrit where he could actually exert his power."

" But he would not, Madeline—*he would not*," answered Vyr, again struggling with his passion. " One nod from Reason, and he would shrink to a puff of smoke and return to his prison in the bottle."

" And I suppose you would even—forgive—"

" No, not *yet*. I haven't risen so high as that. I simply recognize the burning thirst for revenge I felt just now to be a bestial appetite which must be fought against and subdued, if I would realize my highest aspirations. It belongs to a very low stage in development, like the poison fangs of the serpent. It is only in the breast of the savage, wild or ' civilized,' that it is fully developed. He alone can experience more than a momentary joy in its gratification, or escape the remorse and self-scorn which invariably follows in higher natures. No one would suffer more keenly than you, my love, if what you say is your present desire should be carried into execution. I am—going to try—perhaps I may learn to—forgive Peschino."

Madeline rose from her chair, knelt beside him, and leaning her arms on his lap, gazed up into his face in mute adoration. One of his maimed hands stole around her neck.

"You must not give me more credit than is my due," he said with a smile. "I have not forgiven him yet. There is no very great merit in seeking my own best good, is there? If I prefer a lasting, solid happiness to the savage satisfaction of a moment, or to the bitter luxury of an enduring hatred, what greater virtue can I lay claim to than the perfection of selfish wisdom?"

"Oh," she eagerly protested, "you have no right to defame your own great, noble heart. It is blasphemy. It is *not* selfish wisdom; it is Christlike goodness! What more could an angel from heaven do? Your own happiness has nothing to do with it, Hector Vyr—I almost believe you would do the same if you knew it would result in your own misery instead of your happiness!"

"No," he replied, shaking his head. "Not even an angel from heaven would do that. But think of a Being that would! Angels and men may well worship Him!

20

XXIV.

HECTOR VYR VISITS PESCHINO.

PAIN is pain, whoever or whatever endures it.
That the sufferer deserves it does not make it the
more, but rather the less tolerable. In a world
where there is already so much misery, what heart,
human or divine, can rejoice in that which tends to
increase the sum? When we know of some desperate criminal expiating his life-long cruelties, is the
sense of keen satisfaction we feel of the heavens
heavenly? We may satisfy ourselves that it is our
natural love of justice which the God of Justice himself has implanted in us, and which he shares with
us. But justice is only another name for right, and
right is never malevolence. If the pain of others is
to result in greater good to them or to the world, it
is Godlike to rejoice in the good and to accept the
pain for its sake; but it is Satanic to rejoice in the
pain. When we feel our hearts bound with exultation at the recital of richly deserved suffering, is it
on account of the future good or on account of the
present evil? Do our pulses quicken with joy at the
thought of the possible reformation of a criminal or
of benefit to society? If so, we may well rejoice—
we have gone a long way in our journey to the celestial city.

The poetry of justice was but feebly exemplified in the fate of the *Kapitán* Peschino, at least so far as human vision extends. To say nothing of his long years of outlawry, his last act of fiendish cruelty should have been expiated by at least the utmost pain and ignominy the law could inflict, or by a lingering, painful death at the severer hand of Nature. On the contrary, however, whatever his mental experiences may have been, his physical suffering was comparatively slight. The anæsthetic administered to him at the time of the amputation of his limbs, and the unskilful performance of that operation, left him in a state of exhaustion from which he never rallied. Day after day he lay in a semi-comatose condition. Only at long intervals did he awake to full consciousness, and only for a short time at each. It was during one of these intervals that Hector Vyr paid him his first visit. Then, indeed, for a few fearful moments he tasted the retribution he so abundantly merited.

As his languid eyes fell upon the noble countenance he had seen so frightfully distorted, but now so placid, and upon the kingly form he had caused to writhe in agony, but now firm, erect, with every appearance of health and power restored, he recoiled with a look of indescribable horror, and gave utterance to a shriek so wild, so unearthly, that his visitor instinctively retreated from the room. Then a deep but gentle voice came through the nearly closed door:

"May I come in, Peschino?"

"No! no! *Go away!* The very sight of you will destroy me!"

But it was not long before Hector Vyr sat beside his bed, listening to sobs which shook the narrow cot and drew tears from his own pitying eyes.

"It is not as you think, my poor friend. I have not come to torment you."

"You cannot hurt my body," came the answer, brokenly, convulsively—"it is nearly gone already—but you can torment my soul."

"Alas! I have come to do your soul good."

"Good! After what I did to *you!* No, no, no! it is not possible! It was four hours I kept you there—*four hours!* You were very near death when Heaven interposed and saved you."

"Heaven will save you too, Peschino."

"*Save me!*" Words cannot describe the amazement with which these two words were uttered, nor the laugh of wild scorn which followed.

"Yes. Do you think that Infinite Goodness is less forgiving than Hector Vyr?"

"Do *you*—forgive—*me?*"

"With all my heart and soul!" And Vyr's hands, which still showed the marks of the awful cruelty they had suffered, grasped the cold, trembling hands of Peschino.

For a while the wretch did not speak, but lay panting. Then he tore his hands away and with them covered his face. "It cannot be. I cannot receive so much from you. It is not just."

"If I can give, cannot you receive?"

"You—Hector Vyr—really—forgive—Peschino?"

"As I hope that Heaven will forgive me!"

"*O Kyrie eléison! O Christe eléison!*"

During the few days of life that remained to Peschino, he was visited not only by Vyr, but by the others whom he had wronged, and who, influenced both by Vyr's example and by the piteous spectacle of the fallen brigand's weakness and penitence, left him at last with something very like sorrow, if not sorrow itself.

Among his visitors was Tsáras, who besought him to do him a last act of justice.

"Ah," said the dying klepht, "you played your part well; and I am glad you succeeded. There would have been one victim the less. I really believed that you led those people into my snare for a share of the booty. Such things have been done for me. Your cunning did them no harm, but might have done them much good. Yes, Tsáras, I release you from your oath, and I will moreover sign a writing declaring that you were true and faithful to your friends. They will believe even Peschino's dying testimony."

Robert Griffin was the only one of our acquaintances to whom the brigand's death brought unmingled joy. To him the sound of the falling clods was like the sound of music, for they told of lips forever mute. When he learned that the other prisoners had met their fate at the guillotine, and was satisfied that his dark secret had not been betrayed, his breath

came freely again, and he gradually resumed his old
self-assurance. The constant fear and remorse he
had suffered had so engrossed his mind that, for the
time being, he had almost forgotten his passion for
Madeline, and as he had now become convinced of
its utter hopelessness, he had the wisdom to accept
his lot with resignation. It was not many days,
therefore, before he seized opportunities to join in
the counsels of the family, and he even went so far
as to address himself to Vyr with as little apparent
reserve or embarrassment as if he did not deserve
the execrations of the one and the direst vengeance
of the other. In the estimation of his uncle Warren
and of his aunt Eliza he of course stood far higher
than ever before. Madeline's want of enthusiastic
gratitude for the gallant service he was supposed to
have rendered her was a source of profound astonishment and grief to them. She received their reproaches with patience and humility, and promised
to try to feel as she ought.

"Rebellions in Pandemonium!" exclaimed the
major, "what ails the girl? You never failed to
feel as you ought *before*. Are your gratitude and
appreciation so entirely appropriated that you have
none left for this poor, brave boy? Can't you be
satisfied with throwing him over, without cheating
him out of *everything*—even the decent recognition
you would give a beggar who should do for you one-
tenth of what Robert has done?"

But she did not speak of the dark, torturing suspicion that was in her heart; and, although some

trace of her former cousinly manner towards Robert occasionally appeared, they were never again for an instant the congenial pair they had been.

With the now fully recovered victim of his treachery Griffin's relation was most peculiar. A not uncommon effect of wrong-doing is an increasing aversion to the one injured. In this instance the effect was the reverse. The meanest and most cowardly villain is sometimes capable of feeling a sincere admiration for his opposite in character. One of the oldest of sayings is that unlike natures attract one another like the opposite poles of the magnet. When this attraction exists between the good and the evil, the noble and the ignoble, it shows itself on the one side in a longing to reform and elevate the other, and on the other side in a desire, if not to be purified and ennobled, at least to be permitted to contemplate and wonder at that which is as sublime as it is unattainable. A singular attraction certainly grew up between these two, like that between the sun and some frozen, barren planet which it tries to warm into life.

Griffin's animosity to Hector Vyr had been due to a stinging sense of his own immeasurable inferiority as well as to the ill-balanced rivalry between them for the love of Madeline Paul. It was far more than satisfied with the unspeakably atrocious reprisal he had taken, and was now followed by the deepest repentance and admiration, from which every particle of envy was purged. To admiration was soon added genuine friendship, and to friendship an affec-

tion almost like that of a child for its father. In
every way, save that of confession, he did all in his
power to atone for the past. This was, of course,
very, very little; still, if never-ceasing remorse is to
be accounted, it was something.

Vyr appeared to enjoy his friendship and, in a
certain way, to reciprocate it. Although he would
never invite him into his house, he did him many
other favors: he talked with him a great deal, and
frequently took long walks with him; but even in
speech there was a barrier which he never suffered
him to pass: just as he was willing and anxious to
give him free *entrée* to his garden and his outlying
estates, but closed against him every door of his house,
so he admitted him to every subject of conversation
except himself (as to Madeline, Griffin did not dream
of venturing the most distant allusion to her). Whenever Griffin approached the subject of their growing
intimacy or his own sentiments towards him, Vyr
became coldly silent, or immediately diverted his
thoughts to something else. It was evident that,
however much they might have to say to each other,
it was to be only upon things entirely disconnected
with the personality of either.

XXV.

HOW THIS STORY CAME TO BE WRITTEN.

IN spite of Vyr's well-known aversion to every sort and degree of public recognition, a few days after Peschino's death a deputation arrived at Athens, with a request that M. Hector Vyr should present himself at Court, and receive official acknowledgment of the signal services he had lately, and on several former occasions, rendered in rescuing his Majesty's subjects and those of foreign powers from the klephts.

The deputation was courteously received; but the request was positively declined with due gratitude for the honors intended. The only return M. Vyr desired was such as he had formerly received, with permission to continue in the obscurity in which his life had thus far been passed. To this end he humbly prayed that, so far as his Majesty's Government could carry out his wish, nothing should be said or done, either in public or private, which would in any way tend to bring him into further notoriety. Most especially he desired that nothing should be permitted to appear in the public prints bearing directly or indirectly upon him, his acts, or his affairs. If his petition should be granted, he should try to discharge in the future, as he had done in the past, his duties as a private citizen, as a private soldier of his Majesty's army with peculiar privileges and immunities, and as a friend of law, order, and humanity. More than this he trusted would not be required of him.

With this answer the agents of his Majesty's Government were forced to be content.

Accompanying the deputation was Mr. Caleb Goldapple, Secretary of the American Legation, who had special business to transact with his countryman, the guest of M. Hector Vyr. This person, having been invited to Major Paul's private drawing-room, effusively congratulated him on his well-nigh miraculous escape from the brigands, commented on the remarkable qualities of his deliverer and host, and then presented a letter and two cable despatches, all from Josiah Jobling, of the firm of Jobling, Hotchkiss & Paul, Boston, U. S.

Cable Despatch No. 1 was dated September 23d, and stated substantially that all efforts to raise the required ransom had failed, and furthermore that the Western parties had backed out.

"Don't trouble yourselves, you peddling, miserly skinflints!" ejaculated the major, dashing the paper on the floor. "Thank fortune, I had somebody to help me that was worth a thousand hundred million such muck-worms as Jobling and Hotchkiss! But who in the devil are the Western parties?"

Cable Despatch No. 2 was dated September 24th, 10 o'clock A.M., and announced, in substance, that the firm had themselves decided to advance the required sum.

The major reckoned: "September 24th, 10 o'clock
A.M. The despatch announcing my rescue was sent
from Sparta at 2 o'clock P.M. on September 24th. Al-
lowing for all delays, it must have reached Jobling at
9 o'clock A.M. at the very latest—*a full hour before
he sent this!* Ah-ha! ah-ha-a-a! They're a magnanimous pair, are Josiah P. Jobling and Marshall W.
Hotchkiss! a noble, high-souled couple of saints!
an angelic brace of players on the golden harp!
They've decided to advance the whole fifty thousand
dollars, have they? I suppose the Western parties
have backed in! Unprecedented generosity! unparalleled munificence! Was there ever such an exhibition of heroic self-sacrifice since the days of Damon
and Pythias! They ought to have fifty thousand
leather medals struck off and hung round their necks!
Confound the sneaking, hypocritical, Jesuitical humbugs! Going to advance the whole fifty thousand
dollars, are they?—fifty thousand fiddle-sticks! fifty
thousand pop-guns, pepper-corns, rotten eggs, dead
cats, rattlesnakes! Oh, Mr. Goldapple, you just wait
till I get to Boston—won't I reel it off to 'em! won't
I give them a few quotations from Baxter's 'Saints'
Rest!' won't I make their heads hum, buzz, fizz,
sing, snap, sizzle!"

Mr. Goldapple thought it not at all improbable
that he would.

Having thus expended his scorn at, and exultation
over, Messrs. Jobling and Hotchkiss, safe and undeaf-
ened six thousand miles away, the major opened the
letter with a smile of amiable curiosity to see what

further display of phenomenal liberality it might present.

"Boston, August 6, 18—.

"My Dear Paul,—Times are decidedly looking up with us." (Oh, they are, are they?) "The Moseby sales netted us a cool fifteen thousand—I cabled you only twelve, but there was a supplementary order." (By George, that's good news!) "What do you say to _that_, old boy?" (I say it only proves how cussed mean you are.) "Whitlow & Co. have failed, however" (What's this?), "which offsets nearly a third of the Moseby profit." (All an infernal swindle, I'll bet my head!) "The rascally beats paid only twenty-two per cent. Whitlow's wife outshone everybody with her new diamonds at the Toastman jamboree only a week before the failure."

(Here the major stopped reading and effervesced, until the Whitlow failure and the Toastman jamboree were no more to him than a trifling mercantile transaction and an interesting item of society news.)

"But we shall make that all up," the letter went on, "and ten times as much on top of it" (All right; then you will be ready to do something for _me_) "within the next three months." (Ah!) "We have got some responsible Western parties" (Yes, I see) "in tow, who will probably want fifty thousand dollars' worth at the very least." (That's just like Jobling!) "Will let you know by cable the instant the contract is signed.

"Well, old fellow, I hope you are enjoying yourselves among the marble temples and broken-armed 'stone gals.'" (Oh yes! *we've* enjoyed ourselves!) "Don't let your charming daughter" (Confound his impudence!) "fall in love with any of those beggarly Greeks, with their slim waists, black eyes, and straight noses." (Don't *you* fret, Jobling.) "If she does, give them some grape and canister from that twenty-four inch columbiad you call your mouth." (Ha, ha! Jobling isn't such a bad fellow after all, sometimes.) "Griffin will look out for those chaps, however." (Poor Bob!) "By-the-bye, do you suppose he could be persuaded to part with some of his Eastern Pacific if we should get into a particularly tight place? Sound him on that.

"One thing more: don't think of coming home for another solid year. Anybody that has worked as hard as you have for the last twenty-five years" (Oh, slop!), "including your three years of noble self-sacrifice in the war" (What disgusting drivel!), "ought to have a rest of three years at the very least." (Well, I think I *ought*.) "We should all like to see you, of course" (Guess not, if he knew what I've got to say!); "but business is all right, and—well, you know all about that, Paul." (H'm, h'm!) "I have sent you papers by every steamer; hope you have received them all right. Remember us both to Miss Wellington and Miss Madeline. I suppose she will be Mrs. Griffin when we see her next." (Not much, she won't!) "Let us hear from you as often as you can about your travels—don't waste any time writing business. Faithfully yours,
"JOSIAH P. JOBLING."

"Hang me if I believe I shall *ever* go back again!" said Major Paul, throwing the letter down to keep company with the cablegrams on the floor. "They don't want me, and I swear I don't want to see any of their faces again as long as I live! They would have let me and all my family be murdered in cold blood rather than part with their filthy dollars! If there's ever another war, Uncle Sam may find his majors where he can!"

"Don't be ungrateful to Uncle Sam," said the secretary, who had been busy arranging a file of documents. "If the brigands had dared to harm you, there would have been terrible reprisals taken. The world knows well that free and innocent American citizens are not to be slaughtered with impunity."

"Reprisals!" echoed the major, growing suddenly apoplectic from his inability to express himself as the occasion demanded; "that would be *eminently* satisfactory! A man would be unreasonable indeed that should complain of that!"

"But that isn't all," rejoined Mr. Goldapple, looking a little foolish: "you probably will never know the full extent of the efforts which were made in your behalf. The matter was thoroughly canvassed in the House; the lobbies were full of it. But, you see, there were peculiar difficulties—the spectacle of a nation of nearly sixty millions of people submitting to be robbed by a corporal's guard of Greek bandits would have been a little—well, humiliating, to say the least. Still, for all that, it was out of the question to let you die, without doing everything that was possible to save you. If worst had came to worst, there is not the slightest doubt that the ransom would have been raised, either by private subscription or by public appropriation."

"Worst had pretty nearly come to worst," suggested the major.

"Oh no; there was plenty of time. There was talk of sending a military force to rescue you; but that, you know, was the business of the Greek Government. They were importuned enough on that subject, I assure you—witness this pile of letters and documents I've brought for you to examine. You know what the result was: that detachment sent to your relief was the response to your country's demand, Major Paul. To be sure, the movement was not quite as prompt as it might have been; but still it would have been in time, even if it had not been so happily anticipated. I don't think you have anything to complain of, sir," concluded the secretary, with dignity.

"Well, *one* thing is sure, at any rate," said the major, "we are all right *now*."

"And you would have been, in any event."

"I'm not sure of that. I suppose those villains would have cut all our throats before they would have given us up."

"If they had chosen to do that, no power on earth could have prevented them."

"No; you're right, Mr. Goldapple, and for that very reason a ransom would have been better for us than an attempt at rescue. Still, I fully appreciate the objections, and I will not be ungrateful. I presume everything was done for us that could be reasonably expected. I shall always be a true, loyal American wherever I live; but I think it very possible I shall decide not to return to Boston, considering all the circumstances. Athens is not such a bad place for a residence; and now that my daughter—What would *you* think of settling down for life in Athens, Mr. Goldapple?"

"Oh, *I?* Well, my circumstances are very different from yours, you know. I've seen pretty nearly all Europe, and the United States is good enough for *me.*"

"The more I think of it," the major went on, ignoring the secretary's reply to his question, "the more the idea pleases me. Since my wife's death, five years ago, there's nobody in particular that I care for at home. I don't suppose my daughter will ever return—that is, *to stay.* She's more to me, sir, than all the rest of the world put together. I've got capital enough in that firm to keep me going, if J. and H. give me fair play, and I guess there'll be no trouble about *that.* You've lived in Athens a good while, Mr. Goldapple; don't you think there's some pretty fair people there, on the whole?"

"Oh yes, Major Paul, of course there are. Society is rather heterogeneous, however, in Athens. It may be divided pretty distinctly into three classes. In the first place, there are the *Autóchthones,* or true Athenians. You can't get in among *them,* for they despise everything that is foreign; they call all for-

eigners *Heteróchthones*, just as the old Hellenes used
to call everybody else Barbarians.   They swindle and
cheat—"

"Who—the Heterogones?"

"No; the *Autóchthones*.   They cheat and swindle
the poor *Heteróchthones* without the least compunc-
tion—that is, *some* of them do; there are honorable
exceptions, of course—most of the magistrates, pro-
fessors, and merchants, for instance, will compare fa-
vorably with those of any other civilized country."

"Well," said the major, "we have the Automatons
and the Heteroclites—who are the third class?"

"The *Phanáriotes*, or Byzantine Greeks.   They
are generally wealthy and cultivated, have travelled
a good deal and got their minds expanded, you know.
The others are jealous of them—"

"The Heterodoxies?"

"No; the *Autóchthones*—so the *Phanáriotes* are
more apt to be friendly with foreigners—"

"Or Heteropods?"

"*Heteróchthones*.   Their ladies are handsome, accomplished, and are everlastingly chatting—"

"The Pharaohs'?"

"The *Phanáriotes*'.   You will enjoy their *salons*,
Major Paul.   Yes—decidedly your place is among
the *Phanáriotes*."

"All right," answered the major.   "Henceforth I
am a *Phanáriote*."

"No, you cannot be that, for you are not a Greek
by descent; but as a respectable, well-to-do *Heteróch-
thon* you can fraternize with the *Phanáriotes*.   You

21

will not forget, however, that you are an American,
I hope."

"Never! I am an American now and forever,
one and inseparable. Halloo! who is this?"

Happening to glance through the window, Major
Paul had seen a consequential-looking individual in
European dress swaggering up the path, accompanied
by one of the bridge guards.

"Good heavens!" exclaimed Mr. Goldapple, feeling the blood rush into his cheeks, "has that fellow
got in? Well, if that isn't the most monumental audacity I ever saw, even in Yankee-land! He's the
correspondent of the *New York Gimlet*. He tried
to wedge himself in with my party, but we gave him
what he would call the 'Grand Bounce.' He wanted to *interview* your eccentric champion. Fancy
it!"

Major Paul was so delighted that he could not
contain himself. "Let him try it!" he cried, danc-
ing round the room, "let him try it! If he doesn't
get shot up so high that he'll never come down again
I'll eat a year's file of his *Gimlets!*"

The stranger ascended the steps with professional
self-possession, and seated himself on the veranda as
if it belonged to a New York politician's villa on the
Hudson. As soon as the royal deputation had been
dismissed he was ushered into Vyr's "office."

Unabashed by the cool stare of inquiry with which
he was received, he began, with his professional bow,

"M. Hector Vyr, I presume."

"Yes."

"Allow me to introduce myself: J. P. Thumb, of New York."

"What is your business with me?"

"I have been told, sir, that you are a man who hates all kinds of beating round the bush; that there is no use in boring you with ceremonious preliminaries, nor attempting with you any of the delicate finesse which gentlemen of my profession feel obliged to resort to in approaching other distinguished characters. I have been told, in short, that you would see through everything of that sort in a twinkling, and would be simply disgusted with it, if not mortally offended. As that is precisely my own character, I will approach you in a manly, straightforward way, such as I think must appeal to your generous sympathies, and tell you at once, in as few words as possible, my object in calling upon you."

"Go on," said Vyr, with an ominous glance towards the door, then at the window.

"In spite of your reputed efforts to hide your dazzling light under a bushel, sir, your fame has reached even as far as America. However much you may deplore this"—with an ingratiating smile—"it is past remedy now. Your recent act of unparalleled heroism in rescuing my unfortunate compatriot and his family from the brigands has—"

"*Your business!*" thundered Vyr. His voice shook the room. The correspondent felt a peculiar sense of suffocation, as if a cannon had been discharged behind his back.

"I—I beg your pardon—sir. I was not aware that—that—"

"YOUR BUSINESS!"

"Cer — certainly — certainly," stammered Mr. Thumb, breathlessly, sidling towards the door. "I am the representative of the *New York Gimlet*, sir. I—I—the people have learned something of you already—and they wish to know—they have a *right* to know more of the wonderful man who—"

Vyr took one long stride, seized the luckless victim of his own rashness by the collar with one mighty hand, opened the window with the other, and gently set him outside, as if he had been a bag of straw. "Státhas," he said to the guard, "take this person away; and henceforth allow no one to cross the bridge until I have first been informed who he is and what he wishes."

Of course Major Paul and the secretary had been on the lookout, and the air of general collapse with which the discomfited interviewer picked his way down the slope, hard pressed by the guard, afforded them much amusement.

"He will make his report all the same," remarked the major, when they had laughed their fill.

"Of course he will. I fancy I can already see the startling head-lines and double-leaded columns in the *Gimlet*. His eye took in instantaneously everything there was in the room, every article of clothing Mr. Vyr had on; and his walk from the ravine to the house has given him material for a solid column, at the least."

"He won't write so much about his walk *back*," laughed Major Paul.

"Oh yes. His alchemy will find good matter even in that. These magnanimous gentlemen never descend to petty personal resentments. Your champion is doomed to be famous now in spite of himself. Within a month there will be an army of sight-seers besieging his castle."

"And I and my family will be the unhappy cause," moaned the major. "He'll wish he had let us all perish before he opened the floodgates upon himself in this way—blister the whole race of prying, gossiping, goggle-eyed blabbers! What can be done? They'll get small satisfaction—that's one comfort. He will intrench himself, pull in his log-bridge, and woe to the foolhardy gabbler that offers to find another for himself!"

"Well," responded the secretary, "the mischief's done, and it can't be helped. M. Hector Vyr must accept glory, whether he will or no."

"Mr. Goldapple!" exploded the major, as if a new and brilliant idea had popped into his head.

"Well, what now?"

"The mischief is already done, as you say."

"Yes; there's no doubt of that."

"And there's no possible help for it."

"Not the slightest. You can't stop their tongues from wagging now, any more than you can prevent the winds from blowing."

"Then we must countervail them."

"How? What do you mean?"

"Why, if Hector Vyr *must* be talked about and written about, it had better be the truth than all sorts of vile, twisted, garbled, scurrilous, preposterous, idiotic *lies*, hadn't it?"

"I don't imagine there will be any intentional injustice done him," replied Mr. Goldapple, somewhat overcome by the shower of adjectives.

"I don't know. The reception that pitiful, scrubby interviewer got wasn't exactly what you might call *affable*."

"Not exactly," laughed the secretary.

"And I don't believe interviewers are proof against resentments any more than other men. I tell you what, Mr. Goldapple, *you* write his story."

"*I?*" starting back.

"Yes. You can do him justice—at least you tell the *truth*. I'll talk with him about it, and I know he will give his consent. One of the cardinal points of his philosophy is to accept the less of two evils when one is inevitable."

Mr. Goldapple put his finger to his forehead and thought a long time.

"I suppose you could give me all the necessary data?" he asked, at length.

"Of course, of course."

"Well, we'll see."

And that is how this story came to be written.

XXVI.

AU REVOIR.

THE first unmistakable smile that visited the face of Madame Vyr in these days was welcomed with all the enthusiasm that greeted the first doubtful smile of her infancy in that noble old mansion on the Thames. It was a beautiful smile, rather with the eyes than with the lips. She gave it one morning at breakfast, when she was assured that, though Madeline Paul was soon to depart with her friends, it was only for a time. She had conceived a great fondness for the girl, whose splendid vigor and beauty brought back so vividly her own youth; and this sentiment stirring in the depths of her heart, was like a stream of pure, fresh water flowing into a stagnant pool. It is not strange, therefore, that, when she clearly understood the happiness in store for her, her sad, worn face was illuminated with a smile. It was by no means the first happy change that had been observed in her since the advent of the Americans. The general enlivening effect of their visit, the stimulating sense of responsibility she felt as their hostess, and, later and far more than all these, her joy at her son's escape, and at his rapid restoration to health, had wrought a great alteration both in her bodily and in her mental condition. Her step became firm, her large, matronly figure more erect, a little color came into her cheek, and the melancholy, far-away look almost entirely forsook her eyes. But, best of all, she began to express herself freely, and it soon became evident that the poor, distraught creature whose white face and drooping form had haunted the house—moving slowly and silently from room to room, like a restless spirit—had been a woman of superior intelligence, cultivation, and even vivacity. "Ah," said her overjoyed son to his visitors, "now you begin to see what my mother was—and *is!*"

At last the day which the Americans had appointed for the termination of their visit arrived. Without protesting against their departure, Vyr quietly, but with deep sincerity, described the happiness he had enjoyed in their society, and the benefit he had derived from the interruption of his comparative loneliness and from contact with a little delegation from the civilized world. The stirring scenes in which they had all participated had woven ties between them which could never be broken, even if it were not for the infinitely stronger tie that now bound them together.

The evening before their separation the lovers spent in such a blending of heart with heart and soul with soul as only such lovers can enjoy. It was then that Hector Vyr became, if possible, still more thoroughly convinced of the injustice he had done Madeline in harboring the thought that home and friends and the numberless delights of fashionable society could weigh in the balance with life and love with him, even in his mountain solitude.

At Mikro-Maina, Tsáras, armed with his certificate of moral character *signed by the brigand chief* and duly attested, presented himself to Major Paul, with the request that he be reinstated and allowed to finish the undertaking for which he had been employed. His request was readily granted.

Hector Vyr accompanied his guests as far as Sparta. When Robert Griffin came forward to say farewell in his turn, he took Vyr apart from the rest, and said, in a faltering tone, with cheeks flushed and eyes bent downward,

"Mr. Vyr, your treatment of me has been most generous, most noble. But you have never—notwithstanding the respect, the—the *affection* you have compelled me to feel for you—you have never given me a hint—in words, I mean—of your real opinion of me, or of your real feeling towards me."

Although he did not dare to raise his eyes, he felt the power of the look that was fixed upon him.

"Tell me, I implore you," he burst forth, "is there any reason—do you know anything which prevents you from—from—"

Before he could find words to finish his question, the answer came—turning his blood to ice:

"*I know all!*"

XXVII.

A COURT RECEPTION.

"HAVE you been presented to their Majesties?" asked the secretary of the American Legation, addressing a newly arrived compatriot one morning.

"No."

"Would you like to be?"

"I should like it very much."

"Very well. There is to be a grand ball at the palace to-morrow night. I will introduce you to the consul, who will introduce you to the *Grand Maréchal*, and you will receive an invitation."

"But — what shall I wear?" asked the "Globetrotting American."

"Oh, there will be no difficulty on that score. Ordinary evening-dress will do."

At nine o'clock the next evening the secretary and his new acquaintance arrived at the palace, the exterior of which, though of Pentelican marble, was far from imposing. They followed a motley crowd up a narrow staircase, and presently found themselves in a large, lofty hall, whose splendor was in startling contrast with its humble approaches. The floor was beautifully inlaid; an elaborate frieze ran along the middle of the walls; above this were parallelograms of Pompeian painting; the ceiling was

cut into panels, each profusely decorated with red and
old gold; while huge chandeliers and candelabra of
bronze threw a subdued light over all. High Ionic
door-ways of marble opened into two other halls sim-
ilarly decorated, which to one viewing the scene from
a central point gave an effect of almost unlimited
extent.

A multitude of guests in every variety of gay,
splendid, and commonplace costumes surged from
hall to hall, harmonizing admirably with the picturesque decoration of the walls and ceiling: *palikars*
in crimson and gold, officers in uniform, ministers
and consuls in court dress, English, French, and American ladies in elegant Parisian toilets, modest gentlemen in expansive shirt-fronts and swallow-tails, and
islanders in still plainer attire.

Presently a general buzz of excitement arose everywhere, a passage was opened through the crowd, and
their Majesties, with the dignitaries of the court, advanced into the hall. The king, tall, slender, light-
haired, was royally handsome in his citizen's dress
and manifold decorations. The queen was radiant
with smiles, satin, and diamonds. On being presented
the American tourist was favored with the following
extended conversation:

"How long have you been in Greece?" inquired
the king.

"Only three days, your Majesty."

"How do you like Athens?"

"Very much indeed. It is to me, next to my own,
the most interesting city in the world."

The tourist then fell back, and was at once accosted by an old palikar, who was evidently impressed with the attention he had received.

"We are very fond of you Americans," said the palikar. "We have a fellow-feeling with you. Like us, you were oppressed by a tyrannous despotism; like us, you arose in your might and threw off the yoke."

"Yes," assented the American, cordially; "there is a brotherhood between all lovers of freedom the world over."

"We are grateful to you, too," rejoined the palikar. "In our war of independence you sympathized with us, and many a ship-load of provisions came to us from your ports. In our troubles with our brigands since then you have not censured us with the cruel injustice of other nations; you have not insulted us with arbitrary dictation; you have not given us self-contradictory directions as to what to do with the rascals, as England, France, and other European powers have done; you have appreciated our efforts. Sir, the American and the Greek are brothers!"

The tourist gratefully acknowledged the complimentary speech, and turned away to join his friend the secretary. As the two were sauntering through the halls, the stranger's attention was attracted by two ladies who appeared to be holding a sort of minor reception in the centre of an admiring circle. One was a stately matron with a handsome, intellectual face, crowned by wavy masses of white hair; the other was in the very bloom of magnificent womanhood.

"Who are they?" asked the tourist, his face glowing with admiration.

"Ah, you are a stranger. But surely you must have heard of the famous Vyr family?"

"Vere? Are they any connections of the 'Lady Clare?'"

"Neither by name nor by nature. It is V-y-r, not V-e-r-e, and if reports be true, the 'country heart' is to both these ladies 'worth a hundred coats of arms.' It is said they leave their hermitage in the mountains only once a year, and then only from a sense of duty."

"Indeed, this is very interesting. Whose is the 'country heart?' Some simple 'Young Laurence?' some 'foolish yeoman?'"

"Well, upon my word! where have you lived, man? Is it possible you have never heard of the lion of Greece, who might be the lion of the world if he chose, but who shuts himself up in an inaccessible mountain fastness, and stubbornly refuses to be coaxed from his solitude, or to allow any one to intrude upon it? A squad of Bavarian guards regularly patrol the approaches to his castle, and no one can pass them without a written permit, signed by the Minister and countersigned by the old ogre himself."

"Seems to me I *do* remember something of the sort," replied the tourist—"a newspaper sensation three or four years ago. But it subsided very quickly, and I've heard nothing since. I supposed, therefore, that it must have been one of the Sea-serpent series."

"Nothing of the kind," said the secretary, emphatically.

"Then there really is such a marvel as they told about ?"

"Certainly."

"Why don't they keep up the excitement, then ?"

"They *do* in a certain way. There's no end of table and *café* gossip; but the subject is tabooed in the Greek papers. The editors know that Hector Vyr doesn't want to be talked about, and there is a general sense of gratitude and obligation among the people that they know better than to violate. You remember, the newspaper accounts told of his wonderful exploits — how he attacked whole gangs of brigands single-handed, and drove them out of their strongholds?"

"Yes, I remember. He rescued an American family, about whom there was a great fuss made."

"Ah — we'll come to that presently."

"But, of course, nobody believed such stories."

"Nevertheless, they were true in the main. I happen to know all about it. The Greeks believe them, at any rate, and they would demolish a paper that ventured to make the most distant allusion to their hero without his consent."

"Why don't other papers keep up the excitement — English, French, and American papers ? The Greeks would find it a difficult matter to demolish the *New York Herald* or the London *Times !*"

"Don't you know, my friend, no man is lionized very much in these days without his own connivance? The Angel Gabriel himself would have to keep his trumpet blowing, submit to interviews and band serenades—submit? he'd have to *solicit* them! —attend dinners, and make speeches, or he would soon find himself dropping into obscurity."

"But how do you *know*," said the tourist, obstinately, "that it isn't all a fable, a revival of ancient mythology? I should think these Greeks would be up to that sort of thing."

"How do I know? Didn't I tell you I knew all about it? Bless your soul, I've seen Hector Vyr himself, and talked with him!"

"Is it possible!" exclaimed the tourist. "Do tell me all about it."

"Wait till we are cosily seated with our cigars in my library."

"Let's go there now."

"No; we've a great deal to see here first. I want to present you to Madame Vyr, his mother, and Madame Vyr, his wife, when we get a chance. The wife is a countrywoman of ours, a daughter of that very family he rescued from the brigands; so of course she will be delighted to see you. That soldierly-looking old gentleman in the swallow-tail is her father, Major Warren Paul, late of the firm of Jobling, Hotchkiss & Paul. He's what you would call a rabid Philhellene—he's more than that, he's as good a Greek as any old palikar of them all."

Seizing their opportunity, the two Americans wedged themselves through the crowd, and received as cordial a welcome as the secretary had promised.

Madeline had no end of questions to ask in regard to her beloved America, and particularly of her native city, which was also her new acquaintance's home.

Meanwhile the crowd, seeing that it was to be a purely national love-feast, had gradually withdrawn, and were now furtively observing their favorites from a respectful distance.

"Does Mr. Vyr never come to Athens?" asked the tourist, interviewing Madeline in his turn.

"Only when it is absolutely necessary, which is very seldom," answered Madeline. "Then he always comes *incognito*, and goes away as soon as possible."

"Do you spend much time here yourself, madam?"

"No, only a week or two."

"She wouldn't do *that* if she could prevent it," put in the elder Madame Vyr, laughing.

"My husband thinks I must come here at regular intervals to prevent my growing rusty," explained the younger. "Our home is in a very retired situation: we rarely see any one there besides each other and our servants."

"Your friends have difficulty in finding you?" asked the tourist, with affected innocence.

"Yes," answered Madeline, frankly; "very great difficulty."

Major Paul now advanced, to whom the newcomer was duly introduced.

"From Boston, eh?" said the major, shaking his hand warmly. "Glad to see you, sir—tremendously glad to see you. And how are matters at the new Athens?"

" About as they are at the old Athens, if we may judge by this gorgeous display of wealth and general prosperity," answered the tourist, looking around the halls.

" Yes, about the same, I suppose. Plenty of gold and diamonds outside and plenty of nothing inside. If these people would spend less in glitter and more in paying their debts and building up a solid foundation of prosperity, they would be vastly happier and more respected, I keep telling 'em. But, wisdom of Socrates! what do they care for what anybody *says?* As long as they can dazzle your eyes, what difference does it make whether they have anything to eat or not? Go out of this marble palace, and take a walk through the streets : what will you see, eh? And how is it in Boston, sir? Better looking houses and shops, of course—but how large a per cent. of the people do you suppose eat three square meals a day? It's just the same all over the country. With natural resources enough to support a population of six hundred millions in comfort and prosperity, it doesn't half support sixty millions— and all because of your cursed extravagance, sir! Greece is, on a small scale, what America is on a big scale, sir!"

Before the tourist could find words to reply, Madeline said, " You must not mind papa's scolding. He does it only for his own amusement. If there is any country he loves and admires more than Greece, it is his own America."

" And if there's a country," added the secretary,

22

"he admires and loves more than America, it is his own Greece."

"Hold there!" said the major; "America first, always, and forever! But it is always so—I never say a true and honest word but some one must immediately spoil its whole effect by calling it only my scolding!

"But all this isn't what I came to say. I rather think I have some news that will set you ladies to scolding, too—especially *you*," addressing his daughter.

"What is it, pray?"

"The boat went this afternoon."

"This afternoon!" echoed Madeline, in dismay. "Why, it wasn't to go until to-morrow."

"That is very true. All the same, it has gone."

"But it had no *right* to go!" cried Madeline, indignantly.

"True again, my daughter. Still, I can't see that that alters the case. It went as a special accommodation to his Serene Magnificence—or whatever it is—Scrapis Effendi, who had important business at Sparta, admitting of no delay."

Instead of looking in tender sympathy upon poor Madeline's grewsome countenance, her father only laughed at it.

"Never mind, my dear," said Madame Vyr *mère*, "we ought to have become sufficiently accustomed to such things by this time. This is neither London nor Boston, you know. It only involves three more days of gayety in Athens. I think we can reconcile ourselves to that if we try."

Madeline made no further exhibition of indignation or of disappointment until the secretary and his friend had withdrawn, when she indulged in sundry expressions vividly reminding her hearers of her relationship to the doughty major.

"So, so," said the last-named gentleman; "if you find it so hard to submit to three days' enforced exile from your hermitage in the wilderness, what possible hope have we that you will ever make up your mind to the visit to America we have been talking about so long?"

Without noticing her father's question, Madeline only said, while her face suddenly brightened up,

"I'll tell you what we will do, mannáka—we will ask Mr. Goldapple to take us to Gýtheion in his yacht; and Tuesday we shall be at *home!*—think of it, mannáka—номе!!"

It was thus—her hands clasped rapturously together, her eyes brighter than the diamonds upon her white throat—that she spoke of that wildest of solitudes in the Taygetus Mountains!

THE END.

SOME POPULAR NOVELS

Published by HARPER & BROTHERS New York.

The Octavo Paper Novels in this list may be obtained in half-binding [leather backs and pasteboard sides], suitable for Public and Circulating Libraries, at 25 cents per volume, in addition to the prices named below. The 32mo Paper Novels may be obtained in Cloth, at 15 cents per volume in addition to the prices named below.

For a FULL LIST OF NOVELS published by HARPER & BROTHERS, see HARPER'S NEW AND REVISED CATALOGUE, which will be sent by mail, postage prepaid, to any address in the United States, on receipt of Ten cents.

		PRICE
BAKER'S (Rev. W. M.) Carter Quarterman. Illustrated	8vo, Paper	$ 60
Inside: a Chronicle of Secession. Illustrated	8vo, Paper	75
The New Timothy..............12mo, Cloth, $1 50;	4to, Paper	25
The Virginians in Texas	8vo, Paper	75
BENEDICT'S (F. L.) John Worthington's Name.	8vo, Paper	75
Miss Dorothy's Charge	8vo, Paper	75
Miss Van Kortland	8vo, Paper	60
My Daughter Elinor.	8vo, Paper	80
St. Simon's Niece	8vo, Paper	60
BESANT'S (W.) All in a Garden Fair	4to, Paper	20
BESANT & RICE'S All Sorts and Conditions of Men	4to, Paper	20
By Celia's Arbor. Illustrated	8vo, Paper	50
Shepherds All and Maidens Fair.	32mo, Paper	25
"So they were Married!" Illustrated	4to, Paper	20
Sweet Nelly, My Heart's Delight	4to, Paper	10
The Captains' Room.	4to, Paper	10
The Chaplain of the Fleet.	4to, Paper	20
The Golden Butterfly.	8vo, Paper	40
'Twas in Trafalgar's Bay.	32mo, Paper	20
When the Ship Comes Home.	32mo, Paper	20
BLACK'S (W.) A Daughter of Heth. 12mo, Cloth, $1 25;	8vo, Paper	35
A Princess of Thule..............12mo, Cloth, 1 25;	8vo, Paper	50
Green Pastures and Piccadilly..12mo, Cloth, 1 25;	8vo, Paper	50
In Silk Attire......................12mo, Cloth, 1 25;	8vo, Paper	35
Judith Shakespeare. Ill'd.......12mo, Cloth, 1 25;	4to, Paper	20
Kilmeny............................12mo, Cloth, 1 25;	8vo, Paper	35
Macleod of Dare. Illustrated. 12mo, Cloth, 1 25;.	8vo, Paper	60
	4to, Paper	15
Madcap Violet.....................12mo, Cloth, 1 25;	8vo, Paper	50
Shandon Bells. Illustrated.......12mo, Cloth, 1 25;	4to, Paper	20
Sunrise.............................12mo, Cloth, 1 25;	4to, Paper	15
That Beautiful Wretch. Ill'd...12mo, Cloth, 1 25;	4to, Paper	20
The Maid of Killeena, and Other Stories	8vo, Paper	40
The Monarch of Mincing-Lane. Illustrated	8vo, Paper	60
The Strange Adventures of a Phaeton. 12mo, Cloth, $1 25; 8vo, Pa.		50
Three Feathers. Illustrated......12mo, Cloth, $1 25;	8vo, Paper	60
White Heather ....12mo, Cloth, 1 25;	4to, Paper	20
White Wings. Illustrated.......12mo, Cloth, 1 25;	4to, Paper	20

PRICE

BRONTÉ'S (Charlotte) Shirley. Ill'd..12mo, Cloth, $1 00; 8vo, Paper $ 50
  The Professor. Illustrated.........12mo, Cloth, $1 00; 4to, Paper 20
  Villette. Illustrated.............12mo, Cloth, $1 00; 8vo, Paper 50
BRONTÉ'S (Anne) The Tenant of Wildfell Hall. Ill'd....12mo, Cloth 1 00
BRONTÉ'S (Emily) Wuthering Heights. Illustrated.......12mo, Cloth 1 00
BULWER'S (Lytton) A Strange Story. Illustrated..........12mo, Cloth 1 25
                                                          8vo, Paper 50
  Devereux. ....8vo, Paper 40
  Ernest Maltravers ....8vo, Paper 35
  Godolphin ....8vo, Paper 35
  Kenelm Chillingly................12mo, Cloth, $1 25; 8vo, Paper 50
  Leila ....12mo, Cloth, 1 00
  Night and Morning................................8vo, Paper 50
  Paul Clifford....................................8vo, Paper 40
  Pausanias the Spartan...........12mo, Cloth, 75 cents; 8vo, Paper 25
  Pelham..8vo, Paper 40
  Rienzi..8vo, Paper 40
  The Caxtons ....12mo, Cloth 1 25
  The Coming Race................12mo, Cloth, 1 00; 12mo, Paper 50
  The Last Days of Pompeii......8vo, Paper, 25 cents; 4to, Paper 15
  The Parisians. Illustrated.....12mo, Cloth, $1 50; 8vo, Paper 60
  The Pilgrims of the Rhine.......................8vo, Paper 20
  What will He do with it?.........................8vo, Paper 75
  Zanoni ....8vo, Paper 35
COLLINS'S (Wilkie) Novels. Ill'd Library Edition. 12mo, Cloth, per vol. 1 25
  After Dark, and Other Stores.—Antonina.—Armadale.—Basil.—
  Hide-and-Seek.—Man and Wife.—My Miscellanies.—No Name.
  —Poor Miss Finch.—The Dead Secret.—The Law and the Lady.
  —The Moonstone.—The New Magdalen.—The Queen of Hearts.
  —The Two Destinies.—The Woman in White.
  Antonina..8vo, Paper 40
  Armadale. Illustrated ....8vo, Paper 60
  "I Say No".16mo, Cloth, 50 cts.; 16mo, Paper, 35 cts.; 4to, Paper 20
  Man and Wife .. ..4to, Paper 20
  My Lady's Money.................................32mo, Paper 25
  No Name. Illustrated............................8vo, Paper 60
  Percy and the Prophet...........................32mo, Paper 20
  Poor Miss Finch. Illustrated......8vo, Cloth, $1 10; 8vo, Paper 60
  The Law and the Lady. Illustrated...............8vo, Paper 50
  The Moonstone. Illustrated......................8vo, Paper 60
  The New Magdalen...............................8vo, Paper 30
  The Two Destinies. Illustrated..................8vo, Paper 35
  The Woman in White. Illustrated.................8vo, Paper 60
CRAIK'S (Miss G. M.) Anne Warwick...................8vo, Paper 25
  Dorcas..4to, Paper 15
  Fortune's Marriage..............................4to, Paper 20
  Godfrey Helstone ....4to, Paper 20
  Hard to Bear....................................8vo, Paper 30
  Mildred ....8vo, Paper 30

PRICE

GIBBON'S (C.) The Braes of Yarrow.............................4to, Paper $ 20
   The Golden Shaft ....4to, Paper 20
HARDY'S (Thos.) Fellow-Townsmen.......................32mo, Paper 20
   A Laodicean. Illustrated..................................4to, Paper 20
   Romantic Adventures of a Milkmaid ....4to, Paper 10
HARRISON'S (Mrs.) Golden Rod...........................32mo, Paper 25
   Helen Troy...16mo, Cloth 1 00
HAY'S (M. C.) A Dark Inheritance..........................32mo, Paper 15
   A Shadow on the Threshold.............................32mo, Paper 20
   Among the Ruins, and Other Stories.......................4to, Paper 15
   At the Seaside, and Other Stories.........................4to, Paper 15
   Back to the Old Home..................................32mo, Paper 20
   Bid Me Discourse..4to, Paper 10
   Dorothy's Venture...4to, Paper 15
   For Her Dear Sake ....4to, Paper 15
   Hidden Perils ....8vo, Paper 25
   Into the Shade, and Other Stories ....4to, Paper 15
   Lady Carmichael's Will ....32mo, Paper 15
   Lester's Secret..4to, Paper 20
   Missing...32mo, Paper 20
   My First Offer, and Other Stories.........................4to, Paper 15
   Nora's Love Test..8vo, Paper 25
   Old Myddelton's Money ....8vo, Paper 25
   Reaping the Whirlwind....................................32mo, Paper 20
   The Arundel Motto...8vo, Paper 25
   The Sorrow of a Secret...................................32mo, Paper 15
   The Squire's Legacy.......................................8vo, Paper 25
   Under Life's Key, and Other Stories.......................4to, Paper 15
   Victor and Vanquished....................................8vo, Paper 25
HOEY'S (Mrs. C.) A Golden Sorrow..........................8vo, Paper 40
   All or Nothing..4to, Paper 15
   Kate Cronin's Dowry....................................32mo, Paper 15
   The Blossoming of an Aloe.................................8vo, Paper 30
   The Lover's Creed...4to, Paper 20
   The Question of Cain......................................4to, Paper 20
HUGO'S (Victor) Ninety-Three. Ill'd. 12mo, Cloth, $1 50; 8vo, Paper 25
   The Toilers of the Sea. Ill'd ....8vo, Cloth, 1 50; 8vo, Paper 50
JAMES'S (Henry, Jun.) Daisy Miller.......................32mo, Paper 20
   An International Episode................................32mo, Paper 20
   Diary of a Man of Fifty, and A Bundle of Letters.....32mo, Paper 25
   The four above-mentioned works in one volume..........4to, Paper 25
   Washington Square. Illustrated ....16mo, Cloth 1 25
JOHNSTON'S (R. M.) Dukesborough Tales. Illustrated......4to, Paper 25
   Old Mark Langston..16mo, Cloth 1 00
LANG'S (Mrs.) Dissolving Views...16mo, Cloth, 50 cents; 16mo, Paper 35
LAWRENCE'S (G. A.) Anteros...............................8vo, Paper 40
   Brakespeare..8vo, Paper 40
   Breaking a Butterfly......................................8vo, Paper 35
   Guy Livingstone...................12mo, Cloth, $1 50; 4to, Paper 10

PRICE

MULOCK'S (Miss) Olive. Ill'd.......12mo, Cloth, 90 cents; 8vo, Paper $ 55
  The Laurel Bush. Ill'd.........12mo, Cloth, 90 cents; 8vo, Paper 25
  The Woman's Kingdom. Ill'd...12mo, Cloth, 90 cts.; 8vo, Paper 60
  Two Marriages...12mo, Cloth 90
  Unkind Word, and Other Stories............................12mo, Cloth 90
  Young Mrs. Jardine.................12mo, Cloth, $1 25; 4to, Paper 10
MURRAY'S (D. C.) A Life's Atonement....................4to, Paper 20
  A Model Father...4to, Paper 10
  By the Gate of the Sea............4to, Paper, 15 cents; 12mo, Paper 15
  Hearts...4to, Paper 20
  The Way of the World..4to, Paper 20
  Val Strange ....4to, Paper 20
  Adrian Vidal. Illustrated.......................................4to, Paper 25
NORRIS'S (W. E.) A Man of His Word, &c.................4to, Paper 20
  Heaps of Money...8vo, Paper 15
  Mademoiselle de Mersac ....4to, Paper 20
  Matrimony...4to, Paper 20
  No New Thing..4to, Paper 25
  That Terrible Man...12mo, Paper 25
  Thirlby Hall. Illustrated ....4to, Paper 25
OLIPHANT'S (Laurence) Altiora Peto.4to, Paper, 20 cts.; 16mo, Paper 20
  Piccadilly...16mo, Paper 25
OLIPHANT'S (Mrs.) Agnes..8vo, Paper 50
  A Son of the Soil...8vo, Paper 50
  Athelings..8vo, Paper 50
  Brownlows...8vo, Paper 50
  Carità. Illustrated...8vo, Paper 50
  Chronicles of Carlingford..8vo, Paper 60
  Days of My Life..12mo, Cloth 1 50
  For Love and Life..8vo, Paper 50
  Harry Joscelyn...4to, Paper 20
  He That Will Not when He May..............................4to, Paper 20
  Hester...4to, Paper 20
  Innocent. Illustrated..8vo, Paper 50
  It was a Lover and His Lass.....................................4to, Paper 20
  Lady Jane...4to, Paper 10
  Lucy Crofton...12mo, Cloth 1 50
  Madam....................16mo, Cloth, 75 cents; 4to, Paper 25
  Madonna Mary...8vo, Paper 50
  Miss Marjoribanks...8vo, Paper 50
  Mrs. Arthur...8vo, Paper 40
  Ombra...8vo, Paper 50
  Phœbe, Junior..8vo, Paper 35
  Sir Tom..4to, Paper 20
  Squire Arden...8vo, Paper 50
  The Curate in Charge..8vo, Paper 20
  The Fugitives..4to, Paper 10
  The Greatest Heiress in England.............................4to, Paper 10
  The Ladies Lindores...............16mo, Cloth, $1 00; 4to, Paper 20

PRICE

OLIPHANT'S (Mrs.) The Laird of Norlaw ....12mo, Cloth $1 50
   The Last of the Mortimers.....................................12mo, Cloth 1 50
   The Primrose Path...8vo, Paper 50
   The Story of Valentine and his Brother.................8vo, Paper 50
   The Wizard's Son..4to, Paper 25
   Within the Precincts..4to, Paper 15
   Young Musgrave...8vo, Paper 40
PAYN'S (James) A Beggar on Horseback.......................8vo, Paper 35
   A Confidential Agent..4to, Paper 15
   A Grape from a Thorn ....4to, Paper 20
   A Woman's Vengeance..8vo, Paper 35
   At Her Mercy...8vo, Paper 30
   Bred in the Bone... 8vo, Paper 40
   By Proxy...8vo, Paper 35
   Carlyon's Year...8vo, Paper 25
   For Cash Only ....4to, Paper 20
   Found Dead..8vo, Paper 25
   From Exile..4to, Paper 15
   Gwendoline's Harvest..8vo, Paper 25
   Halves..8vo, Paper 30
   High Spirits..4to, Paper 15
   Kit. Illustrated...4to, Paper 20
   Less Black than We're Painted................................8vo, Paper 35
   Murphy's Master..8vo, Paper 20
   One of the Family...8vo, Paper 25
   The Best of Husbands..8vo, Paper 25
   The Canon's Ward. Illustrated ....4to, Paper 25
   The Talk of the Town...4to, Paper 20
   Thicker than Water............16mo, Cloth, $1 00;   4to, Paper 20
   Under One Roof...4to, Paper 15
   Walter's Word..8vo, Paper 50
   What He Cost Her...8vo, Paper 40
   Won—Not Wooed..8vo, Paper 30
READE'S Novels: Household Edition.   Ill'd. ....12mo, Cloth, per vol. 1 00
   A Simpleton *and* Wandering Heir. | It is Never Too Late to Mend.
   A Terrible Temptation. | Love me Little, Love me Long.
   A Woman-Hater. | Peg Woffington, Christie John-
   Foul Play. | stone, &c.
   Good Stories. | Put Yourself in His Place.
   Griffith Gaunt. | The Cloister and the Hearth.
   Hard Cash. | White Lies.
   A Perilous Secret...12mo, Cl., 75 cts.; 4to, Pap., 20 cts.; 16mo, Pap. 40
   A Hero and a Martyr..8vo, Paper 15
   A Simpleton..8vo, Paper 30
   A Terrible Temptation. Illustrated...........................8vo, Paper 25
   A Woman-Hater. Ill'd.......8vo, Paper, 30 cents; 12mo, Paper 20
   Foul Play ....8vo, Paper 30
   Good Stories of Man and Other Animals. Illustrated...4to, Paper 20
   Griffith Gaunt. Illustrated ....8vo, Paper 30

PRICE

READE'S (Charles) Hard Cash. Illustrated....................8vo, Paper $ 35
   It is Never Too Late to Mend............................8vo, Paper   35
   Jack of all Trades.......................................16mo, Paper   15
   Love Me Little, Love Me Long ....8vo, Paper   30
   Multum in Parvo. Illustrated....................4to, Paper   15
   Peg Woffington, &c.....................................8vo, Paper   35
   Put Yourself in His Place. Illustrated..........8vo, Paper   35
   The Cloister and the Hearth....................8vo, Paper   35
   The Coming Man.....................................32mo, Paper   20
   The Jilt...32mo, Paper   20
   The Picture...16mo, Paper   15
   The Wandering Heir. Illustrated ....8vo, Paper   20
   White Lies..8vo, Paper   30
ROBINSON'S (F. W.) A Bridge of Glass..............8vo, Paper   30
   A Fair Maid ....4to, Paper   20
   A Girl's Romance, and Other Stories...........8vo, Paper   30
   As Long as She Lived................................8vo, Paper   50
   Carry's Confession...................................8vo, Paper   50
   Christie's Faith.......................................12mo, Cloth 1 75
   Coward Conscience..................................4to, Paper   15
   Her Face was Her Fortune.........................8vo, Paper   40
   Lazarus in London...................................4to, Paper   20
   Little Kate Kirby. Illustrated....................8vo, Paper   50
   Mattie: a Stray.......................................8vo, Paper   40
   No Man's Friend......................................8vo, Paper   50
   Othello the Second..................................32mo, Paper   20
   Poor Humanity ....8vo, Paper   50
   Poor Zeph!...32mo, Paper   20
   Romance on Four Wheels...........................8vo, Paper   15
   Second-Cousin Sarah. Illustrated ....8vo, Paper   50
   Stern Necessity......................................8vo, Paper   40
   The Barmaid at Battleton.........................32mo, Paper   15
   The Black Speck......................................4to, Paper   10
   The Hands of Justice ....4to, Paper   20
   The Man She Cared For.............................4to, Paper   20
   The Romance of a Back Street....................32mo, Paper   15
   True to Herself.......................................8vo, Paper   50
RUSSELL'S (W. Clark) Auld Lang Syne ....4to, Paper   10
   A Sailor's Sweetheart...............................4to, Paper   15
   A Sea Queen..............16mo, Cloth, $1 00;   4to, Paper   20
   An Ocean Free Lance................................4to, Paper   20
   Jack's Courtship...............16mo, Cloth, 1 00;   4to, Paper   25
   John Holdsworth, Chief Mate ....4to, Paper   20
   Little Loo ....4to, Paper   20
   My Watch Below......................................4to, Paper   20
   On the Fo'k'sle Head................................4to, Paper   15
   Round the Galley Fire..............................4to, Paper   15
   The "Lady Maud:" Schooner Yacht. Illustrated........4to, Paper   20
   Wreck of the "Grosvenor".....8vo, Paper, 30 cents;   4to, Paper   15

PRICE

SCOTT'S Novels. See *Waverley Novels.*		
SHERWOOD'S (Mrs. John) A Transplanted Rose............12mo, Cloth	$1	00
TABOR'S (Eliza) Eglantine.....................................8vo, Paper		40
Hope Meredith.......................................8vo, Paper		35
Jeanie's Quiet Life................... ....8vo, Paper		30
Little Miss Primrose ....4to, Paper		15
Meta's Faith.......................................8vo, Paper		35
The Blue Ribbon..................................8vo, Paper		40
The Last of Her Line ....4to, Paper		15
The Senior Songman................... ......4to, Paper		20
THACKERAY'S (Miss) Bluebeard's Keys ....8vo, Paper		35
Da Capo.......................................32mo, Paper		20
Miscellaneous Works ....8vo, Paper		90
Miss Angel.......................................8vo, Paper		50
Miss Williamson's Divagations...................4to, Paper		15
Old Kensington. Illustrated ....8vo, Paper		60
THACKERAY'S (W. M.) Denis Duval. Illustrated ....8vo, Paper		25
Henry Esmond, and Lovel the Widower. 12 Ill's ....8vo, Paper		60
Henry Esmond......................8vo, Pa., 50 cents ; 4to, Paper		15
Lovel the Widower.................................8vo, Paper		20
Pendennis. 179 Illustrations ....8vo, Paper		75
The Adventures of Philip. 64 Illustrations ....8vo, Paper		60
The Great Hoggarty Diamond ....8vo, Paper		20
The Newcomes. 162 Illustrations ....8vo, Paper		90
The Virginians. 150 Illustrations.................8vo, Paper		90
Vanity Fair. 32 Illustrations.....................8vo, Paper		80
THACKERAY'S Works. Illustrated ....12mo, Cloth, per vol.	1	25
Novels: Vanity Fair.—Pendennis.—The Newcomes.—The Virgin-		
ians.—Philip.—Esmond, and Lovel the Widower. 6 vols. *Mis-*		
cellaneous: Barry Lyndon, Hoggarty Diamond, &c.—Paris and		
Irish Sketch-Books, &c.—Book of Snobs, Sketches, &c.—Four		
Georges, English Humorists, Roundabout Papers, &c.—Catharine,		
&c. 5 vols.		
TOWNSEND'S (G. A.) The Entailed Hat.......................16mo, Cloth	1	50
TROLLOPE'S (Anthony) An Eye for an Eye...................4to, Paper		10
An Old Man's Love................................4to, Paper		15
Ayala's Angel....................................4to, Paper		20
Cousin Henry ....4to, Paper		10
Doctor Thorne. ....12mo, Cloth	1	50
Doctor Wortle's School ....4to, Paper		15
Framley Parsonage..............................4to, Paper		15
Harry Heathcote of Gangoil. Illustrated ....8vo, Paper		20
He Knew He was Right. Illustrated.................8vo, Paper		30
Is He Popenjoy?.................................4to, Paper		20
John Caldigate.................................4to, Paper		15
Kept in the Dark ....4to, Paper		25
Lady Anna......................................8vo, Paper		30
Marion Fay. Illustrated ....4to, Paper		20
Phineas Redux. Illustrated........................8vo, Paper		75

PRICE

TROLLOPE'S (Anthony) Rachel Ray..........8vo, Paper	$	35
Ralph the Heir. Illustrated..........8vo, Paper		75
Sir Harry Hotspur of Humblethwaite. Illustrated......8vo, Paper		35
The American Senator..........8vo, Paper		50
The Belton Estate..........8vo, Paper		35
The Bertrams..........4to, Paper		15
The Duke's Children..........4to, Paper		20
The Eustace Diamonds. Illustrated..........8vo, Paper		80
The Fixed Period..........4to, Paper		15
The Golden Lion of Granpere. Illustrated..........8vo, Paper		40
The Lady of Launay..........32mo, Paper		20
The Last Chronicle of Barset. Illustrated..........8vo, Paper		90
The Prime Minister..........8vo, Paper		60
The Small House at Allington. Illustrated..........8vo, Paper		75
The Vicar of Bullhampton. Illustrated..........8vo, Paper		80
The Warden, and Barchester Towers..........8vo, Paper		60
The Way We Live Now. Illustrated..........8vo, Paper		90
Thompson Hall. Illustrated..........32mo, Paper		20
Why Frau Frohman Raised her Prices, &c..........4to, Paper		10
(Frances E.) Among Aliens. Illustrated..........4to, Paper		15
Anne Furness..........8vo, Paper		50
Like Ships Upon the Sea..........4to, Paper		20
Mabel's Progress..........8vo, Paper		40
The Sacristan's Household. Illustrated..........8vo, Paper		50
Veronica..........8vo, Paper		50
WALLACE'S (Lew) Ben-Hur..........16mo, Cloth	1	50

WAVERLEY NOVELS. 12mo. With 2000 Illustrations.

THISTLE EDITION..........48 Vols., Green Cloth, per vol.	1	00
Complete Sets, Half Morocco, Gilt Tops..........	72	00
HOLYROOD EDITION..........48 Vols., Brown Cloth, per vol.		75
Complete Sets, Half Morocco, Gilt Tops..........	72	00
POPULAR EDITION..........24 Vols., Green Cloth, per vol.	1	25
Complete Sets, Half Morocco..........	54	00

WAVERLEY NOVELS. 12mo. With 2000 Illustrations.

 Waverley; Guy Mannering; The Antiquary; Rob Roy; Old Mortality; The Heart of Mid-Lothian; A Legend of Montrose; The Bride of Lammermoor; The Black Dwarf; Ivanhoe; The . Monastery; The Abbot; Kenilworth; The Pirate; The Fortunes of Nigel; Peveril of the Peak; Quentin Durward; St. Ronan's Well; Redgauntlet; The Betrothed; The Talisman; Woodstock; Chronicles of the Canongate, The Highland Widow, &c.; The Fair Maid of Perth; Anne of Geierstein; Count Robert of Paris; Castle Dangerous; The Surgeon's Daughter; Glossary.

WOOLSON'S (C. F.) Anne. Illustrated by Reinhart..........16mo, Cloth	1	25
For the Major. Illustrated..........16mo, Cloth	1	00
YATES'S (Edmund) Dr. Wainwright's Patient..........8vo, Paper		30
Kissing the Rod..........8vo, Paper		40
Land at Last..........8vo, Paper		40
Wrecked in Port..........8vo, Paper		35

www.ingramcontent.com/pod-product-compliance
Lightning Source LLC
Chambersburg PA
CBHW021750110726
47902CB00006B/1466